# LUNACIA

**AERLEON**

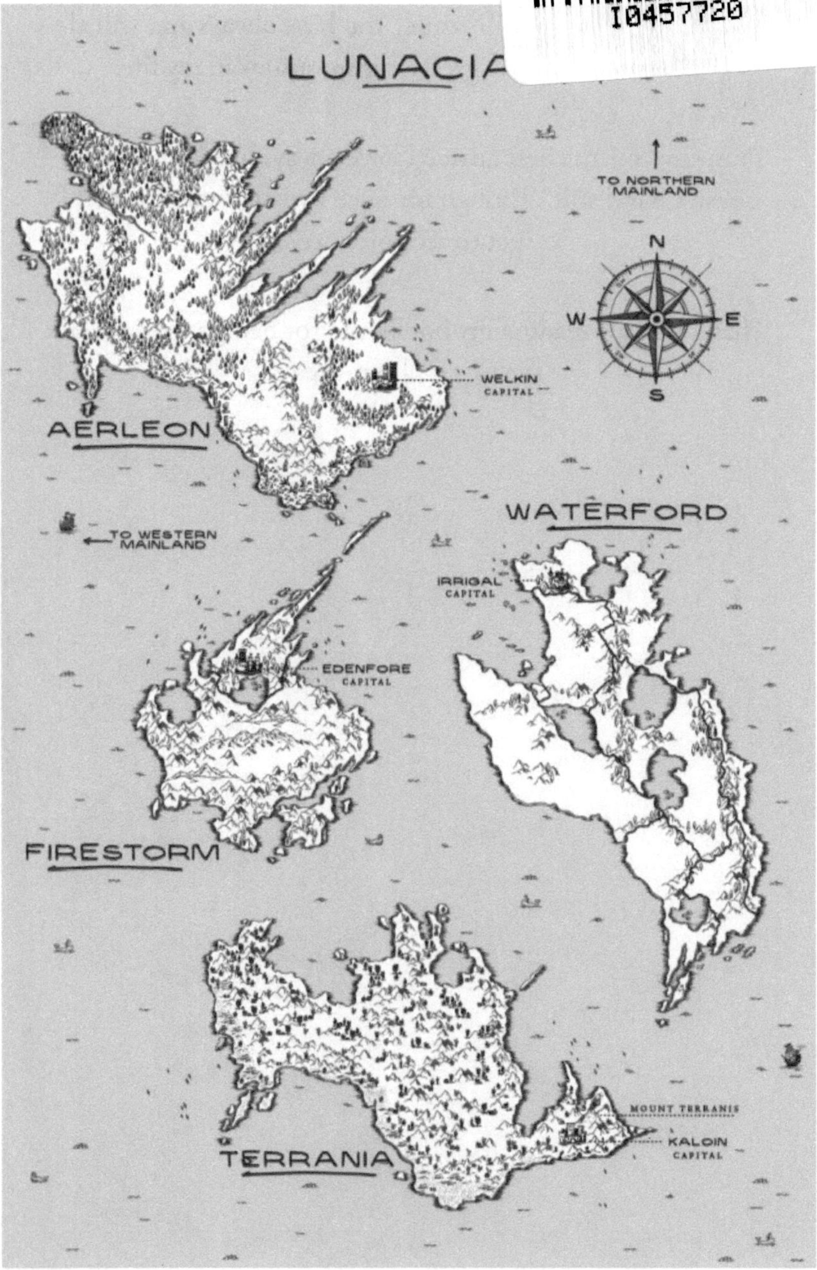

WELKIN
CAPITAL

TO NORTHERN
MAINLAND

N
W E
S

**WATERFORD**

TO WESTERN
MAINLAND

IRRIGAL
CAPITAL

EDENFORE
CAPITAL

**FIRESTORM**

**TERRANIA**

MOUNT TERRANIS

KALOIN
CAPITAL

For my Grandmother 'Narnie'. You have always and will always be one of the greatest inspirations in my life.

You gave me the best advice I have always lived by - "Time doesn't stand still." Though for once I wish it would when I get to see you next.

Thank you for reading my books and for being more excited than I am about them.

First published by Kathryn Lee 2020
Text - ©2020 Kathryn Lee
Cover design – Hannely Micu
Cover images - ©Shutterstock
Map – Natalie Simmonds

This book has been typeset in Draft2Digital
ISBN: 978-0-646-82355-3

# Also by Kathryn Lee

**The Lunacian Chronicles**
Kingdom of Stone
Flower of Solitude

**(Not so) Average Addie**
And the Secrets to Science

Power twice does destruction hold,
born on the full moon it was foretold.
One Elemental heart forever torn,
to do what's right and be reborn.

...

# 9 Days 'til Invasion

...

# 1

Nanu stood with the Queen on the balcony overlooking the harbour, the morning sun glistening over the eerily calm water. Almost three hundred ships and boats had arrived over the past twelve hours, and still more were arriving by the hour.

The citizens of Aerleon and Waterford were seeking safety inside the stone walls of Edenfore. But the capital of Firestorm could only hold so many - and it was near capacity.

"We can't turn people away," Queen Isabella said shaking her head. "But where do we put them? We haven't enough food to sustain this many people for more than a few weeks. And Luna knows how long the siege will last."

When the maid had returned from the Northern Mainland just over a week ago, she was just in time to help Izzy's baby come into the world. The stress of dealing with the All-Powerful Child had sent Izzy into labour. Thankfully though, the birth was event free and the news of the new Prince's arrival had sent the citizens of Firestorm into the streets to celebrate. Everyone was happily rejoicing, that is until word began to spread that their home would soon be invaded by soldiers from the Northern Mainland. The revelry quickly turned to fear and panic.

People began locking themselves in their homes – only venturing out to get the necessities like firewood and food. Three days after giving birth to the new prince, Izzy ventured out. While walking the streets of Edenfore she didn't meet a single soul to speak to besides the blacksmith who was putting out the fire in his forge.

The wind howled through the tall stone buildings along the streets and whistled through the treetops – Izzy felt uneasy. Gone were the cluttered and noisy market stalls, the children running around playing. The threat of an invasion wounded Izzy's pride to the core. *What kind of ruler can't even keep her people safe?*

But on the balcony looking out over the water, Nanu held the Queen's hand placating her with promises that everything was going to be okay.

"There's no way you can know that," said Izzy still looking outwards.

Nanu let go of the girl's hand and put an arm around her shoulders. Pulling her in close, she said, "I do not know very much about a lot of things little one, but I do know that while there is air in your lungs and a fire in your soul, everything *will* be okay."

A voice from behind them spoke, "I've evacuated all the elderly from the outlying villages." Constance had entered Izzy's chambers. It seemed as though she'd adjusted well to her role as Princess and Izzy couldn't imagine being without her.

The Queen turned, "Thank you, Constance. And what of the children?" she asked.

"I'm still waiting on a report from the guards still in three of the villages, but it seems as though everyone is accounted for so far."

"Good," Izzy said. "We will lock the castle gates tomorrow night once we are sure everyone is inside."

"I'll let the Guard Master know," Constance said.

"Thank you," said Izzy and Constance took her leave.

"You are doing everything you can little one," Nanu said. "No one could expect you to do more than you already are."

Izzy sighed, "I wish there was more I *could* do though. I just feel helpless," she said – her shoulders sagging. She felt the weight of everyone's expectation that she could miraculously save them from what was coming.

There had been reports from returning fishing boats that there were twenty-seven ships bound for Lunacia. Each ship holding nigh on five hundred men, it was more than the Lunacian army had in its ranks.

There had never been a need in the past for a large army. Until now the army had merely been for the royal family's protection and crowd control at public events – not that there had been many since her mother had passed when she was younger.

"But for now, you need to show your people that you are here for them. Go, visit them," Nanu said. "Go and show them you care and that you will stand with them in this battle."

"Maybe I should," said Izzy.

"If anyone should be feeling terrible it is me little one. He is my brother. I tried my hardest to stop him, to talk him out of invading our country but he wouldn't listen," Nanu said.

Izzy took the maid by her shoulders and pulled her face close to her own, "Now you listen here," she said with much conviction, "I don't want to hear anything about you feeling responsible. He is a grown man, and he has made his own choices."

The older woman nodded, and Izzy went back to looking out over the water, "It's been awfully calm the last few days," she said. "Maybe with so little wind, it will take the ships longer to get here?"

"I wouldn't count on that," said Nanu. "Just because there is not much wind between the islands, doesn't mean there isn't wind out on the open ocean."

"And the Guard Master is sure that they'll arrive in nine days?" she asked.

A slight nod was all Izzy got in response – the maid's gaze fixed on the horizon.

MAKESHIFT BEDS AND living quarters had been set up in every empty room of the castle, as well as the buildings inside the castle walls. The people were filing into the castle, Aristide wondered if the line of people would ever end. He and Xander had been helping to oversee the evacuation of the villages. Gypsy tribes were now the last to arrive.

Inside the walls, it was clear where people had come from. They had all begun staking out space amongst those from their own communities. Small disagreements were breaking out all over the place- which group had set up somewhere first or how much space another community had been distributed. Consequently, Ari and Xander spent much less time distributing the essentials like food and water and more time settling squabbles between communities.

The greatest issue that seemed to arise was that none of the Elemential villager groups wished to be housed anywhere near the Gypsies. Understandable of course, but it's not like there was much of a choice. Space was limited and time was running out.

An evacuation on this scale had not previously been attempted as far as Aristide knew. He had now read most of his ancestor's journals and to his knowledge, Lunacia had never come under threat from an outside force before. There were no policies or procedures in place for an event like this.

The Council had a meeting with all the royals when Nanu first told Izzy of the Emperor's plans. King John wanted to go on the offensive suggesting they take the ships out and meet them in the open water. The only problem with that idea, Lunacia only had five war ships. Five against twenty-seven was never going to be good odds. Plus, the ships from the Northern Mainland were exceptionally large and outfitted with many cannons. Lunacia's naval fleet was no match for them.

This was the reality that Queen Isabella was now facing. Whatever was to happen, there weren't enough soldiers, there wasn't enough food and there wasn't enough time to do anything about either problem. For Lunacia, the waiting game had begun.

"Did you direct the southern Gypsy tribe to the dressing hall?" Xander asked one of the guards posted near the gate.

"As requested, Your Majesty," he replied.

"And what about the western tribe, did they go with them?"

"Some of them did. The others chose to remain just outside the castle walls. They said something about not being able to walk on stone for fear of losing their connection to nature," the guard rolled his eyes.

"Just keep an eye on them okay?"

"As you wish, Your Majesty," the guard said before returning to his post.

Xander rubbed his temples. Tension plagued his neck which sent sharp pains up into his head. He'd been running on little sleep for the past few days trying to organise everything that Izzy couldn't. She'd been torn between spending time with their new baby in the nursery and trying to resolve the many questions from her people. But Xander knew his wife needed the help and agreed to work with Constance to manage the evacuation process.

Constance had left to update the Queen on their progress, so he'd asked Aristide to take a break from dealing with the Council so he could come down and help him at the gates. With the sheer amount of people that were coming through the gates he needed all the help he could muster to avoid it all descending into chaos – although from the outside it looked very much like chaos.

"You need to take a break," Aristide said, walking up to Xander. "You've been out here all night."

The Fire King looked at his cousin, he somehow still managed to look like he'd had a full night's sleep – even though he'd been sailing to and from Waterford ferrying citizens across the channel all night.

"I think we all need a break, but it isn't exactly an opportune time to take one," Xander said. "Besides, we're almost done here.

The scouts said there isn't anyone left in any of the villages or Gypsy camps."

Ari nodded, "All the people from my island are accounted for except for the guards who are staying behind to guard the castle," he said.

"How many?"

"Eighty-three."

"Good. Okay, well once this last lot of people have come through, I'm going to find Izzy and see if we can get some rest," Xander said yawning.

Ari smiled, "Sounds like a good plan."

"DID YOU GET WHAT I requested?" Constance asked the man at the end of the shadowed alley.

"I did, but you have to know, this is the last time," he said.

Constance took the small package from him and tucked it into her cloak, "I won't need you again anyway, so you needn't worry about getting caught," she said.

"No pun intended young miss, but you're playing with fire. If the Queen were to find out..."

She cut him off. "The Queen won't find out unless you open your big fat mouth about it."

Constance left the man standing there and rushed out of the alley towards Aristide who was working only a short distance away. Thankfully for her, Ari had not seen where she'd come from. He offered her a warm smile and a wave as she approached him.

"Is everything going okay down here?" she asked – her hand traced the outline of the small package through the layer of her cloak. As if to check it was still safely tucked away.

"We are just finishing up here," he replied shifting a bag of grain from one wagon to another.

Constance's eyebrows rose. "That's a lot of grain," she said with a slight nod towards the wagons.

"It's not nearly enough," Ari said. "This will probably only last about a week with everyone that's now here."

"Well we will just have to get more then, won't we?" she said in her overly chipper voice. "I'll go see if I can organise another wagon."

Aristide grabbed her arm as she went to walk off. "There isn't anymore. This is all there is," he said. "Well, this and what's already been taken inside to the storage area."

Constance scoffed. "What do you mean this is all there is? Surely there is enough food- didn't people bring their own from the villages?"

Ari pursed his lips and let out a huff of air through his nose. "No one has the ability to be able to tend their gardens while they're locked inside the castle walls Constance. All the fresh food they've brought with them will rot in less than a week."

Aristide was getting a little bit tired of having to explain things to the new princess. She wasn't exactly stupid, just naïve – and she didn't think. He supposed it was also due to her age and lack of proper upbringing for a royal. But it still annoyed him to no end.

"Oh," was all she could say.

The Water King could see she was looking for something to do to be helpful and suggested, "You can go, make sure everyone inside is okay. See if the guard numbers inside are sufficient? We have a couple of the Gypsy tribes that have taken refuge in one of the halls with a few of the citizen villages."

Constance nodded and strode off towards the main castle.

THE NOISE WAS DEAFENING. Shouts and screams from each side of the room echoed back from opposite walls straight into Constance's ears. She shook her head trying to think straight. What she saw; Gypsies on one side of the room, and Elemential citizens on the other – a clear divide between them down the middle. The loudest yelling came from a Gypsy Elder who had hold of a basket of carrots – he was lobbing them at the Elementials.

Constance looked back and forth to each side. The Gypsies would throw a piece of food at the citizens – the citizens would throw something else back. It looked like a massive food fight.

"ENOUGH!" she shouted as loudly as possible, her voice echoing off the back wall of the room.

To her shock, every single person in the hall stopped mid throw – *a princess was in the room now and everyone should cease their ridiculous bickering or else,* she thought.

After a moment of quiet – everyone staring at her, including the guards who had no idea she could yell so loudly, Constance walked slowly up the middle of the room to the steps at the other end.

It was a dais of sorts – more of a platform though.

She turned around slowly to face the crowd. What was she going to say? She'd not had to address people like this before. Constance had only been referred to as a princess by Izzy for about a week by this point, so she was still in the habit of her old way of thinking – that she was useless and insignificant and anything she had to say would be disregarded because it had come from a child. But she was a child no longer.

Her hands started shaking and sweat started forming along her brow. Nerves rose from deep within her stomach. She wondered if this is how Izzy felt every single time she had to speak to a large crowd.

A loud creak came from her right. A murmur spread through the crowd and Constance turned her head.

*Oh, thank the stars for that,* she thought as she saw Izzy walk in accompanied by two of her guards and Nanu.

The Queen – in all her grace, joined Constance up on the platform. Izzy sent a small smile the girl's way and turned to the crowd.

"This is how it's going to be," she said. "In case it has escaped your notice, we are about to be at war. We do not, I repeat, *do not* have the luxury nor the resources to entertain the notion of wasting food, no matter the circumstances. You *will* clean up this mess, you *will* try and salvage any of the food that has been thrown around the room, and you will *get along*," the last two words were said through gritted teeth.

The Gypsy man who was loudly yelling earlier tried to say something to the Queen, but she held up her hand to silence him and continued. "It is not by choice that we find ourselves in this situation. And it is not by choice that we are having to cram everyone inside the castle walls for protection. But hear me now, anyone who is seen to be disturbing the peace will find themselves with a very sore rear end from landing on it as my guards throw you out the gates," and with that, she left. Head held high and Constance trailing right behind her.

A LETTER HAD COME IN with one of the last fishing ships taking refuge in the harbour. It was from the Emperor. Somehow, the fishing ship had crossed paths with the fleet on its way home and had come out unscathed, only because they needed a messenger.

One of the castle's guards rushed into the throne room where Izzy was waiting to meet Xander and Aristide. The two of them had sent word that they were nearly finished at the gate and would meet her for lunch shortly.

The guard clutching the letter in shaking hands handed it to the Queen.

The seal was unbroken. The Queen ran one finger across the red wax. It was still intact – a fierce-looking dragon with flames spewing from its mouth stared up at Izzy.

She broke the seal – the soft crack the only sound in the room as the other nobles looked on, eager to know what the letter held.

Izzy was tempted to walk out of the room taking the letter with her. She would have also been just as happy to throw it in the bin. But alas, as Queen she knew she could not.

The paper was thick, but it was not smooth in her hands as she unfolded it. Scanning the contents, she audibly gasped. Xander had arrived moments after she received the letter and rushed to the Queen's side peering over her shoulder as she read it.

Izzy's eyes darted around the room, silently weighing the importance of one against the many.

"What does it say?" asked one of the noblemen stepping into the middle of the room.

Xander shook his head, a warning to Izzy not to read it aloud. But she couldn't keep this from her people. Her heart was torn, her love and loyalty fighting with reason and duty. She knew which one she had to follow as much as it would hurt.

She began, "It's from the Emperor – signed by his own hand."

Nanu stood – a quick intake of breath the only sign she was worried about what was to come next. It was obvious that a peace treaty wasn't to be expected, but even still the maid had only spent a brief time with her brother and in that time, she'd learned he was not a man to play games with.

"It says that my Uncle Maximus is still alive," Izzy said trying to fight back tears. She wasn't sure the source of her tears though – were they joy or sadness?

"What does he want in return for bringing him home?" King John had been irritatingly silent throughout the entire process of organising the citizens. Leaving Izzy to make all the decisions and preparations.

"It's not something we can give," she said as she lowered her head and handed the letter to her uncle who now stood before her.

The Earth King took the letter and skimmed the scratchy writing, "How do we even know he is telling the truth?" he said shoving the letter into Xander's chest.

"We don't," replied Izzy. "But can we really take that chance?"

The nobleman who spoke earlier pressed further, "Would either of you care to tell us what he wants? I know I'd like to see Prince Maximus home."

The gathered crowd in the throne room mumbled their agreement with the nobleman.

Izzy looked towards her uncle who gave a slight nod, "He wants me to surrender Lunacia to his rule, in exchange he will release Maximus."

The nobleman was silent – as was every other person in the room.

Xander was the first to speak, "We will not sacrifice our lands for the possibility that he is telling the truth," he looked to Izzy for her approval – she nodded. "There is no way to tell if the Emperor is just using the Queen's emotional attachment to her uncle to gain control here, or if he actually has Maximus alive. It's been five years since Maximus and his ships left our harbour. We know from King Christian's trial with the evidence that was presented, that he had a hand in Maximus's fleet being overrun by the Emperor's men. Who's to say that Maximus hasn't been dead this whole time," he paused to take a breath. "We just can't take that risk."

"And not to mention," Izzy continued where her husband left off, "There is no way we would ever relinquish the control of our lands to this madman."

The Queen snatched the letter from Xander and tore it to pieces throwing them into the air and setting them on fire. Ashes rained down over her ebony hair – her eyes held a fury only those who bore witness to her Uncle's demise would have recognised.

"These are our islands," she said loudly enough so that even those in the far corners of the grand room would be able to hear her clearly. "I will never see them in the hands of that blood sucking insect. I give you my word, as I stand here before you, I will fight until my dying breath to protect every person that lives in Lunacia. As my father, King Theodore, did before me. I will fight until the life leaves my eyes and the spark leaves my soul. He will never add Lunacia to his list of conquests."

"Here, here," the nobleman shouted – to which the crowd echoed.

"One more thing," the Fire Queen said. "I'm going to get my uncle back – one way or another."

# 2

"Why are we coming down here again?" Agnes asked as she followed Izzy to the dungeons.

The Queen lifted her dress slightly, so it didn't drag in the mud and replied, "I still have questions. Questions that didn't get answered because things happened so quickly. We sort of just threw her down here and didn't give her a second thought."

Agnes pursed her lips and stared the Queen down hoping she would reconsider. "It's not wise to be talking to prisoners. You should have your guards question her if you need to know so badly." She picked up a torch from the wall, "What sort of questions do you have anyway?"

"Firstly, I want to know who her parents are. Or how she came to have this sort of magic. Was she born with it?" Izzy wondered if that was the case for all of the All-Powerful Children. Were they all born with powers like the Elementals were?

That would've been the most logical answer and Izzy really hoped that was the case. She couldn't begin to fathom the problems that might arise from magic that could be acquired.

*I wonder if that's why the Emperor wants Lunacia so badly. Does he know something I don't?* she pondered.

The air was stuffy and smelled of moss and excrement. The girls weren't sure if the smell was from animals or humans as the pig pen was right outside the vent holes to the dungeons. Either way, the stench was foul and nauseating.

Mud stuck to Agnes's shoes – she tried to scrape it off as they moved from the dirt path to the cobbled area leading to the dungeons, but it was gluggy and stuck like glue. She tried hard not to think of what could be in the mud to create that consistency.

"I don't think you're going to get many answers from a girl you knocked out and have had locked up ever since," Agnes gestured around. "It's not exactly a palace down here."

Izzy frowned, "I know, and I'm sorry for that. But she must understand that she came in threatening me and my people. I wasn't really left with much of a choice. If it weren't for Jackson, there wouldn't be much left of me right now I don't think."

"I guess you're right," the other girl conceded.

The guards unlocked the back gate so they could enter – the screech of the hinges sent a chill up Izzy's spine.

They walked down the passage and Izzy was reminded of her visit to Ashin all those months ago. He had been held in the Terranian dungeons, nonetheless, it felt eerily similar. Prisoners pleaded and reached through the bars towards the Queen. Water ran down a drain channel between the path and the cells and Izzy was thankful for the separation – even though the channel was only narrow.

The cell where Nova was being held was right down the end of the west section of the dungeons. The guards told the girls how they hadn't heard so much as a peep out of her since they locked her in there. They said she would calmly come to the bars for her food and return to her bed without speaking. Granted, they'd left her wrists shackled – a fact Izzy was just discovering now as they approached the cell.

"Guards," Izzy turned on them angrily. "Why is the prisoner still shackled? There is no way she can use any form of magic inside these walls. You know this!"

The guards exchanged a look of guilt with each other and then both turned back to the Queen. "I don't know. We only just came on shift here this morning, Your Majesty. We would normally be working at the harbour," he said. "But with the invasion coming, we were moved here."

Izzy rolled her eyes, "I do not want to hear the excuses and blame shifting. Undo her shackles this instant. She is in a cell that blocks all magic, shackles are completely unnecessary," the Queen sighed and looked at the girl sitting on her bed watching the conversation- a scowl cemented on her face.

The guards did as they were told and relocked the cell. Just because the dungeons blocked all magic, didn't mean the girl wasn't still a threat outside her cell. The Queen might be brazen coming down here to talk to Nova, but she wasn't stupid enough to be inside the cell with her – even non-magical hands could still do a lot of damage, and Izzy wasn't exactly used to physical confrontation.

Nova stayed sitting on her bed rubbing her wrists – scowl still held firmly in place. Izzy wondered if perhaps they had been too tight.

"Hello," the Queen said. "Is it okay if I ask you a few questions?"

The girl didn't respond, nor did she break eye contact.

"I don't think she is very fond of you," Agnes said quietly to the Queen.

Izzy made a soft sound of agreement before saying, "I think perhaps we should start over. My name is Isabella Lunakeep, Queen of Firestorm," she paused. "I understand your name is Nova?"

Still with the scowl – the girl nodded. This was a start.

"And you blame me for my father drugging you all those years?"

Again, Nova nodded.

It might've been annoying to only get nods in return, but at least it was a start to conversing with the girl.

"Who are your parents?" Izzy asked. "Do I know them?"

Nova cocked her head to the side and narrowed her eyes but gave no sign she planned to answer this question.

Instead she asked, "Where's my necklace?"

"What necklace?" Agnes asked.

The girl stood up from her bed and made a show of moving her sheet around on the mattress, "When I was brought here, I was wearing my necklace. I had it when I woke up after the first," she paused, "Problem. But when I woke up this morning – it was gone."

"We aren't in the business of stealing people's necklaces, Nova. I'm sure it will be in there somewhere if you came in with it."

Nova shook her head. "No. You're wrong. When I went to sleep last night, I know I had it on because I was playing with it. But when I woke up this morning it was gone."

"Maybe you just need to take another look?" Agnes offered.

The girl huffed and turned to sit back down, "You really aren't very bright, are you?" she directed at Agnes. "Don't you think I've looked already? This cell is only so big, and I don't exactly have much to keep me occupied during the day. I have been looking. It's not here. Someone stole it!"

Izzy looked at Agnes. Hoping her friend would gather the meaning behind her look of, '*Why would anyone want to steal her necklace?*' – Agnes shrugged her shoulders.

"I'll look into it. Now will you answer my question?" the Queen asked.

"Not until you bring my necklace back. It's all I have left of my family," Nova said, "Then I'll answer any questions you want."

That was it, Izzy knew the girl would stay true to her words. The two girls started walking back out past the other cells. There was no way Nova was going to answer any more questions without her necklace being returned. But the Queen couldn't think why anyone would want to steal it – let alone anyone who could get in and out of the noisy cell gate without waking Nova up.

As if Agnes was thinking the same thing she said, "Peculiar isn't it that she didn't wake up when someone came into her cell?"

Izzy nodded in agreement – her mind reeling over the possibilities. *Who could have done this? Was Nova lying? No, surely not. She wouldn't lie about something like this. It makes no sense.*

"So, what are we going to do?" Agnes asked.

Izzy shrugged her shoulders, "I'm not sure to be honest. I'm going to ask around though – see if the other guards on duty last night saw anything."

Agnes placed the torch back in its holder and sighed. "Why is it that I always seem to find myself in the middle of all the drama that happens in this castle?" she smiled ruefully.

"Ha!" Izzy laughed. "Just remember you're the one who begs to come along. If you somehow get involved that's your own fault."

The other girl stopped walking and said, "I just don't want a repeat of what happened last time. With all this magic inside us and yet we were all standing there not knowing how to protect you from her." Her eyes darted back towards the dungeons where Nova sat quietly in her cell.

Izzy inhaled deeply. She knew why Agnes was worried – and how could she not be? Nova was unpredictable and no one really knew the depths of the power she inside her. Luna forbid she escaped somehow. "I don't think you need worry yourself, Cousin," the Queen said knowing that they all had every reason to worry. "She isn't going anywhere anytime soon," *I hope*, she finished in her head.

"I DON'T REALLY THINK it's something I'm interested in right now," Aristide said to Xander as they made their way down the balcony corridor towards the Council meeting room. Xander had been pressing to find out when Ari was going to marry the girl he was promised to. "I don't even know her."

"You've got your entire life to get to know her," the Fire King said.

Ari raised an eyebrow at his cousin, "And you would've been perfectly content to just marry whoever was picked out for you? What if it wasn't Izzy? Would you still have been happy with any old girl?"

"That's not the point," Xander replied defeated. "I got lucky. I hadn't been promised again since the first one failed so miserably. Besides..."

But his sentence was cut off by a body coming towards him. He was barrelled to the ground, intertwined in the yards of excess fabric that was the girl's dress.

Aristide just stood there laughing of course and not helping.

The girl managed to straighten out her bright orange dress and untangle herself from the Fire King when he noticed that it wasn't just any girl. It was Constance.

"You need to watch where you're going," he said a little more gruffly than he intended.

The girl looked at him sheepishly as she inspected a small rip in the bottom of her skirt, "I'm sorry. I wasn't looking where I was going."

Constance started frantically looking around on the ground for something.

"Did you drop something?" Ari asked as he saw the girl relax when she found the small box she'd dropped.

Constance quick as lightning snatched it up and hid it away in the folds of her dress.

"What is it?" Xander asked.

The eyes of a guilty person never stay fixed for long as she answered him, "Nothing. It's nothing. Just one of my necklaces I sent out to get cleaned."

Ari and Xander glanced at each other suspiciously – their arched eyebrows and side eyes revealing much about the look that passed between them.

As if she could read each of their minds, she proffered the box to them, "Seriously, that's what it is. See?"

As she opened the box, the two boys looked in. Sure enough, there was the necklace she often wore. Shiny and silver, the crescent moon pendant sparkled under the rays of the midday sun that filtered in under the awning.

"Look, I have to go. But it was nice bumping into you," she said with a giggle.

Aristide gave a mock bow to the princess as she toddled off.

"Did you think that was as odd as I did?" he asked Xander.

"Just a little bit," he replied picking up a couple of pieces of paper that he'd dropped in the fall. "But as I was saying, you probably should try and at least get to know some of these girls," Xander gestured to the list of names he held.

Ari rolled his eyes and accompanied it with a groan. "Fine," he said. "But remember this moment when I come back to you after a year of marriage asking you to help me get out of it because she's desperately unhappy."

Xander laughed, "I would think that any girl that ended up marrying you wouldn't complain," he said. "Haven't you heard? You're Lunacia's most eligible bachelor right now."

"Just perfect," Ari replied sarcastically.

"WHY DON'T YOU COME to bed?" Xander asked his wife. "It's late."

He'd found her holding their infant son in the nursery. Her eyes were glassy, a sure sign they had not long since been full of tears.

Izzy looked up from their son's face and met her husband's gaze. "I just wanted to squeeze in one more cuddle before bed," she said.

Xander sighed. "You're not going to be any good to anyone unless you get some sleep," he said. "The nursemaid will look after him tonight."

The Queen had taken an unusual approach to being a mother. It was the norm for Queens and noblewomen to have a wet nurse, but Izzy had decided that she wanted to feed and raise their son herself. His nursery was adjoined to their chambers, so it wasn't far for Izzy to go to tend to him if he woke during the night – which he often did. Even people without children know that tending to a baby throughout the night is exhausting, let alone for a Queen that is trying to figure out how to save her kingdom from being invaded.

Izzy shot her husband a look that said, *'Do you really think I'm going to listen to you?'* before she placed the sleeping babe back down in his crib.

The fireplace crackled quietly, and Izzy wandered over to the balcony to look out across the water. A chill was drifting in from the sea and she wondered if it was Luna's way of telling her their enemies were getting closer.

"What do you think will happen to our son if they manage to sack the city?" she asked.

Xander walked up behind her and reached his arms around her. "That's not going to happen," he said. "They might have weapons, but we have magic on our side. The Emperor has no idea the power we hold."

Izzy craned her neck to look back up at him. "I picked a name today."

His eyes lit up. "You did?" A smile spread quickly across his face showing his unbridled joy.

She nodded. "Emory. It means home strength and industrious leader."

Xander held his wife a little tighter. "I think it's perfect," he said. "And very fitting for these trying times."

"Emory Cole," she said. "Cole after your father."

A tear formed in the corner of Xander's eye and rolled down his cheek. "I'm sure he would've been very proud to know that."

Izzy nodded and returned her gaze to the ocean that stretched out from the cliffs.

The Firestorm castle wasn't built along the shore's edge like the Irrigal and Kaloin castles. No, Edenfore was constructed slightly inland from the coast to avoid the violent tides and harsh winds. But as nothing was built between the castle and the water, there was a clear view to the huge and rocky passage between Firestorm and Aerleon.

The Queen and her King summoned the nursemaid, once she'd arrived, they headed towards the door that led to their chambers. *Perhaps,* she thought, i*t was time she got a good night's sleep. Luna only knew how long it would be before that opportunity would come around again.*

Izzy laid her hand on the doorknob to their adjoining room, "Did you talk to Ari about it being time for him to find a bride and marry?"

Xander laughed. "I did, but somehow I don't think he was too excited about the prospect."

The Queen rolled her eyes, "Of course, he isn't, but he really needs..."

She was interrupted, a man burst into the nursery room. Izzy instinctively conjured a large ball of fire in her palms and coated it in lightning sparks readying to hurl it at the man if he dared to go near their son.

"A message," was all the man managed to choke out as he huffed and puffed. Clearly out of breath from climbing the eight flights of stairs it takes to get up to the royal chambers.

Xander ran to the man and took the paper from him – Izzy right behind him.

The Fire King opened it, quickly read it, and looked to the Queen.

"Well," she asked. "What does it say?"

Xander turned to the messenger and told him to leave.

"You really need to tell me what's going on," said Izzy her panic mounting.

"I don't know how to say this," he said. "They found Jenta dead in her chambers."

Izzy stared at her husband unable to speak. The Councilwoman had long been a supporter of the young Queen's reign.

"It says that she was brutally murdered. We need to go," said Xander.

"IF WHOEVER DID THIS can get past the guards to a Council member, then no one is safe," Ari bellowed at Jackson who'd attended the scene to investigate.

Izzy and Xander burst into the room and were confronted with the horrific scene of Jenta's dismembered body. Her torso lay on the bed, but her head was nowhere to be seen.

Aristide addressing Jackson, "I'll deal with you shortly. Don't go anywhere." He took a step to position himself between the bloody scene behind him, and the clearly distressed Queen.

"Who would do something like this?" she pleaded in the hopes that she'd be told they had already found and arrested the monster responsible.

Ari shook his head, "We don't know yet." He glared at Jackson who was now studying the remains of the well-loved Councilwoman.

Izzy pushed her cousin aside and walked over toward the bed where she lay. Dried blood stained the sheets and Council paperwork lay strewn across the rest of the bed. The Queen fell to her knees – Jenta's corpse now at eye level.

"Izzy," Xander calmed his wife with a touch to her shoulder. "Come away. You don't need to see this."

"She was my friend," she said. She could barely find the strength to tear her eyes away from the carnage before her. A hollow sensation in the pit of her stomach, the nausea rising to the back of her throat. Izzy placed her hand on her stomach and pursed her lips in the hope of holding back the bile.

Xander looked back at Ari for support and the Water King moved closer. "She was friends with us all," he said.

"Then why...who?" she wailed. Words escaped her and tears ran down her cheeks unable to be controlled any longer. The kohl eye-liner staining her cheeks and jaw line. Her bottom lip quivered from the threat of unleashing a flood of emotions.

The Fire King, worried that Izzy might let her powers explode from within led her back to their rooms where Nanu, her ever-present confidante was waiting for her. He asked the maid to draw a bath for the Queen so she could wash the dried blood from her feet. Izzy hadn't even stopped to put slippers on before rushing to the Councilwoman's chambers.

Aristide later spoke with Jackson to try and figure out exactly who was on guard duty in Jenta's residential section and anyone could have committed such brutality undetected. All the nobles and Council members shared a wing with a handful of guards to patrol the corridors. It was likely the guards were at the other end of the wing when the murderer came to the Councilwoman's rooms- a scenario that Ari believed entirely plausible.

Jackson vowed he would not rest until the killer was found and brought to justice. But Ari told him that even though he was upset earlier, everyone, especially the Master of the Guard, needed to be well-rested with the looming invasion. Unfortunately, finding Jenta's murderer would have to wait for now.

Jackson was clearly feeling the pressure of his position. He had not been leader of the military for long and this was his first real failure. If the culprit wasn't captured, then surely people would be expecting him to be stripped of his position.

"So, what have you found out so far?" Xander asked when he returned to the scene after settling his wife into bed.

Jackson used a cloth to wipe the sweat from his brow. "We don't know much, but what we do know is that whoever did this didn't leave a single shred of evidence. The sheer ferocity of Jenta's slaying surely, they would've been covered in blood? But there are no footprints, no smudge marks in the blood and no sign of anyone entering or exiting. The doors were also locked from the inside," he said.

Ari shared a troubled look with Xander. How were they supposed to find a killer that left no evidence behind?

# 3

"Are you joking?" Ari asked Xander incredulously shortly after they had left Jenta's rooms.

A sly smirk crept across the Fire King's lips. "Not in the slightest," he said. "Irrespective of what else is going on, I'm serious about you needing to find a wife."

The Water King put his palm to his forehead in disbelief. "Now is not the time Xan. We have other things on our plate to worry about first."

Xander gave Ari a playful shove. "There's no harm in meeting her," he said.

Ari's eyes grew wide. "What? You've already organised it?"

The smirk quickly spread into a full-sized grin. "You bet. Tomorrow morning. She's coming to Edenfore to meet you."

"Do I know her?" he asked.

"I don't think you've met this one. I know you've met her sister. You spectacularly rejected her when your mother paraded her in front of you," said Xander.

Ari rolled his eyes. "So, it's Manta's sister?"

A slight nod from Xander said yes.

Manta was introduced to Aristide at one of the many balls his mother used to host. It was about five years ago before everything went sour between them. Ari's mother decided that she would choose who he was going to marry. Of course, the Water King had a different opinion on the matter. She became pushy and it drove a wedge between her and her son. Ari got so sick of hearing his mother nag at him day in and day out that he sent her to live on the other side of Waterford under the guise of them needing her extensive experience overseeing trades and export. That was all a lie of course, but he'd quite honestly had enough. At least this way she was out of his way and given that she really didn't have any reason to come to the castle – that, and Ari was rarely at home on Waterford as he spent much of his time on Firestorm, the two rarely had cause to see each other.

There wasn't anything wrong with Manta. Not really. Ari just wasn't in the mood to strike up a relationship with someone so soon after losing his father. And he thought perhaps his mother pushing him so much was her way of coping with the grief of losing him also. That aside though, he had been rather rude to her when they last met. And now with Xander having set up a meeting with her younger sister, Ari wasn't quite sure the girl would be too interested in him for any other reason besides the fact he was a king – which is exactly the kind of woman Ari had simply no interest in.

Ari had long dreamed of meeting a girl the traditional way. That is, without it being a set up. He believed that true love could never blossom by force. He was starting to rethink that given his younger sister Hela had fallen madly in love with her new husband. But that surely was an exception. There is no way that Ari could see himself falling in love with a girl because he was told to.

"She's apparently very smart," Xander cut into Ari's thoughts.

Aristide shot him a foul look. "Is that code for she's not very pretty but she makes up for it in brains?"

Xander let out a full-blown belly laugh. "Something like that," he said still laughing.

As they walked along the dimly lit corridor to their chambers, servants and nobles alike gathered in the halls. They'd come to see if they could find out any more information about what happened to Jenta. So far, the rest of the palace had only been told that something had happened to her. They didn't yet know what, why or how.

"Look at them all," Ari said disgusted. "They're like vultures. The second there's any kind of gossip or news to be spread, it's around the castle in no time."

Xander hummed in agreement before saying, "If news gets out that she was murdered, we are going to have a situation on our hands."

"In case you haven't noticed, we already have a situation on our hands with the number of citizens and gypsies taking up residence inside the castle walls," Ari said giving Xander a pointed look.

A silent nod was Xander's response.

"Our list of suspects just grew exponentially. Jenta was the one to pass the law that prohibited Gypsies from owning land on Firestorm," said Ari.

"There's no way a Gypsy could make it that far into the castle unnoticed though," Xander replied.

"Not unless they had help."

Xander let out a massive sigh that sounded more like a whine. "Why does everything have to be so complicated? Why can't we all just get along?"

"We wouldn't need Kings and Queens if we could all get along now, would we? And we certainly wouldn't need a Council."

They'd reached Aristide's door and he reached his hand for the doorknob, "I'll see you in the morning," he said as he turned it.

"Bright and early in the parlour. Your new bride will be waiting," Xander teased.

"Ugh, fine. But you owe me," Ari said. "I think a month of you doing all my paperwork should suffice. And that still doesn't mean that I'm going to marry her. I'm just agreeing to meet her."

Xander waved goodnight to his cousin and continued down the hallway laughing to himself as he made his way to his room where his wife was waiting.

WATER TRICKLED DOWN the bricks next to Nova's head, and for the first time since her imprisonment she felt awash with despair. The Queen hadn't given her any hope of when or even if she would ever be released. Feelings of dread started building deep within her. Would she be locked up here for the rest of her days?

But after a while she realised that feeling deep within her wasn't dread. It was the gentle rising of something else – something deeper and more elusive.

Sitting on the cot in the corner of her cell, Nova brushed the droplets of water from her forehead with the back of her hand. Her clothes were now covered in filth and grime – a far sight from the intricate detail of the gypsy skirt that was buried beneath.

She ran her fingers over the cracks in the mortar and a spark jumped from the tips of her fingers to the wall. It was as if the wall itself was feeding off some kind of magic and the cracks began to mend themselves. Nova followed the mending fissure to the window that loomed high above her head. Outside, the stars twinkled on the blanket of darkness that was the night sky.

The girl remembered a time when she was much younger, laying for hours on the roof of her caravan staring into the sky's infinite oblivion. Life had seemed so much easier, then she made the worst decision of her life- taking her anger out on a Queen. A Queen who really hadn't done anything against her.

Nova's stomach twisted, the sparks from the wall danced toward her in tendrils of light mixed with darkness.

She stood, looking at the sea of wispy, vine-like strings of light, seeking her out. Nova reached out her hand– her fingers drawing nearer to them as if being pulled by some invisible force.

The tip of her finger brushed against them and a rush of what felt like pure energy ran up her arm and deep down into her very core.

A noise behind Nova startled her, she whipped around only to realise it was just the two guards entering her cell the same as had happened every night since her imprisonment.

Turning back toward the wall she saw that the tendrils were gone, vanished into thin air as quickly as they'd come. *"Did I just imagine all of that?"* she wondered.

"Oi, girl," the taller of the two guards said. "You know the drill. Get over here."

Without making a fuss, Nova picked up the chair from the opposite corner and placed it in front of the two guards before taking a seat.

Nova had tried to fight them off the first few times they'd entered her cell, but it always ended the same way, with her being beaten into submission. Their beatings were enough to cause her pain, but they were never vicious enough to leave a mark that couldn't be easily healed by the Medica and his salve. Just before the change of shift, the guards would call the Medica from his quarters. The old man would sigh and shake his head, but he wouldn't say a word. His only task was to apply the magical salve that made her still forming bruises, from the nightly beatings, vanish. Although the salve may have taken away the visible signs of the bruising it certainly didn't heal the pain they caused underneath.

Nova was beginning to wonder if she should've eaten some humble pie when the Queen had come to visit her. Were these beatings happening by her orders in the hopes of loosening her tongue on other matters?

But Nova was determined to stand her ground. She wanted her necklace back. It had been blessed by her mother and grandmother on the day of her birth. It was her only connection to her home. The half-crescent pendant, she was told, was the source of her magic.

Nova had long since known she was special. She was told from an early age that her magic was not like the magic of the Gypsies – nor was it like the magic of the Elementials. It was something different – something far more dangerous. Her mother always told her that no one knew what she was capable of because powers like hers had not been seen in someone entering adulthood since ancient times.

There was little documentation of a power like Nova's and most of it was only survived by way of fireside songs and children's stories. Nova wondered if the Elementials possessed records of another like her.

When the guards and the Medica finally exited her cell, she climbed into her cot and pulled up the covers, desperate to hide from what lay beyond the warmth they brought. But the feeling had returned. Her stomach was twisting, and her hands felt clammy. She pulled her hands out from under the blanket to see that her palms were now almost glowing blue. The blood rushed through the veins on the back of her hands – she could feel her heart beating in her throat.

Nova sat up and shoved the covers down. She was suddenly far too hot, and she felt like the walls of her tiny cell were closing in on her.

A magnificent light burst from her in every direction – the most electrifying blue. Illuminating not just her cell, but the night sky outside her window was enveloped with a beam of light. The brick work around the small window began to shift and crack. All the self-healing it had done, was now coming undone in a matter of moments.

A drop of water from the bricks above, landed on her forehead waking her from what she then recognised was just a dream. She looked down at her palms which were now of course just the normal tan colour they always were – albeit still covered in a layer of dungeons grime.

For the rest of the night, Nova sat on her cot with her back up against the wall staring at the palms. How much of what just happened was a dream? She wasn't sure if she'd dreamt about the guards coming in or if she had been dreaming when she saw the tendrils of light coming from the walls. But one thing she did know, was that the feeling of magic in the pit of her stomach was still there, as if it was waiting for something. Was it waiting for her to open herself up and welcome it – or was the magic waiting for its moment to consume her?

# 4

Why did it have to be so bright first thing in the morning? Aristide certainly wasn't made for getting up with the sun. Bleary eyes and tousled hair greeted him when he found his reflection in the looking glass. A splash of water would hopefully take away the obvious signs of little sleep.

It had been a rough night for all the royals. No one truly slept – not with Jenta's killer still on the loose in the castle somewhere.

The image of her corpse just lying there lingered in his mind's eye. Like a brand it was seared, showing itself to him like the sun shows itself to the land in the morning – inescapable. His cousin's terror-filled scream rang loudly in his ears – her voice cracked as the air she tried to breathe in escaped her reach.

As Ari turned from the basin, he shook his head trying to shake loose the image from his mind. He looked towards the chair where his shirt lay haphazardly cast aside from the night before. Spots of blood on the cuff the only evidence it wasn't all a freakish nightmare.

Shrugging a clean shirt on well, mostly clean, Aristide left his rooms and padded down to the dining hall. His stomach was screaming out with hunger. After what they'd all seen the night before, his usual midnight snack was forgotten about – not that he would've been able to eat anything anyway without being sick.

A guard opened the great wooden doors for him to enter, and as they creaked open Constance appeared at his back.

"Good morning," she said with an all-too cheerful tone in her voice. "Did you sleep well, Your Majesty?"

Ari narrowed his eyes at the new Princess. "Why in Luna's sake would you think I could sleep well?" the tone in his voice was a tad sharper than he intended but, nonetheless, he had a point.

Constance put her hands up. "No need to get grumpy with me," she said. "I was just being polite. But I won't ask you how you are in the future if you're going to snap at me like that."

*Oh, for the love of Luna.* Ari thought as he brushed his hair back out of his face with his palms. He wasn't in the mood to deal with her chirpiness, so he just said, "Sorry, no. I did not sleep well."

"Fair enough," Constance replied as she skipped around the Water King and into the dining hall.

He sighed. Not only was he not in the mood to deal with Constance's relentless smiling and happiness, he was supposed to go and meet this Luna forsaken girl that Xander was trying to set him up with. Ari wondered how Xander could still be wanting to continue with this considering Jenta. But he'd made a promise to meet at least one girl from Xander's list. Nadia's family was very wealthy and supported much of the kingdom with their meat production, so they wouldn't take kindly to their daughter being stood up after they'd gone to all that trouble of sending her over to Firestorm for this meeting – even if he was a King.

"Did you even look at yourself this morning?" Xander teased. "Or did you just think that Nadia would find it endearing that you look like you spent the night in the pig pen?" he asked with a laugh.

Ari only grumbled something under his breath as he grabbed a pastry from the table and dropped it onto his plate.

"Look, she's waiting in the courtyard for you for when you've finished your food and you're in a better mood," Xander said.

Ari looked up, "She's here already?" He hadn't expected the meeting to be first thing this morning. It was barely twelve hours since he'd even agreed to be introduced to someone. "You knew you'd get your way and you asked her to come here before I'd even agreed?!"

A smug look crept across Xander's face. "And what if I did?" the smug look slowly morphing into a smile.

"That's very bold of you. What if I'd said no?"

"Well then I would've had to work on you until you had said yes," Xander said as he stood up from the table. "Now get your act together, finish your food and come with me to meet her."

IT WAS SPRING, SO EVERY single flower imaginable was in full bloom around the castle. The Queen's private courtyard was presently the only place within the castle walls that didn't have people making camp on every single inch of the luscious grass. Izzy had decided to keep this one area for her quiet reflection in case she needed some alone time that wasn't inside the dreary stone walls of the castle.

"She's shown great promise in the running of her father's trade enterprise," Xander said to him as they meandered down the pathway.

Ari nodded in agreement, his mind elsewhere still thinking of how Jenta's killer managed to enter her rooms without so much as moving a latch on a window.

"Nadia's also taken to being the spokesperson for the Bill the Aerleon kingdom is trying to pass that will integrate the Gypsy folk into the Elemental society."

Xander's words washed over Ari. Why was he even here right now? Not only did they have an enormous amount of work to get done to prepare for the invasion in just over a week, they also had to work out who killed Jenta to prevent them harming anyone else. He didn't have time for this.

"Xan," Aristide said grabbing hold of his cousin's elbow and pulling him up. "I really think we should..."

"Good morning," a sweet voice cutting him off mid-protest.

The two young Kings turned their heads to see Nadia standing there dressed in a light blue dress that hung loosely off her curvy figure.

"Good morning," Xander greeted her. "I hope your journey to Firestorm was a gentle one."

She bowed her head in agreeance and then looked to Aristide, whom up until this point, had been still as a statue eyes fixed on the maid beside Nadia.

The girl was gorgeous. Breathtakingly, stunningly gorgeous. Aristide's hands grew clammy at just the thought of being able to reach out for hers. Her eyes shone as if reflecting each star in the night sky.

Auburn hair with more red hues than blonde in magnificent curls nestled delicately just below her waist. Pulled back behind her ears, a single diamond nestled in each hair clip was no match for the radiance that emanated from her perfectly glistening smile. The dress she wore was... her body was.... even her feet looked delicate in their beaded silk shoes. Ari had never in his life been left speechless by the beauty of a girl... That was until this very moment. He didn't know where to look. His eyes wanted to ravish every single inch of her body, but propriety dictated that was inappropriate.

So instead, he bypassed Nadia and extended a hand to the maid.

"I'm Aristide," he said sheepishly.

"Ari," Xander whispered reprimanding his wayward cousin. "That is Nadia's maid. What are you doing?"

But with his other hand, Aristide gave Xander a shove that told him he knew exactly what he was doing. Nadia simply stepped aside and stood next to the Fire King.

"I'm so sorry," Xander said to Nadia.

A warm smile grew on her face. "Did you know that Emily has been my maid since we were both very young girls?" she asked.

"No, I didn't" Xander replied.

Nadia looked sideways at him. "She's also been rather unlucky in love the past few years. It's been quite some time since someone looked at her the way that His Majesty just looked at her then."

"Won't your father be unhappy that the king has taken a liking to your maid though?" Xander asked.

Nadia shook her head. "He sees Emily as his own daughter. Since the passing of her parents some years ago from Neeto, he's been like a father to her. And I am certainly not going to stand in the way of letting something blossom. Besides, Emily has had a thing for Aristide since she first laid eyes on him at the games. She won't stop talking about him to be honest."

"Did you have any intention of starting a courtship with the king?" he asked his eyebrow raised.

"Oh goodness no. He is so far from my interests," she said. "But how could I pass up the opportunity to let Emily meet him?"

Aristide had since walked Emily down to the fountain, and they were giggling and chatting as though they'd known each other their entire lives.

"I never thought that he would look past me to her though. So that's rather a shock," Nadia continued. "I'm not the prettiest of girls, I know that but generally I have suitors lining up to say two words to me."

Xander laughed. "But we both know that's because of your father's wealth."

"Which he certainly won't care for because he has enough of his own," she chuckled.

"Would you care for a cup of tea?" Xander asked. "Izzy usually comes down from the nursery around this time looking for food, maybe we could meet up with her? I'm sure she would love to see you."

"I'd love to see her. It's been far too long since I was last here." Nadia took Xander's arm and they left Emily and Aristide in the courtyard to go in search of a warm cup of tea. It may have been a spring day with the sun shining, but an unusually crisp chill lingered in the air. Far too cold to stay outside for too long. "And I'd most dearly love to meet your little Prince. I hear you've named him Emory. What a lovely name for a prince," she said as they made their way inside.

"DID YOU EVEN READ JACKSON'S report?" Izzy asked, frustrated with the lack of answers from the alchemists about Jenta's murder. "It's impossible to have no clues so that we can catch the killer," she continued rifling through the pages of the report. Each one more useless and uninformative than the last.

The alchemist lowered his eyes, "I cannot conjure evidence out of thin air, Your Majesty," he said.

Izzy looked up at him and huffed out a breath. "Do better," was all she could muster.

"But, Your Majesty," he tried to argue. The Queen held up her hand as she saw Jackson entering the room.

"Any news?" she asked.

The Commander shook his head. "Nothing new, Your Majesty."

"Oh, for Luna's sake!" Izzy exploded throwing the paperwork into the air. "I just want to know how they got away with it!"

A confused look crossed Jackson's face. "Who, Your Majesty? Do you know who did this?"

"No, but we should. Didn't you feel the residual magic in the air last night?" she asked, an almost pleading look on her face.

The alchemist who stood listening on but clearly completely forgotten used his Air magic to silently collect the papers back into a pile on the Queen's desk.

"I'm not as sensitive as you are, Your Majesty," Jackson replied.

"Oh, just stop it with the '*Your Majesty*' this, and '*Your Majesty*' that," she snapped. "Did you feel it or not?"

"No, Your M...No," he said quickly correcting himself. "I didn't."

"Well I sure did. I was almost sick it was that strong. And I don't know of anyone that holds that kind of power inside of them except for Nova, and she is safely contained in the dungeons."

Jackson's eyes narrowed, "Are you saying you think there is another All-Powerful Child running about the castle?"

The Queen sat back down and folded her arms across her chest. "Can you give me a better explanation? Because thus far I can't think of another plausible cause."

The Commander took the seat opposite the Queen and put his elbows on the desk. "The journals never said anything about there being two at the same time though."

Izzy shook her head, "No, they didn't. But I was going through the journal of the old court Oracle, I didn't think anything of it at the time, but have a look at this and tell me what you make of it?" she grabbed a journal that was sitting off to the side and slid it across the old oak desk.

Jackson reached his hand out to steady the page and after a moment of studying the disorderly scrawl, he looked up at the Queen, eyes wide with a mixture of shock and intrigue.

"I know," she said. "That was my reaction too.

"What does it say?" the alchemist enquired gingerly. Izzy completely forgetting the old man was still in the room- on reflection she may well have chosen not to start this conversation with him in earshot.

Izzy read, "Power twice does destruction hold, born on the full moon it was foretold. One Elemental heart forever torn, to do what's right and be reborn."

"What do you think it means?" Jackson asked.

"I have no idea, but it wouldn't surprise me if it meant there was a second All-Powerful Child running free in the castle," she said.

Jackson rubbed his eyes, another victim of sleep deprivation. "This is ridiculous! Oracles were proven to be false over a hundred years ago."

Izzy made a side-long glance at the alchemist who was still listening on intently. "Then why is it that everything else that this particular Oracle has foretold has come true then?"

The Commander reached for the old journal again. "Does it say anything else?"

"Only that the Elemental who's heart is forever torn will basically sacrifice themselves in order to stop the destruction- whatever that is."

"So, what now?" he asked. "Can we actually do anything with this information?"

"I want to set up an examination station so that every single person inside the castle grounds will be checked. I want to know the affinity of each citizen's element. We need to have a record of who wields what. Honestly, I don't know why we don't have something already. The record *should* point us straight to the All-Powerful Child that is trying to hide in plain sight," the Queen said lacing her fingers together on the oak table before her.

The alchemist chimed in, "But Your Majesty, we haven't used the power serum in generations."

"Does it not work?" she asked pointedly. "Does it not make the person who ingests it reveal their elemental affinity whether they desire it or not?"

"It does, but it's barbaric," he said. "Forcing people to do something like this is the reason why the people revolted against your family generations ago. Your family was lucky to retain the leadership of Lunacia."

"DO NOT QUESTION ME!" she bellowed as the alchemist shrank away from her. "We have much larger threats coming our way than people's opinions of me. If they don't like it, they can leave. Simple as that."

The alchemist bowed his head and Jackson stood readying to carry out the Queen's instructions, "I'll make the preparations, shall I?"

"Let the people know it is optional. But, if they choose not to take part, they are choosing to leave the castle grounds and the protection and security that comes with it at once. Is that understood?"

Jackson nodded, bowed to the Queen, and exited her study.

The alchemist turned to Izzy, "You left out something, Your Majesty," he said.

"I know," she responded. "But I see no need to create more panic. I have an heir."

"Just because you have an heir, doesn't mean that he, an infant child is ready to take the throne. Why didn't you tell him the part of the prophecy where it says that the one to sacrifice themselves is the Queen?" he asked. "I've been studying these journals for years, Your Majesty. I know what the text says.

"I didn't think it was necessary. We don't even know if any of this will come to pass. I am merely trying to be prepared, but my focus right now is on finding Jenta's killer."

She turned her chair to face the window behind her and said without looking back, "That will be all."

"Yes, Your Majesty," he replied making to leave the room but as he did the Queen addressed him once more.

"And Alchemist, you will not breathe a word to anyone about what was said inside this room today, is that understood?"

The man replied, "Not a word, Your Majesty," as he turned and exited the study.

# 5

Wind rustled through the leaves high up in the canopy – birds could be heard singing their sweet morning song in their nests. Frost glistening on the dry leaves strewn across the forest floor crunched with each step Nova took. And as she looked around at the sunlight passing through the branches, she wondered if her life would always be like this.

Her mother had sent her out into the thick of the forest to find a special type of moss that only grew under one waterfall which lay deep into the unknown. The moss was used by her mother to make a special slime that when mixed with a few other special ingredients, would be rubbed on the boundary trees to the settlement. The slime would induce vivid hallucinations to ward off intruders. It would only work of course if the intruder touched the slime – which of course they inevitably would- they'd lean up against a tree or log to rest at some point during their trek. But the Gypsies always knew which trees were marked.

But there was always one part of the entire process Nova never understood- why was she the one who had to go and collect the moss. Her mother always told her she was special but being special felt more like being her slave. She felt like her mother's errand girl existing solely to do her bidding.

Nova pulled her drink out of her satchel and took swallowed a mouthful. Water always had a strange aftertaste when it came from her calf-skin flask – not like water straight from the creek that was cool and refreshing this had a tangy taste that never quite felt satisfying to her thirst. Her mother insisted however that she must always drink from this calf-skin flask and not any other – something about it being specially blessed for her. Nova didn't really believe in all that magic stuff though. She'd never seen any real evidence of it from the Gypsies. She'd seen the Elementals of course, but they lived so far away, they weren't wandering through camp every other day.

As she led her horse to the lake at the bottom of the waterfall for a drink, he whinnied happily at the lizards basking in the sunlight along the rocky edge. Nova tied his rope to a fallen branch and slipped off her boots. She stepped into the water and its icy coolness shot through her toes making her feel alive. Stars and fire crept up her legs and she stopped, just for a moment, to revel in the feeling the sudden shock sent through her whole body.

The moss lay behind the blanket of the fall, she placed the rest of her over clothes neatly behind her on the warm rocks and slowly lowered the rest of her body into the freezing water.

After returning to camp, she sought out her mother and gave her the satchel of moss, there was a lot this time. Last time she had ventured out to find some the weather was too dry and the waterfall wasn't flowing fast enough so it was slim pickings.

"Nova, what took you so long?" Theodora asked as she stepped out of the wagon.

She sighed, "I took a swim. Is that not okay?"

With a huff, the Gypsy elder took the bag from the girl and said, "You knew I needed this straight away. You had one task. I specifically told you to not get distracted and you couldn't even manage that."

"I'm sorry Mother. I only swam for a few minutes," she said. But when the girl looked around, she noticed it was not even mid-mealtime, the sky beginning its daily sunset show.

By her calculations, the trip out of the camp and back should've only taken three hours total and considering it was barely dawn when she'd left, there was certainly about eight hours of her day that were now unaccounted for.

"Mother?" Nova called to the old woman meekly.

A huff was all she got in answer.

"What's happening to me?" she asked, "I got to the lake, took a sip of water, got the moss, returned to camp, and the next thing I know I've lost over half the day."

Theodora looked her up and down. She motioned for her daughter to come and sit beside her at the making table, "I think it's time," she said.

"Time? For what?" Nova said as she sat beside her mother.

"Time you were told about your powers."

"HOW LONG ARE WE GOING to watch this awkwardness?" Izzy asked Xander as they looked over at Aristide who was gracelessly trying to make a good impression with Emily.

Xander stifled a laugh, "Oh come on. Let him have this. He has been working himself to the bone for the past week."

Izzy rolled her eyes and smiled, "I'm not saying he can't have a relationship," she said, "Just that we have more pressing issues to deal with than watching him flounder."

Ari was trying to show Emily the ancient paintings that lined the Great Hall. She didn't look the least bit interested in what he was saying, so things were not going well. But she kept hold of his arm as they walked along dutifully listening to the history of each painting- one bizarre story after another; someone who fought a boar and a knight from the olden-days that slew a dragon.

Emily looked up at Ari and asked, "Did you say dragon?"

"Oh, here we go," Izzy said under her breath on the other side of the room. She knew that the mythical dragon story was one of Aristide's favourites.

"Did I miss something?" Xander asked her quietly.

Izzy nodded towards the lovebirds, "You wait. This is about to get very animated."

Aristide launched into a story, arms waiving wildly as he began to regale Emily with the tale of the dragon who used to live in the cave at the top of Mount Eldur – the highest mountain on the island of Firestorm.

*"Before the Moon Goddess had a fight with her sister the Sun Goddess, the two co-existed in the same sky. There were many hours of each day where the two goddesses came together to celebrate their fecundity. This caused the sky to turn dark for only an hour at a time. It was then that the dragons would venture from their lairs.*

*One day, when the Moon Goddess Gea went to her sister, the sky again grew dark. But this time, the Sun Goddess Surya, was angry with her sister and pushed her away. Gea didn't understand why her sister was so upset with her and begged for Surya to tell her what was wrong. The Sun Goddess refused and disappeared behind the horizon never to be seen in the same sky as her sister again.*

*The land grew dark – all except for the small amount of light coming from the Moon Goddess's tears that made its way down to the land to relieve the people and animals of the suffocating pitch black.*

*The villagers would shut themselves in their homes, knowing that the darkness would pass, allowing them to come out again soon. The dragons didn't have time to venture down into the village before the light returned, but the people refused to take that chance and protected themselves anyway.*

*Except this time the darkness didn't recede.*

*In the cave atop the highest mountain – Eldur – lived Fireheart the Restless. He was the oldest and largest dragon ever known to have existed. The ridge along his back was covered in red and black pointed scales which were tipped with a poison that would kill any mortal who dared cross him. He had not been seen in many centuries and was thought to have long since returned to the dust from which he came. No mortal was brave enough to venture to his cave to find out for sure though.*

*Fireheart the Restless awoke and smiled, his eyes fluttering open as his mouth yawned wide revealing his poison coated fangs. Fire rumbled in his belly and as he lumbered his large body from his cave for the first time in many centuries, his claws scraped across the stone like the scratching of a bow across the strings of a violin.*

*The villagers heard this from the bottom of the mountain, and many decided to flee their thatch and mud brick homes in search of better shelter.*

*The darkness persisted for many hours and word was sent to a nearby castle that the great dragon had awoken.*

*A band of knights was assembled and given specially crafted spears to slay the dragon that would surely reign terror down on these poor villagers. One of those knights was the great Batal Lunakeep.*

*The knights rode to the base of Mount Eldur to await the return of the dragon. Many of the smaller dragons that inhabited the nearby lands were placid and could be easily trained like a dog. Not all dragons had wings, the dragons that the knights ride were the land-dwelling type. Completely wingless and as docile as a babe.*

*Fireheart stood at the edge of the cliff at his cave and sniffed the air. He could smell the fear pouring off the knights below- well all but one knight.*

*The great dragon leapt down from his cave and beat his wings to land softly in front of the now fleeing Knights. Their smaller dragons had made a run for it the moment they smelled Fireheart, leaving the knights with only their spears.*

*Fireheart huffed smoke from his nostrils and leaned his head down lower to the ground toward the knights. Batal Lunakeep stood at the front of the group – his spear at the ready, his shield in place.*

*But the large dragon only cocked his head to the side and let out a whine. Batal cast his shield aside and gripped his spear with two hands.*

*Fireheart crouched down further, and, in his throat, the glow of his fire gland brightened.*

*Batal struck the dragon beneath his jaw and drove the spear up be-*
*tween the eyes and watched the life leave them.*

*He had killed the great dragon and was hailed a hero for protecting*
*the villagers.*

*When the tyrant who had control of the country eventually died*
*with no heirs – the people of the land came together and proclaimed*
*Batal Lunakeep their first legitimate King."*

Emily screwed her face up in disgust. "So, you're telling me that
this Batal guy killed a dragon that was kneeling to him in peace?!"

Until that moment, Aristide had idolized this ancestor, he'd never thought the dragon capable of being peaceful.

"I think I've heard enough," she said and walked away from the
Water King. Aristide stood there alone beside the painting of Batal
and the head of the dragon looking both confused and dismayed.

Xander crossed the floor laughing hysterically, "Smooth moves,
Cousin."

Ari shot him a murderous look, "Oh shut it," and stalked off.

"HAVE YOU DECIDED WHAT you're going to do with all the
people crammed in the castle?" Jackson asked Izzy.

Izzy was still standing with Xander after Aristide tried to woo
Emily when the soldier came in.

She turned to him, "To be completely honest, I haven't even decided what I'm going to do in five minutes from now."

Jackson gave a curt nod. "The only reason I ask is the Elementials
are becoming restless being so close to the Gypsies."

"They've been more than restless since this all started," Xander
added.

Izzy rubbed her face, as if trying to wipe the frustration away.
"Do they not understand? Gypsy blood or Elemental blood – we

will all die if we don't come together in this battle against our common enemy?"

Screams echoed down the hallway that runs alongside the Grand Room.

"I think they've just reached boiling point," Jackson said breaking into a run toward the noise.

Izzy and Xander followed the soldier. It was a good thing that the Queen had decided to wear brown riding pants and a sensible button-down blouse rather than a large cumbersome dress. She thought her crown looked out of place no matter what she was wearing, but it looked especially odd with her current ensemble.

Entering the room where the yelling was coming from, they were met with Elementials and Gypsies facing off once again.

*Not again*, thought Izzy.

The shouting was so loud Izzy clamped her hands over her ears. Men from the Gypsy clans were holding an Elemential man by the hair, forcing him to his knees in front of them. Gypsy women lined themselves in front of their men holding their hands out in warning to any Elemential that dared advance to free him.

The Queen hurried over to the man on his knees. As she was stepped toward him a Gypsy elder blocked her path preventing her from getting any closer.

"Let me through," the Fire Queen said hoping she sounded commanding. The Gypsy man standing before her was twice her size. He looked down at her menacingly with his pointed nose and square chin.

"This does not concern you, Your Majesty. Kindly leave us be," he said crossing his arms in front of him.

Izzy shot him an incredulous look before straightening herself up and squaring her shoulders. She may not be anywhere near this man's size, but she was the Queen, this was her castle, and she will be obeyed.

"Would you like me to have you escorted to new accommodations? My dungeons have ample space for you to cool off, *Sir*," she said as patronisingly as possible. "It seems you haven't noticed, but you are currently standing in my castle, on my land, in my country. You may call this island your home just as I do, but you are not in charge in here."

"You don't have the authority to lock me up. I am a Gypsy elder. It's against the law to imprison a Gypsy elder unless a mortal sin has been committed. But you already knew that didn't you?" he matched her tone.

The Queen took a deep breath trying to calm her nerves. After all the man was right. Unless she wanted to break the ancient law, she couldn't imprison him for this. Even if he was in her castle going against her wishes.

"So, if you don't mind," the man continued sensing her hesitation. "We will continue with our negotiations."

Izzy looked past the Gypsy to the man being held captive. It was one of the Council members whose son just happened to be the Master of the Dungeons and Holder of Keys.

"What is it you want?" the Queen asked steeling herself for his response. Izzy had a fair idea she already knew the answer that was coming.

Yet another Gypsy elder had come to stand before her and she said, "We want the release of our Nova from the dungeons in exchange for this man's life."

"I can't do that," Izzy replied.

"You're the Queen, aren't you?" the gypsy woman asked condescendingly.

Izzy had had just about enough of this. She scanned the room for Jackson who by now was standing in front of the Elementials trying to stop them from escalating the situation more. He looked at the Queen and shook his head. This was not going well.

"I will see you in my study to discuss terms."

The Queen couldn't afford to have a civil war inside her castle. If releasing Nova meant peace between the Gypsies and Elementials, then perhaps she might just have to give in.

The man nodded. But as he did, an Elemential man broke through the line Jackson and his men had formed and rushed at the Gypsies.

He had a crazed expression on his face and a fury in his eyes. And then he stopped. When he'd reached the Gypsies holding the Council member, he stood stock still. The man's eyes grew wide and his skin turned pale.

One of the Gypsy women stepped toward him her hands still raised in front of her. Her lips were moving as though she was talking but Izzy was too far away to hear what was being said.

The man dropped to his knees and fell forward landing face down. Behind Jackson a woman- Izzy assumed was the wife of the Elemential- screamed. The room fell silent except for the murmurings of the Gypsy woman whose chant could now be heard as clear as the river's water passing over rocks.

"A curse I lay upon you, a curse you shall endure. Until our daughter returns to us, the magic of the sun and moon will find you and consume you," she repeated over and over.

"What is she doing?" Izzy screeched at the elder in front of her.

"Our demands were not met in a timely fashion. She has cast the sleeping curse," he said as if Izzy should have understood this without being told.

Izzy pushed past him and ducked under his arm to run towards Jackson who was now comforting the wife.

"Get him moved out of here to the Medica's rooms, immediately!"

Jackson just stared at the Queen. His eyes like glass.

"Jackson!" Izzy yelled as the soldier fell to the ground. Victim to the same curse as the Council member.

Izzy realised what was happening as she scanned the room. Not all of the men, but the majority of the Elemental men in the room were now splayed out on the floor with glazed eyes.

Izzy spun on her heel to face the gypsy woman who laid the curse.

"We have a war about to land on our doorstep and you've just taken out able bodied men. You're either incredibly confident in your magic and ours or you're the most stupid woman I've ever laid eyes on."

"Return our Nova. You have twenty-four hours, or this sleep will be permanent," was all the woman said. She turned and walked off taking the other Gypsies with her.

The Councilman who was now asleep, slumped to the ground as they let him go. The women and Izzy, along with the five men in the room that remained standing silently looking at each other. What could any of them say in this moment?

*Xander!* Izzy remembered that her husband had entered the room with her. The Queen desperately searched the men spread out on the floor.

Did Xander manage to leave unharmed? Was this castle-wide or isolated to this room? She had no idea.

But then she spotted him. Eyes closed, laying near the entrance to the room. He'd hit his head on the doorway on the way down. A trickle of blood ran down his cheek and dripped to the floor.

"Xander!" she tried to wake him, but he didn't budge.

In one fell swoop she'd lost her personal guard, about a hundred able bodied men, and her husband. Only women, children, and a few men who she now saw were elderly or disabled remained awake in the room.

*And all this before lunch,* she thought with a laugh. Because if she didn't laugh right now, she would cry. They were running out of time before the Emperor and his army arrived. She didn't have time for this.

The Queen sat beside Xander for nearly an hour. A million thoughts were running through her head.

*How do I wake them up?*

*I can't release Nova – can I?*

*What would happen if I did release Nova? I don't have any way of controlling her. We don't have any more powder.*

Izzy looked up and saw Agnes standing in the doorway across the room – her mouth agape in shock.

"Agnes," Izzy said getting the girl's attention. "Is it the same out there?"

A nod was all she got in return and Agnes began to cry.

# 6

"When does the ship leave?" Emily asked the shadowed man.

"In an hour," he said taking the letter from her hand. "That's if we can leave unnoticed. They've tightened the port's security since news broke of the Emperor coming."

Emily sighed, "I heard. Where is the ship anchored?"

The man looked over his shoulder. "North of Terrania, hidden by the rocky outcrops off the coast."

"Good," she said. "Make sure the Emperor gets it. He needs to know that the Gypsies have played right into our hands and that we're ready for him as soon as he can get here."

"Do you want me to give your mother a message?" he asked.

Emily shook her head, "I think the Emperor's mistress has enough to contend with right now, don't you?"

"I heard that the Empress and her children stayed behind," he said.

"As well they should. War is no place for a frail old lady and her weak children."

The man started to leave but turned back to say, "She's proud of you, you know."

"It's been many years since I've seen my mother. And last time I checked she didn't give a wit about me. That is why she sent me to this backwards nation. I will do my duty to the Emperor and nothing more. You'd better be going," she paused looking toward the port. "It looks like your small boat is ready earlier than you thought. You wouldn't want to miss it."

"ARISTIDE, WHAT ON EARTH am I supposed to do?" Izzy asked Aristide.

The pair had retreated to her study. Izzy had been overcome with sheer relief when she found Aristide hadn't been affected by the Gypsy curse. At the time of its casting he'd been down at the port trying to find Emily. Izzy was grateful to learn that only those within the castle walls had been affected by the curse, but that still included most Firestorm's military forces. They'd been inside the walls trying to calm the Gypsy clans, as well as sort out where everyone would be housed until the siege ended.

Aristide absentmindedly twirling a pencil around his fingers said to no one in particular, "I just don't understand where she could've gone. One minute she was walking down the pathway – the next she'd rounded a corner and was gone. I was only five seconds behind her. I got to the corner where she'd turned, and poof nothing. I don't get it."

Izzy rolled her eyes and sat back in the old leather chair her father had sat in for years before her, "Can you concentrate for even just a second Aristide, please? For Luna's sake, the girl didn't even seem that impressed by you. I don't have time for your non-existent love life right now, so can we get back to the current crisis? Please?"

He immediately snapped out of his musings and looked sympathetically at his cousin. Gently placing the pencil on the desk, he said reluctantly, "You could just let her go."

She looked at him gobsmacked. "That's your solution? Just let her go?" Izzy said waiving her arms in exasperation. "Nothing would be solved if I simply released her. I'd probably be more likely to result in my death than peace between our peoples."

"Well, I am not sure what other suggestion I can make," Ari hmphed. "Contrary to popular belief, I don't always have all the answers, Izzy."

"But you're all I have right now," Izzy lamented. "Xander and Jackson are down, and I have no idea where my other guards are. Agnes is busy moving those affected by the curse to a safer place until we can work out what we are going to do with them. And Constance, I haven't seen her all day."

"Constance was down at the wall this morning looking for something to do."

"How does that help me right now?" she quipped.

The Queen sighed, "I'm sorry. I just feel so overwhelmed right now."

"Have you checked on Emory?" Ari asked.

She nodded. "Nanu is with him. I sent for him as soon as I'd left Xander, but I was told that he was safe with Nanu. The nurse had just finished feeding him and they were settling him in the nursery for a sleep."

Izzy sighed turning her chair around to look out the window. "Do you think I'm doing the right thing?"

"No. Yes. I don't know," Ari answered.

"Well that was a helpful response."

"I'm sorry. This is unfamiliar territory for all of us. I've left my island virtually unguarded because we both know that he is only after Firestorm. He won't touch Aerleon because Christian created such a large military force there and his idiot of a son has further fortified the castle walls since his death. I'm surprised they can even breathe in there it's been locked down so tight," Ari said.

Izzy let out a small laugh. "I wonder what my father would say if he was here?"

"He'd probably tell you how much of a horrible job you're doing and then try doing it himself before realising that any decision you make is like being between a rock and a hard place."

The Queen nodded in agreement.

The two of them just sat there in silence for the longest time. There wasn't anything they could do and little left to be said about their current situation. If they were to release Nova, she would most certainly come for the Queen again. They couldn't just free her and let her go back to live with the Gypsies because they were all inside the castle walls.

Finally, Izzy breaking the silence faced Aristide once again and said, "I'm going to go see her."

"See who?" Ari said. He was now studying the spine of an old volume of trade laws that was sitting on the edge of the desk.

Izzy rolling her eyes replied exasperatedly, "Who do you think? Nova. I'm going to go see Nova," she said standing up. "Are you coming?"

"If I must," he replied.

WET GRASS SQUELCHED under Izzy's feet outside the dungeons entrance. It would seem the groundskeeper had neglected this section of the grounds – which wasn't surprising given the current situation. Long stems of grass seeds swayed like a curtain caught in a light breeze that filtered between the buildings. Aristide grasped the Queen's hand to help her over a particularly muddy patch before arriving at the iron gates that led to the dungeons master's quarters.

Constance suddenly appeared giving them both a start.

"What are you doing down here?" Ari asked noting that she'd just come from inside the dungeons.

The new princess looked back and forth from the Queen to the Water King before saying, "I was bringing food to Nova."

Izzy narrowed her eyes. "Why?"

"I wanted to check on her and see how she was going. But she was asleep, so I just left the tray and came straight back out," Constance said tugging at her dress that was now getting mud all over it.

"Okay, but you shouldn't be coming down to see any prisoners without permission, Constance," Ari chided.

Constance agreed and left the two standing at the gate.

Aristide rang the bell that sat high upon the brickwork and the two waited patiently for someone to come.

After a few minutes of waiting, he rang again and still, no one came to answer their call. It was nearing midday and even in the dead of night, this gate was never to be left unattended.

Panic mixed with bile began rising in Izzy's throat. If the men inside the dungeons were affected by the Gypsy curse, then no one would be able to get food to the prisoners. They'd be locked in. Unless the Dungeon Master had stepped out for a moment by some miracle – all the keys would be inside the dungeons.

The Queen shot a panicked look at her cousin, "You don't think..."

But a rattle of keys from inside the gate cut her off from finishing her sentence and an elderly man limped his way down the five steps to the gate.

Izzy's felt a wave of relief wash over her, the tension leaving her shoulders. "Sir are you the only one awake inside?" she asked still with a hint of the earlier fear creeping into her voice.

The old man jingled the keys until he found the one for the gate. He wiped the large iron key on his tattered and dirty shirt before putting it into the rusted lock on the side of the entrance.

"Eh?" he said looking up, squinting his eyes to look at the pair before him.

"Are you the only one awake?" Aristide repeated rather loudly to the man before whispering to Izzy, "I think he's fairly deaf."

He shook his head. "Oh no," the old man said. "No earthquake here. This lot would've slept through it anyway. Can't wake 'em up, the lazy imps."

Well that answers that question. Thought Izzy.

The man opened the gate, tucking the keys back into the brown leather belt slung around his waist.

Isabella and Aristide carefully stepped into the dungeons walking up the stairs to the guard's room.

The Queen took a moment to check on the men that were 'sleeping' while Aristide convinced the old man to give him the keys. As it turned out, the man didn't even know about King Manu's passing, so he was reluctant to believe he was talking to the Waterford King. Fortunately, Ari's smooth talking and genial nature won him over.

"How are they?" Ari asked when Izzy joined him again. Aristide had poured the man a cup of water which he accepted gratefully.

Exhausted she sat down on the dusty sofa next to the man, "They're okay I guess," she said. "I'm just worried what's going to happen if they're left like this for too long. They need to eat."

"That's a good point," said Ari. "Shall we go and talk to Nova and find out if releasing her is going to be a really bad idea?"

Izzy nodded and standing she brushed the dust from her pants she thanked the elderly guard and told him to rest a moment before joining Ari at the next gate which led to the cells.

Just as she remembered from her earlier trip down to the dungeons with Agnes a few days ago. The putrid smell hit her with the same ferocity as a bull breaking out a pen. Aristide clearly didn't have as sensitive a nose as she did because it was all she could do not to empty the contents of her stomach right there and then. Thankfully, she had a scarf in her pocket that she'd worn during the chill of the morning air and she pressed it to her nose and mouth to try and filter the horrendous stench.

Just like before they arrived to find Nova sitting on the cot in her cell.

"Nova?" the Queen called to her. "May we speak, please?"

The girl slowly stood and sauntered over to the bars where the pair stood – a foul look on her face as she looked fixedly at the Queen.

"Are you being treated well?" Izzy asked.

Nova turned her gaze to Aristide. "Did you know that the salve your people invented is being used in the dungeons to treat prisoners after they're tortured and beaten?"

Ari's eyes widened in shock. "What?"

"The salve," Nova reiterated. "Did you know it's being used here to hide bruises that your guards are leaving on your prisoners after beatings?"

Izzy looked to Ari in horror. "Aristide?"

"I didn't know. No," he said looking Nova right in the eyes.

"And did you know," she continued this time talking to Izzy, "that I requested yesterday to speak with you? But no one came."

Izzy looked down, "I'm sorry."

"Wow. I've never heard royalty apologize before. That's new," a vindictive smile tugged at the corner of her mouth as she tilted her head to the side.

"Oh, just stop it," Izzy blasted. "I came here to discuss your possible release, and this is how you greet us?"

Nova grabbed the bars and lurched forward pressing her face between them, "Your guards have been beating me every single night since I arrived, and you tell me you had no idea. And you," she spat at Ari. "Your Island has been supplying vast amounts of a supposed rare salve to the dungeons Medica and no one noticed?"

Ari didn't know what to say. He hadn't noticed. He knew of the salve, and he knew it was made from the oil harvested from the Rainbow Salaman fish, but he didn't know that it was being smuggled out of Waterford. It was usually only reserved for the direst of ailments. Even as a member of the royal family who had been training a little too hard, he had never once considered applying the salve to cover his bruises before making public appearances. The idea was ridiculous to him so to discover it was being used to hide abuse of prisoners was infuriating and distressing to discover.

"I am going to investigate how this happened, you have my word," said Izzy. "And I'm deeply sorry for the pain that has been caused since you have been here. Please know, that was not ordered by me and it is not something I condone."

Nova nodded. "Have you found my necklace?"

"Not yet," Izzy had completely forgotten about the girl's necklace.

"Then I have nothing further to say to you," Nova said turning back towards her cot.

"So, you don't want to be released?" asked Ari disbelief etched in his voice.

She turned her head back. "If I believed you actually intended to release me then I might consider speaking with you. But I don't believe you do."

Izzy put her hand out to Aristide. "Give me the keys."

He obliged albeit begrudgingly and Izzy tried key after key until one clicked and the door to the cell swung open.

"Please don't try and kill me," the Queen said. "I've had a really long few days and I'm not in the mood. I'll continue looking for your necklace but for now, go see my maid Nanu. She will give you a room."

Nova just nodded. At that moment Izzy noticed that there was no tray of food in Nova's cell.

"When was the last time you ate, Nova?" she asked.

"Yesterday when they threw me some bread," replied Nova.

As Izzy turned to leave, she said. "May I ask one more thing of you, Nova? Please tell your Gypsy friends to release my people from their curse. I have done as they've asked."

And the Queen left. She was eager to eat some lunch and sit with her son to process the morning's events before she sought Constance out. She was determined to get the entire story behind her visit to the dungeons.

"HAVE YOU SPOKEN TO Constance yet?" Aristide asked Izzy sometime later when he saw her in the hall.

The Queen was snacking on one of her favourite delights out of the castle's kitchen, a pastry filled with sweet apples. "No. Not yet," she said. "I'm on my way to her rooms now to speak with her," she said as she finished the last mouthful- as she brushed her hands to get rid of the sugary powder and crumbs.

Ari nodded. "What are you going to say to her?"

Izzy took a seat on one of the benches lining the hall and laid her hands in her lap. "To be honest, I haven't really given it much thought," she said. "Why in Luna's name was she even down there in the dungeons?"

"I have no idea," Aristide said as he moved to sit beside her. He distractedly played with a bubble of water in the air between his hands, shaping it into different creations. "They're the same age, you know. Maybe she was just looking for a friend. There aren't many other girls her age around here for her to talk to."

The Fire Queen looked at her cousin and sighed, "There are plenty of people she can talk to. Seeking out a prisoner in the dungeons is not the proper place for a Princess of the royal families to go to, to make a friend. Surely she's not *that* lonely for company."

"I wouldn't think so," he said eyes fixed on the water floating higher and higher towards the ceiling.

Izzy raised her hand, and with the crook of her finger the water dissipated into steam. "Aristide are you even listening to me?" she said shoving with her elbow into his ribs.

"Ow. Yes, I am," he said rubbing his now sore side. "What do you want *me* to do, Izzy?"

"Well, she's your cousin too. Can't you help me out a little bit here? You know how much I am dealing with already."

Aristide's shoulders dropped. "Well, she's not technically my cousin, but you're right. I'll go see Constance."

The Queen rolled her eyes. "No. That's not what I'm saying," Izzy said sighing. "Just do me a favour, go check on Xander and the others who are still passed out or cursed or whatever the Gypsies have done to our people, and while you're doing that see if you can find that Gypsy Elder who placed the curse on them. I did as they asked, I released Nova. I want to know why our people aren't awake yet."

"Done," he said standing up.

"And Ari," the Queen stopped him and looked at him with pleading sincerity and the hint of a smile. "Please, don't get distracted."

The Water King echoed her smile and strolled down the hall towards the quarters housing the cursed Elementials.

CONSTANCE WAS LAYING sprawled over her bed playing with a curl in her fiery red hair when she heard a knock at the door.

"Constance, it's me Izzy. Can I come in?" the Queen asked, her voice muffled through the thick wood.

The new princess raised herself up onto her elbows and called to Izzy to enter.

Opening the door carefully the Queen stepped in. "Can we talk?" Izzy asked as she peered around the door.

Constance remained as she was on her bed and motioned with a nod of her head for Izzy to join her.

"I feel like you perhaps didn't tell me the whole truth when we saw you down at the dungeons earlier," she said.

The younger girl sat herself up, adjusting herself – her sweaty palms leaving a wet mark on her silk dress. "I was just taking food to the prisoner."

Izzy took a deep breath. "And that's where I don't think you told me the whole truth," she paused. "You said to me that you'd left a tray for her because she was sleeping but there was no tray in her cell, nor anywhere near it," she said shifting her weight to face the other girl. "I don't wish to start an argument with you, but I'd like the truth. The whole truth."

"I don't know what to say," Constance said shrugging her shoulders. "You won't like the real reason I was there."

"Can you tell me, please? I promise not to get angry. I just need to hear the truth," Izzy prodded.

Constance again wiped her palms on her skirt, more sweat forming on her brow. "I've run out of my tea. And since you told me that it was impractical to get anymore from Aerleon because we are no longer doing any trade with them, I've been trying to source it on my own."

Izzy narrowed her eyes at the girl. "You went to see Constance to get more tea?"

She nodded. "I overheard one of the Gypsy elders in the great room yesterday. They were talking about how Nova hasn't had any of her Uvvweeya tea since she's been locked up. I wondered if it was the same tea. So, I asked the elders and they told me I must have misheard them, and they had no idea what I was talking about. But I could tell they were lying. I know what I heard."

"So, you went straight to Nova to ask her instead of coming to Aristide or myself?" the Queen asked.

Constance nodded sheepishly, "I'm sorry. I didn't get any information from her though."

"What do you mean?"

"Well when I got there, she gave me one look, then went and sat on the other side of her cell. I asked her who she got her tea from and she denied drinking any type of sort of tea. She told me I must be mistaken," said Constance.

Izzy rubbed her temples. First the threat of the Emperor, then the Gypsy and Elemental issues, then Jenta was brutally murdered, half the castle's men had been put under some Gypsy curse – and now this? She needed a break.

The tips of her fingers started to grow warm with her increasing frustration. "So, what was the plan after you found out Nova doesn't drink this tea?"

"I don't know. I just know I need to get some today. I ran out last night and I already don't feel right," Constance said rubbing her hands together.

Izzy looked down seeing the wet patch on the girl's dress, "I think maybe you should just go without from now on. I'm not sure it's good for you. If I didn't know any better, I would say you're already in withdrawal, Cousin."

"No!" Constance yelled springing to her feet.

"Calm down," said Izzy positioning herself between Constance and the door.

"Don't tell me to calm down!" she yelled again. "I want my tea! I *need* my tea."

"I think it's best you stay here in your rooms for the foreseeable future, Constance. Or at least until you get these urges and your anger under control," the Queen said moving for the door. "I'll have food sent to you and if you need anything, I'll have one of your maids stationed just outside the door."

Her exit was met with incoherent screeching and the sounds of vases and anything else Constance could lay her hands on hitting the door as it closed behind her.

*I think I'm going to have to start asking people to take a number and telling them to stand in line with their issues,* Izzy thought. *Was this what my father had to deal with his entire life? No wonder he was short tempered.*

Izzy shook this latest issue from her mind and made her way to the nursery to spend some quality time with her son. Just another issue to add to the growing list but her son was one of her few safe havens amidst all this chaos and she needed the peace of his presence in this moment- Luna only knows how many more peaceful moments lay ahead of them.

# 7

"**Y**ou can't keep me here!" Constance screamed after the Queen.

She knew full well Izzy could most definitely keep her locked in her room, but that was beside the point. Looking around the girl couldn't see a way out. Flashbacks to her time living with the Emperor came rushing back to her and panic gripped her tightly in the chest.

*"Get out of bed!" yelled the Emperor's Head Maid. "You'll get another beating if you're late for your training session."*

*A bleary eyed eleven-year-old Constance silently protested as she was forced to leave the comfort of her toasty warm blanket.*

*"What am I even training for?" the girl asked.*

*The maid slapped Constance across the back of the head and threw her training outfit on the ground next to her feet. "Hurry up and put this on. I don't want to hear any backchat from you while doing it. The Emperor has been very generous in giving you a place to live when neither of your parents wanted you. Behaving like a good little girl is the least you can do."*

*Constance nodded and quickly put on her gear.*

*She was marched down to the training arena and while waiting for the Master of Training to arrive, the maid handed her a nice hot cup of her special tea, its warmth soothing her freezing hands.*

*"Drink this quickly, you don't want to keep Master Tinto waiting when he gets here. He will be eager to get started."*

*The tangy liquid scalded her throat when it reached her stomach, the familiar sense of nothingness washed over her once again.*

*"He's here. Get up girl," the maid said as she shoved Constance into the dirt arena.*

Back in the present Constance's eyes started to water remembering the first of many hundreds of training sessions she was made to take. She never did learn what the training was for, but each time she had failed to pick up a new skill, a beating was sure to follow.

She ran her jagged, half-bitten nails over the scars on the back of her arm. Each welt a reminder not to cross the Emperor.

There was no way Constance wanted to face him again. She'd barely escaped with her life when she left the Northern Mainland. He'd decided he had no more use for her, and by the Emperor's will she had never learned why. But Constance wasn't going to pass up free passage home to Lunacia.

Suddenly she was hit with a twinge of pain behind her eyes, her vision punctuated by stars. More memories pushed themselves forward threatening to open what felt like a flood gate of emotions.

*"You're weak!" the Emperor yelled at fourteen-year-old Constance.*

*The girl stood in front of his throne weeping into her hands.*

*"Take her away. Twenty lashes for being insolent, and another twenty for being weak," he said to her captor before looking back at her. "You will respect my authority, and you will do what you are told. Those men were prisoners. They were worthless."*

*Earlier that day, whilst in training, the Emperor had brought six refugees out from the camps. Camps was a far too polite term for what they really were. They were in truth make-shift jails at the edge of the town. Barbed wire ran along the top of the iron sheeting made sure no one was tempted to try and escape. And if that wasn't deterrent enough, armed guards were posted every twenty feet along the perimeter.*

*The Emperor gave Constance a sword – its blade reflecting in the light so brightly tiny spots formed in her vision. He told her to pick it up, to prove to him that she was ready. Ready for what? she thought.*

*"You will kill these prisoners, girl. They are worthless rats," he spat.*

*Constance looked at the refugees before her- each of them sharing the same chocolate skin tone as the Emperor.*

"Son," the Emperor's father spoke quietly into his ear. "Don't you think this is going a bit far? She's just a girl. A child."

"Keep out of it, old man," he said as he shoved his father backwards.

A look of pity flashed across the older man's face as he looked at Constance, and he did as he was told.

"Lift up the sword girl," the Emperor said again this time through gritted teeth.

Constance looked down at the sword in her hands. The hilt was set with jewels and decorated with intricate carvings felt heavy in her hands. She dropped it to the ground and looking up at the Emperor said, "No."

The Emperor stopped for a moment – unable to believe someone would so openly defy him. "What did you say?"

The girl straightened her back and lifted her chin. "I said, no. I won't kill these innocent people to pass your test. Not when I don't even understand why I'm being tested."

Constance shot a look at the old maid that was standing behind her. She stood looking at Constance, both hands covering her mouth. What had she done? To challenge the Emperor like that in front of other people. She would surely be put to death, she thought.

But no. The Emperor spoke quietly to the guard who stood behind him and the guard handed over his sword.

With a single motion the Emperor slit the throats of all six prisoners kneeling before him. A note of satisfaction on his face at the efficiency of the blade he wielded.

An audible gasp rose from the arena as onlookers tried to digest what they were seeing. But Constance wasn't given any time to take in what had happened as she was taken away to spend at least a night in the hot box as punishment for defying the Emperor.

But that wasn't to be her only punishment. The lashes sent excruciating pain through her back – each strike slicing into the skin leaving it a bloody mess.

Tears fell down Constance's cheeks as she remembered how many weeks and months it took for the lashes on her back to heal – only for them to be reopened the next time the Emperor was unhappy with her.

As more tears fell, Constance felt the pit in her stomach shift. It was a strange sensation – surely from her lack of tea. It almost felt as if something within her had come alive. Constance had not been this long without drinking her tea for as long as she could remember.

A spark flew from the wall, joining itself to the tip of her finger. Constance raised her arm and it followed as she waved her hand back and forth.

Something had been awakened inside her. Something dark, but also light and it sang to her. It beckoned to her.

Constance followed the tendril to the window frame from its starting point, touching her fingertip to the wood, the spark disappeared. She looked out the window thinking that it went outside, but it wasn't there.

As she looked out the window though she did see something, or rather someone. Nova was walking on the path below her window. She was being escorted to the residential rooms by one of the castle's maids.

"HAVE YOU SEEN THIS?" Agnes was biting her lip as she handed Izzy a parchment scroll bearing the seal of the Emperor. She smoothed her hands down her purple silk of her dress hoping to wipe away the angst she felt wondering what it said. "A messenger left it with your lady's maid a short time ago."

The Queen held it in her hands a moment before running the pad of her index finger over the red waxy seal. The dragon had large spines down its back that ran to its tail which curled up around and over its head. As Izzy traced its outline, a cold shiver ran up the back of her neck.

Cracking open the seal- breaking the formidable dragon in half – Izzy took a quick look around to make sure no one was watching her besides Agnes. Who knew what people would think if they found she was receiving correspondence from the approaching enemy? She wasn't ready to put herself under the scrutiny of the Council by holding another meeting.

The cream parchment crinkled in her hands as she unfolded it. Words of anger and hatred flew from the page, it was an immediate assault to her eyes. Izzy knew without reading on any further that this was a letter filled with pure loathing and contempt for her as a Queen – but of course, it was her duty to read on.

*Young impudent girl,*

*I have given you plenty of warning to give up your frivolous mission to save your worthless country. My spies tell me that there is much upheaval inside your castle walls. I am expecting an update from one of my spies later this week which will confirm my suspicions that everything is going to plan for my conquering of your supposed nation.*

*Your efforts thus far to assemble what you call military forces is laughable. I wonder if they're all asleep by now. That was an interesting piece of information I happened to come across. I didn't realise that your prisoner was so valuable to the gypsies.*

*But perhaps we can come to an agreement, after all. If this prisoner is so valuable – why not send her to me in exchange for your uncle.*

*I will still be conquering your feeble excuse for a country.*

*When I have my army come ashore, I will make sure they make a pile of rubble out of your castle and put your pathetic throne on top for good measure.*

*I warned you not to cross me and yet you continue to defy me. Either you are very brave, or very stupid. I'm gathering it's both.*

*I'm offering you a chance to save your people here. Forfeit the prisoner and I will spare your people. You will die a quick and clean death by my best swordsman. I'm sure your uncle will enjoy watching that.*

*A word of warning, your response should be hasty. Give your reply to my lovely ex-resident Constance. She will know what to do.*

*Emperor Chino.*

Izzy's skin turned the colour of flour – pale and dull. Tiny sweat droplets started to form on her brow and her mouth felt as if she'd eaten cotton. She searched the hall for a water station but found there wasn't one. Agnes stood in front of the Queen with her hands wringing the life from her poor embroidered handkerchief.

"What did it say?" Agnes asked with almost hope in her eyes.

Her father had gone back to his island and barricaded himself and their people on Terrania the moment the last letter was received from the Emperor. Agnes doubted he'd even remained long enough to have heard about Jenta's murder since it happened so late at night.

All the Terranian ships had left the Edenfore port by the night's end leaving only Aristide's fleet of ships, the local fishing boats, and the few privately owned vessels.

Izzy's knuckles were white as she balled the parchment up in her hands, "That man..." she paused to gather her thoughts beyond the blinding rage that was building deep within her. "He will *never* set foot on my shores."

"But what did he say?" prodded Agnes nervously.

"He says I am to die to spare my people. But I won't give him that satisfaction."

"What are we going to do? He's to arrive in just over a week," Agnes whined.

Izzy started to walk back towards Constance's rooms. If the Emperor wanted her to give her response to the new Princess, there had to be a reason. The Queen wondered if the girl was aligned with that wretched excuse for a man.

And there was only one way to find out.

It only took Izzy ten steps to get back to the girl's door and with a sharp knock she pushed open the door, not waiting for an invitation to enter.

Constance was standing at the window staring out with a blank look in her eyes.

"We need to talk," Izzy told her cousin.

The new Princess didn't respond, but instead continued to gaze through the weather-worn glass.

"Constance," the Queen prodded, daring to take a step closer.

Biting her lip, Constance turned. A look of worry now replaced the look of nothingness. Her eyes were sunken and her face gaunt.

"What's wrong?" asked Izzy reaching for her cousin's arms.

Constance recoiled from her touch and stepped around the Queen. "Please don't. I don't need, nor want your sympathy," she said moving toward her drinks trolley set near her washroom.

Izzy raised an eyebrow, watching her cousin frantically searching the drawers for her tea.

"Can I help?" she asked.

Constance shot her a glare. "You're the one that banned me from getting any more. Now you want to help?"

Realisation dawned on Izzy- Constance hadn't just reached the last dregs of her supply, she had completely exhausted her supply of special tea. She sighed and cautiously took a step toward her cousin, hoping she didn't come across threateningly because she could see how fragile the young girl was.

"Constance, I truly don't think you need it anymore. It's really difficult for us to source given our strained relationship with Aerleon," Izzy tried to explain once again.

Izzy picked up a small towel that had clearly been slung on the side of the trolley after use, folded it and placed it on the shelf above the drawers.

The new Princess' shoulders drooped in resignation. "You don't understand. I've been drinking this every day for as long as I can remember. It reminds me of home."

"Home?" Izzy was confused.

"Yes. Home," Constance said. "My time living with the Emperor might not seem like it could ever be my home to you, but it was all I knew and it's all I remember. And by The Emperor's will, I was well taken care of- even knowing now I was just a trophy to him."

Izzy wasn't sure what to say, so she just said, "I see."

"I would sit there in the morning looking over my balcony out into the bay with my tea. I'd watch the men getting their fishing boats ready, the women working the markets down by the dock..." she sighed. "And I'd drink my tea and feel relaxed and calm before I was whisked away to do whatever daily task the Emperor had me do."

This tidbit piqued Izzy's interest. "What sort of tasks?"

Constance hadn't been particularly open about her time with the Emperor thus far. After all, she'd only been on Firestorm for just a few weeks and with everything else happening, Izzy hadn't had the time to delve into conversations about her cousin's childhood.

The Queen followed Constance into her washroom and watched her pick up a facecloth and dunk it in the bowl on the bench. The looking glass in front of them showed two young girls – one a Queen, and the other a seemingly lost Princess. But beneath all the finery, their ancestor's features played out on their faces in similar ways. Izzy saw their matching small noses with freckles sprinkled across the bridge and over their cheeks.

"Constance? I want you to talk to me," the Queen said.

The other girl took a deep breath in and let it out slowly – the wet washcloth in her hand dripping water onto the marble bench. "What do you want me to say?" she said resigned. "I was tortured, beaten, and forced to do things that make me sick and give me nightmares. I know the tea is some sort of drug, I'm not stupid. But it was the only thing that stopped me feeling. It made me numb. I can't face what I've done," as she crumbled into sobs.

"You know that as a Queen, but more importantly as your cousin I can't allow you to continue to ingest something that I know isn't good for you."

Constance spun on her heel to face the Queen – daggers in her eyes. "How would you know that? You don't know anything," she spat.

"Calm down. I'm just trying to say that I know you think it helps, but you have no idea what the tea is doing to you. Yet you drink it anyway."

She rolled her eyes before storming past her cousin back out into her room. "You don't know a thing about me. My father was the one who insisted I drink the tea."

The fury in the Princess' eyes grew and Izzy's patience was starting to wear thin.

"Are you still in contact with the Emperor?" the Queen asked pointedly.

"Are you kidding me?" Constance retorted. "I ran away from that horrible tyrant the second I could. I ran back here because I thought my father would be able to help me," she paused. "That was until I got to the Firestorm dock and found out you'd murdered him."

There it was. Constance was angry with Isabella and blamed her for her father's death.

"You know I had no choice," Izzy countered.

"You always have a choice," more sobs escaped from Constance, despite her attempts to prevent them by covering her mouth with her hands.

"He was a dangerous man. You must know this. He was tried and convicted for his crimes and I did what I had to do. I'm not proud of it, but I honestly had no choice," said Izzy, trying to convince herself as much as she was Constance. "Now answer my question. Are you still in contact in any way with the Emperor?"

"Get out of my room!" Constance screamed throwing the sodden washcloth back through the washroom door.

"Answer my question," Izzy said as calmly as she could. She could feel her frustration manifesting itself as warmth in her stomach threatening to come rushing out. Her palms growing warmer with each moment her cousin refused to answer her.

"No!" she yelled. "I'm not. I thought of all people you would be able to see that I do nothing but help you and this stupid kingdom. I've been working myself to the bone for weeks and for what? For you to still doubt me?" she sunk to the floor and continued to sob hysterically.

Izzy inched closer but Constance held up her hand to stop her.

"Don't touch me."

"Okay," said Izzy. "But you need to understand that trust is earned. It is not just given. I will give you the benefit of the doubt this time. But if I ever have another reason to doubt you, you can go right back to the Northern Mainland and live out the rest of your days there," and with that she left.

BIRDS SANG IN THE TREES of the Queen's courtyard and the last of the water left over from the gardener lingered on the blades of grass beneath Izzy's feet. The late afternoon sun had started to sink beneath the horizon throwing off magnificent orange and pink hues. After speaking with Constance, if that's what you could even call their exchange, she needed a moment to gather her thoughts.

The Emperor might be many things, but he had never been one to make false claims. When Izzy read the letter claiming that Constance was somehow involved with his machinations the Fire Queen feared there was no one she could trust. Perhaps that was his plan all along – to sow seeds of distrust amongst her closest allies.

Izzy ran her palm across the top of the hedges that lined the stone path as she walked down to the platform overlooking the harbour. Taking a step onto the marble tiles she gripped the wooden railing with both hands she bowed her head. The Queen took a deep breath in and let it out slowly, just trying to find composure.

Her people were still 'asleep,' and with minimal guards left unaffected by the Gypsy casting the likelihood of something else coming crashing down today felt like an inevitability – Luna, fate and bad luck were all converging. Nova – unbeknownst to Izzy was currently unguarded in her room, as was Constance. The maids that were stationed outside the new Princess' door had to leave to perform other duties normally performed by the butlers.

"How did everything go so wrong?" she said to no one in particular. "If Father were here, he would've done everything so differently."

The harbour was full of ships of all sizes – people bustling around preparing them to be warships. Izzy could see fishermen and dock workers alike installing cannons onto even the smallest of ships.

Some of them were large fishing boats at best. She put her head in her hands, "What have I done? I should've just surrendered."

A voice from behind said, "No one ever seized power with the idea of relinquishing it."

Izzy turned, tears streaming down her cheeks.

Before her stood Xander. He was awake – leaning on a crutch but awake, nonetheless.

Running up to him, he enveloped her in his arms. "I'm sorry you've been going through this alone," he said smoothing her hair down with the gentle caress of his fingertips.

"How is everyone else?" Izzy asked, her mind immediately going to the others.

A look of despondency flashed so briefly across Xander's face that Izzy almost missed it. "They're still sleeping," he said letting go of her waist and taking hold of her hands.

Izzy looked him over from head to toe. "Then how is it you're awake?" she asked.

Xander shrugged, "I'm not sure. None of the Gypsies will speak with us anymore."

"But I did what they asked," she said growing more infuriated by the minute. "Now they're giving us the silent treatment. They are being protected by my castle walls. Honestly," she huffed. "Didn't they ever get taught you don't bite the hand that feeds you?"

The grimace on Xander's face told Izzy that there was more to this than what he was letting on. "What?" she asked with one eyebrow raised.

"Oh, nothing," replied Xander walking past his wife to stand at the railing her found her at.

Izzy whirled around and stepped in beside him. "Don't make me order you. You know I can, and I will."

Xander sighed. "They're now upset that Nova won't speak with them."

"Is that why they woke only you up?"

He shook his head. "No. I actually don't think they meant to wake me. Or maybe they did. I'm not sure. I don't think they have any control over when the curse will lift."

"Hang on," Izzy said shaking her head. "You're saying they can't lift this curse and I let Nova out of the dungeons on the supposed good faith that they would?"

"Unfortunately, yes," Xander said. "I don't think it was intentional though. A few of the Gypsy Elders were speaking with Agnes when I overheard them. I had just awoken, and I only caught a bit of what they were saying. But it seems as though the curse the woman put on goes on moon cycles. Or so they think."

Izzy needed to process all of this and with everything else that had happened since the morning and the night before, it was as clear as mud.

She rubbed her temples and smoothed her wispy raven ringlets back behind her ears. "Do they know why you were the only one to wake up then?"

"Not a clue. But I'm not complaining," he said putting his arm around his wife.

"No, I guess not," Izzy said. "Still, I think we should get you back so you can at least sit. You've gone awfully pale and you don't exactly look stable on your feet."

Xander went to protest but Izzy cut him off. "Do I need to make it an order?" she said smiling.

# 8

Nova sat on the floor in front of the unlit fireplace. She imagined it filled with wood crackling away under the intense heat that Lunacian hardwood brought. But alas, this one had nothing but dust and cobwebs from the charred remains of the last fire.

One of her most favourite activities back at the gypsy camp was to sit by the fire feeling all cosy and warm. This room however felt damp and cold like a used dish sponge. Moisture collected on the inside of the windows signalling that the air was cooling outside. Soon it would be the end of autumn, the trees outside had lost their leaves. Those that did remain had changed from green and alive to brown and dry, ready to detach from their trees and caught by the approaching wintry winds.

Leaning back on her hands, Nova tilted her head back to look out the window at the waning sunlight. A deep sense of regret passed through her as she recalled the previous night's dream. Although at this point, she wasn't so sure it was a dream anymore. She'd heard tales of powerful gypsy children who had the ability to astral project – though they were aware of what they were doing. Nova though, was almost certain that her hatred manifested subconsciously.

Whilst being ushered to her room, she overheard a few of the maids speaking of the Councilwoman's demise the night before. How her head was no longer attached to her body. The same maids also spoke of how there were no points of entry and the guard had no leads pointing them to who killed the poor woman.

A tear dropped from her right eye and down her cheek to rest on the corner of her lip. And as she wiped it away, a conversation that was had by the Gypsy Elders when she was just a child came to the front of her mind.

"They can't do this to us," Darius the eldest Gypsy man cried. "This is our land. We might move from here to other parts of the island seasonally, but we always come back here. It has been our home for generations."

Theodora shook her head in defeat. "I don't think we have much of a choice. They want to use this area for training grounds for the Lunacian military," she said.

Darius paced back and forth from the central fire to the log upon which the other elders were sitting. "We have been here for generations longer than the Elementials," he pointed out.

"But might I remind you," Theodora's sister Rosa interjected. "That it doesn't matter how long we have been here. The Elementials take whatever they want when they want it. Generations ago we had a camp in the place that they now call their harbour. That didn't stop them from claiming it for themselves. It was our main source of fish."

Darius let out an exasperated noise and shook his head. "But now there is a law. They want to tell us that we cannot own any land. Not just now, but ever!"

A young Nova hid behind the spokes of a wagon wheel, trying desperately to understand what she was hearing.

Rosa continued. "Jenta has gone too far this time. Ever since your son," she shot a pointed look at Darius. "Played with her heart, she has been passing one law after another inhibiting us from leading our peaceful lives."

"I didn't know there were other laws passed," Theodora said biting the corner of her lip.

Rosa nodded. "There is a lot you don't know my younger sister."

"Like what?" asked Darius.

The older woman stood, moving closer to the fire to warm her hands. "Not only can we not own land, but she is also the reason why our magic has been deemed a crime against the crown. Although I'm not sure how they plan to watch us all the time to make sure we aren't using it. And since our magic comes from the land and the animals as well as the sun and the moon, I don't think they really can. Just like their magic, sometimes we don't always control if we use it or not."

"Jenta will pay for this," Darius said. "Mark my words."

Nova, only hearing up to that point and not staying to hear what the Elder's plan was going to be, was so infuriated by what she'd learned that she ran to the clearing close to the camp to talk to the Moon Goddess.

Out of breath and sweating from the muggy air, Nova raised her hands to the sky to invoke the Moon Goddess.

"Moon Goddess, I ask that you shine your wonder upon me and grant me the power to unlock my hidden powers. I am not yet of age, but my cause is noble."

As it has always been, a gypsy girl wouldn't come into her powers until her sixteenth birthday. But Nova, at this point being thirteen, thought she was ready, and wanted to access them to save her people, and rid them of the oppression that was Jenta. The Councilwoman was on a mission to destroy the man who broke her heart. Even though law prohibits Gypsies and Elementals from marrying and having children, there have been many cases of Gypsies and Elementials having flings. Most of the time the Gypsy man would woo the Elemental woman and make promises of running away together to the Northern mainland where they can live happily together forever. But when things get too serious, the Gypsy man will more often than not, simply fade into the forest leaving the woman broken-hearted and alone.

"I ask that you bless me with my ancestral powers so that I may bring justice for my people."

But nothing happened. Her mother found her crying in the clearing sometime later and brought her back to the camp – gave her a drink of her special sweet tea and sent her off to bed.

Nova remembered what it felt like to have no power thrumming through her veins, and she didn't like how it felt. She'd felt empty and resented the Moon Goddess for withholding her powers for as long as she did.

But that feeling of guilt crept back, and she knew that she was the one who had astral projected into Jenta's room and had taken the woman's life – all while she slept deep down in that dungeons cell.

LATE AFTERNOON SUN streamed into the temple through the stained-glass windows high above Aristide's head as he entered. He'd spent the afternoon searching for Emily and had finally discovered that she had come to the temple to pray with Nadia.

The two young women sat in the pews closest to the front, their heads bowed, and both were deep in prayer.

He paused for a moment, just absorbing the beauty that radiated off her golden hair. As he breathed in, the air in his lungs felt cool – and wet. His powers pulsed through his body and his heart raced each time he saw Emily.

Ari had to know her, be with her – and this time he was determined not to make a fool out of himself by getting too carried away telling her a story about a dragon. It should've been obvious to him that any self-respecting lady wouldn't like a story about an animal that ends in its death. Even if that animal was a vicious dragon that was going to burn the entire country to ashes.

His crown suddenly felt heavy on his head. Sweat gathered underneath the silver metal that formed the band and he wiped away the droplets that escaped onto his cuff. The water King could see the gems in his crown reflecting fractals along the brickwork of the temple – brilliant blues and whites in shards of sharp angled lines.

As he turned his head back to Emily, he realised he'd been noticed. Emily stood facing him – still next to Nadia who was still deep in prayer.

"Your Majesty," she said dropping into a curtsy.

Ari hated that people bowed and curtsied before him. He knew it was just the way things were done, but that didn't mean he had to like it. He didn't see consider himself above anyone. For Ari he liked to believe he was their equal, except he was born into the privileged position of having power to make a change.

"Please don't do that," Ari said extending his hand to help Emily up.

Nadia broke from her prayer and proceeded to curtsy before Aristide. "I don't want you to curtsy either," he said embarrassedly.

"Apologies, Your Majesty," Nadia and Emily said in unison.

"Nadia, may I steal Miss Emily away to accompany me on a walk through the garden to watch the sunset?" Ari asked Nadia.

Nadia smiled at her friend, "Not at all. Emily would be delighted, wouldn't you?" The last sentence sounded more like an order than a question which made Aristide more than a little uncomfortable.

Emily glared back at Nadia, but then turned to face Ari who looked absolutely besotted. "Of course, I'd love to, Your Majesty," she answered as she walked out from the pews and took his arm.

Sounds of crickets buzzing and bird songs could be heard in the gardens around the temple in the afternoon light. Emily hadn't been on Firestorm long so Ari thought he would show her how beautiful the sunsets could be. That, and he wanted to spend as much time as possible with her. He'd never felt like this before. His powers were fluctuating with each beat of his heart. Every time she looked into his eyes he felt as if he was swimming in the coolest waters, yet at the same time his body felt like it was boiling over with the heat of his affections.

All those feelings and he'd not even known her a full day yet. Ari wondered if this was what love at first sight felt like?

"Do you believe in love at first sight?" Emily asked. Unexpectedly breaking the silence as if she was reading his mind.

A moment of sheer terror rushed through Aristide all the way down to the pit of his stomach before a dawning realisation. "You're a Sense user, aren't you?"

Emily laughed, "Unfortunately yes. But don't worry, your secret is safe with me."

Ari looked confused, "Secret?" he asked really hoping that there wasn't an actual secret that he'd been keeping at the front of his mind.

"I also believe in love at first sight," she said. "But I've never found it with anyone, let alone a King. So, my heart is quite guarded as you can probably understand."

Relief, sweet relief.

"Is that all that you're reading from me?" Aristide asked, really hoping that his other more important secrets were still locked away tightly in his mind. This conversation gave Aristide insight into why his uncle, King Theodore had thought it was a clever idea to send the Sense users away with Max. There was a real risk that one of them could read something they weren't supposed to, which could get people in powerful positions, like him, in a lot of trouble.

"There are other things," Emily giggled obviously trying to show a lack of interest in what she may accidentally discover. "But I'm only interested in how you feel about me. All the other things I perceive from people like you, powerful people, tends to be mind-numbingly boring really."

"And now that you know how I feel about you," said Ari biting his lip. "How do you feel about me?"

Emily let go of his arm and continued walking along the garden path. She called back over her shoulder with a coy glance at him, "I'm not sure yet. But I do want to see where it goes, don't you?"

Aristide could see the smile tugging at the corner of her mouth as she reached her delicate hands out to caress the flowers growing at the top of the hedges.

As the Water King followed Emily through the garden, his mind raced ahead to what they could become – husband and wife. He pictured them in the Aerleon castle with her holding their babe in her arms while he danced with their older daughter in front of the fire. So many images of a hopeful future played out in his head – all of which required him to stop being such a coward and actually speak to her openly about things other than the weather and the garden.

That was easier said than done though. The last time he grew close to a girl, she was ripped from his side by his wicked uncle as he'd later found out. It only made the pain resurface when he'd learned that Christian had her murdered – or lost at sea as was the story.

"Emily?" he called to her. "May we talk?"

She turned to him; the light blue silk dress rippled like water when a stone broke through its surface.

"What..." he paused, not knowing how exactly to start this conversation. "I need to know how you feel about me."

Emily smiled, and to Aristide it was as if the light of the sun had smothered the darkness of the night. "I like you very much, Your Highness," she said taking careful steps toward the King.

This wasn't exactly going how he'd planned it to. In his mind he'd played it out that she would turn and profess her undying love for him. But of course, they'd only just met. How could she have such feelings for him this soon? Was he crazy for feeling this way already? She'd already said that she believed in love at first sight. Why was it so preposterous that it had actually happened?

"I would like to officially begin a courtship with you," Aristide breathed out in a rush of words.

Emily looked away over her shoulder, panic in her eyes, "I'm not sure this is wise, Your Majesty."

"Why not?" Ari asked closing the gap between them and taking her hands in his. "I'm a King. It's wise if I say so."

Emily let out a sigh. "I'm of common birth, Your Majesty. It wouldn't be proper to dilute the royal bloodline with someone of my standing. And, as much as I could see us being incredibly happy together, I do not have a dowry. I have nothing I can give you."

She let go of his hands and clasped her own behind her back before continuing. "I must take my leave and return to my Lady, Your Majesty."

Ari tried to interject, but she silenced him saying, "I thank you for your attentions, it is very flattering. But please do not pursue me."

Emily found her way along the path and back into the temple leaving the Water King looking forlorn and alone next to the hedge with the fragrant flowers that she had just moments before been running her hands over.

"I'VE CALLED THIS MEETING because quite frankly, I've had enough," Izzy said to the noblemen gathered in the throne room. As most of them were now elderly, they'd not been affected by the curse. The ones who were affected however, were the nobles Izzy was hoping would back her with this ludicrous plan she was about to reveal.

Aristide and Xander stood each side of her – Xander's hand resting on his wife's shoulder affectionately giving her much needed unspoken support.

The morning had been a tough one for Izzy, the toughest so far since becoming Queen. She felt like she was being pulled in a thousand directions. Her heart and mind were torn between wanting to protect the Elementials by ordering the Gypsies out of the castle grounds because they cursed her people. All the while her mind was telling her that even though they are Gypsies, they are still residents of her country who need and deserve her protection. But what protection could one young Queen offer to tens of thousands of people? Most of her meagre army was still sleeping because of the curse, and those who were awake were left navigating the mounting tensions between Elementials and Gypsies.

All of this prompted Izzy to devise a plan that she hoped would ease those tensions and her ever heightened stress levels. The Emperor's ships were coming, there was no doubt about that, and when they arrived, it would be nothing but carnage.

Izzy looked past her husband to the window – the same window she once stood at with her father all those years ago. But it was not like it was years before, rain was not pouring down and masking the harbour from view. Darkness blanketed Edenfore, broken only by the lanterns on ships and the glow of the fire pits along the dock.

"Our people," she started, looking back at the gathered crowd. "Have no hope of beating the Emperor if we stay locked up here like animals in cages. Our castle can withstand a siege, but for how long? We don't have enough provisions to survive more than two weeks."

The rumblings of discontent grew louder with every second that passed. Side conversations were breaking out amongst the crowd and she was losing their attention.

Izzy had been taught how to project her voice in large rooms when addressing crowds, but she was just so tired that even speaking loud enough for the person directly in front of her to hear was a mammoth effort.

"Quiet!" Aristide yelled. "Let the Queen be heard or find yourself on the other side of the castle walls."

Instantly they were silent, and Izzy was thankful for her cousin's interjection. She just didn't have the energy to deal with everything she already had going on let alone trying to placate dissenting nobles who believe they know better.

"Thank you, Aristide," Izzy said. "Provisions are a big issue, we know this. But an even more pressing issue is if our walls are breached. Edenfore is an old city with old walls. I cannot guarantee that it will stand up to a siege because we simply don't know the strength of the Emperor's forces."

The eldest of the nobles Sir Hindol piped up, "We've gotten this far believing we will be safe enough inside the walls. Why change things now?"

Sounds of agreement warbled behind him.

Izzy rolled her eyes, "You think the Emperor and his men are just going to up and leave after two weeks. Oh look, they're out of provisions – let's go home now." The Queen stood shooting a pointed look at the old man, "How naive can you be? They'll wait us out and we'll either die in here from starvation or we will die at their hands when they breach the walls."

It was Agnes who spoke up next, having been silent up until that moment. "So, what do you propose we do?"

Izzy gave her a small nod and a smile. "We train, we prepare, and we fight."

"But all our best men are still cursed," Agnes countered.

"That they are, but last time I checked, some of our most powerful Elementials are women are they not?" Izzy crossed her arms ready for whatever argument the old men were about to come up with.

This was not a popular statement and Izzy knew it. The old men didn't like to think of their wives and daughters as having more power than them – but it was the truth. Whilst the male Elementials did have substantial power, it was the women who showed the most skill at their elemental ceremony.

The old men also didn't want to send their wives and daughters out into the fight, but at this point Izzy knew there wasn't much choice if she were to remain Queen and they were to survive what was coming.

"Are we all in agreeance that we need to gather our forces?" Aristide asked the restless group.

Murmurs of agreement trickled out in the group, but it was obvious they were ill at ease with this proposal.

"Very well," he continued. "I also have an announcement."

Izzy looked at her cousin quizzically. This wasn't in the plan.

"It's okay," he whispered to her and then turned back to the crowd. "For the foreseeable future, I will be stepping down from my position and title as King of Waterford."

Shock and horror could be seen on the suddenly silent faces before him.

"That is," he said, "for now and until we can deal with the threat of the Emperor. I will be leaving Queen Isabella in charge of Waterford and its forces so that they can join with the Firestorm forces seamlessly. I have spoken to King John and he agrees that it is for the best, and he will also be stepping down on Terrania temporarily."

A voice from the back yelled, "What about Aerleon?"

Aristide nodded towards the voice. "As you already know, Aerleon's royal family have distanced themselves from the rest of Lunacia since Christian was exposed as a traitor and put to death. We cannot count on their help, nor can we count on them to continue to be part of our nation."

"Have you lost your mind?" Izzy hissed at Aristide.

"It's better this way," he said through gritted teeth whilst trying to maintain a smile to the rest of the room.

"You've got to be kidding me?" Izzy slumped down into her throne rubbing her temples with her thumb and fingers. "Don't you think I already have enough on my plate and here you've decided to add two more countries and their military to it?"

Aristide continued in his hushed tone, "I would've discussed it with you, but I knew you'd protest. I know how busy you are cousin, but that's the price you pay for being the Queen of our largest island with the biggest forces. Amalgamating with Firestorm is Waterford's and Terrania's best chance of making it out of this. As it is for everyone."

"Ugh, I don't even want to deal with you right now. I know why you've really done this," she said still seething. "You want to spend more time with that Emily girl. I heard you got rejected because you're too high born for her. Is that how it happened, or will you correct me?"

Aristide rolled his eyes. Isabella was right, in some ways but terribly wrong in others. He did want to spend more time with Emily, but since she'd rejected his advances, he felt there wasn't much he could do right now.

"You're not right and you know it," Ari said trying to convince himself that Emily wasn't the reason he was giving up his throne. "It's best for Lunacia that we have one leader right now. We don't need conflicting orders circling around."

"Conflicting orders?" Izzy's hands were growing hot, so she curled them under her legs. "I thought we were working together in this Aristide. I thought that we were working well together. I haven't once thought that we didn't work well as a team. I don't know how you could put this all on me without even discussing it with me first."

The same voice from the back of the room rang out again. "What about the Gypsies? They've got powers too."

"You seem to have everything figured out, why don't you handle this one?" Izzy spat at Aristide.

Xander motioned to Ari to sit down. "It's okay, I've got this," he said to them both. "We've given it much thought. Granted their magic is different to ours, and we don't really know much about how they use it or how powerful it is, but we believe they can be of help to us and there is a place for them in this fight beside us. I've written a letter to the Elders stating that every able man and woman is duty bound to take part in the battle training which we will be doing over the coming days. If they do not wish to take part, then they won't be offered shelter when the Emperor and his ships arrive."

Agreeance from everyone in the room – finally.

"And on that note," Izzy said getting to her feet. "I'm going to go see my son and get a good night's rest. We have a terribly busy day ahead of us tomorrow. And apparently, I now have two more countries to run," the last few words were directed at Aristide. Xander got to his feet, "Shall we?" Izzy asked him.

Xander reached for his wife's hand, but instead of taking hold of it, Izzy shoved her hands deeper into her pockets. Xander hadn't seen his wife this livid since having to deal with her Uncle Christian. He wondered if her hands were singeing the insides of her dress yet or if she'd managed to put a lid on it. Either way, he'd need to talk her back down from this ledge very quickly. *Perhaps*, he thought, *spending time with our son was what she needed.*

Izzy didn't turn towards the nursery when leaving the throne room though. Instead, she turned towards her father's – now her - study and the hallway that still held the half-burnt picture of her mother.

# 9

"How could you do this to me?" Izzy was in her chair facing the window behind her desk looking out toward the water. She knew without turning around that it was Aristide who'd walked into her study behind her.

She'd been furious with her cousin and spent the last twenty minutes seething watching her hands pulsate through the different shades of red and orange as her temper flared up and down.

"Let me explain," he said nervously.

Izzy spun around leaning back and putting her feet up on her desk most unladylike. "Is there any point?"

Aristide crossed the floor quickly and took the seat opposite. "Do you really think I'd just give up my throne like that?"

The Fire Queen scoffed. "At this point Cousin, I have no idea what's going through your head. Today has been a mess. I don't know what to think or how to think anymore. I finally come up with a solid plan on how we are going to survive this, and you drop this bombshell on me. Did you not think you should maybe speak to me about it first?"

"I didn't get a chance," he countered. "And it isn't my choice."

"What do you mean 'not your choice'?" said Izzy disbelievingly. "It sounded very much like it was your choice half an hour ago when you told the nobles what you were doing. Or what you aren't doing I should say."

"Would you just listen please?" he half yelled in frustration slamming his palm down on the desk.

Izzy looked down at where Aristide's hand was, crossed her arms and shrugged. "Go on then."

"I got given a letter."

"And..." she prodded raising her eyebrows.

"A letter threatening to expose who my real father is unless I relinquished my throne immediately," he said.

"What? Who sent it?" Izzy asked taking her feet down and sitting forward to lean over the desk. "You still should've come to me so we could discuss what to do first. We could have made an announcement saying that no matter who your true father was, that I support you as King and there's no one better for the title than you. Ari, you've been a prince all your life. You've been trained to be King. I don't think anyone could argue that you aren't the right person to be sitting on that throne. And besides," she continued. "Who else would run Waterford if not you?"

"I understand all of that, but they threatened my mother," he said wiping a tear away from his cheek with the back of his hand. "Whoever sent it, is holding her captive and they said they wouldn't release her until I gave up my throne. They didn't say who I had to give my throne to though. Just that I had to give it up. So, I gave it to you because I trust that one day, you'll give it back."

Izzy was speechless. Until this point, she'd simply assumed that Aristide was being fickle stepping aside. She'd thought that maybe all the pressure of the invasion was getting too much for him to handle and that he just wanted to run off into the sunset with Emily and be done with royal life.

"Is she safe now?" the Fire Queen asked as she reached out to take her cousin's hand.

Aristide placed his other hand atop hers before saying, "I don't know. The letter said that she would be released the moment that I stepped aside. But I guess it will take time for news to make its way back to Waterford."

"So, she's being held on Waterford then?" asked Izzy.

Aristide took a deep breath in, "I'm not exactly sure. But they sent her broach with the letter as proof that they have her."

"Do you have a way of contacting them to find out if they've released her?" she asked.

He shook his head. "I found the letter in my coat pocket. I'd left it laying over the back of a chair, so someone must've slipped it in while I wasn't looking."

"And you have absolutely no idea who has her?" Izzy brought her hand back and rested her chin on her fist.

Ari pursed his lips. "I have a couple of ideas. But nothing solid. I'm working on it though."

"Working on it? You mean when you find out you're going to go and do something stupid, don't you?"

His silence confirmed Izzy's suspicion. She knew her cousin very well, and he might not be a fighter, but if pushed she had no idea what he was capable of.

IZZY KNEW THAT LEAVING Aristide to his own devices wasn't exactly the best idea, so before turning in to bed for the night, she sought out Agnes.

"I want you to keep an eye on Ari for me," the Queen said after finding Agnes in the kitchen.

Agnes was halfway through swallowing a mouthful of buttered bread and tilted her head to the side in confusion.

Gathering the meaning of the look, Izzy continued. "I need to tell you something."

The Queen sat her cousin down and told her all about the kidnapping of Aristide's mother and the threat of dethroning him. Agnes was caught off guard with Aristide's true reasons for stepping aside as much as Isabella had been. So, it began to make much more sense to her now that she had been made aware of the terrifying reason behind Aristide's impulsive decision.

Heat from the hearth was stifling and Izzy wiped the sweat from her brow. The silk of her dress becoming stained with each pass.

"You don't think he would try and get on a ship to Waterford this close to the invasion, do you? He may not make it back in time?" Agnes asked worriedly.

Izzy pursed her lips. "That is my greatest concern," she said. "He's not one to seek out fights, but I'm worried that if he seeks this one out, he won't return."

"So, you want me to keep an eye on him? I can't exactly stop him if he does choose to leave." Agnes said taking another bite of the bread roll.

"There is no one else I trust with this information right now Agnes. If he does try to leave, please come, and get me immediately, okay?" Izzy stood up and grabbed one of the rolls from the table and Agnes nodded.

After the Queen left the kitchen, Agnes sat for a long moment before getting up to fetch herself a drink. Whilst pouring it, she heard someone walk in the room behind her.

"Ari," she said startled. "What are you doing here?"

Izzy had not long left and Agnes was worried that Aristide had overheard the conversation.

"Just getting some food," he said lifting his bag onto the long wooden table in the centre of the room.

Agnes put the jug and cup down and walked closer to her cousin. Ari was packing in roll after roll as well as pieces of fruit and cured meat. "Going somewhere?" she asked trying to keep her voice light.

"Look," Aristide said flatly. "I heard you and Izzy talking, so you know full well what's at stake here. She's my mother Agnes, I have to go."

Agnes let out a sigh. She did know that he needed to go, but she couldn't ignore a request from Izzy to inform her he was leaving.

"Please don't put me in this position," was all she could say but her voice was clearly etched with worry.

"I'm not putting you in any position. It's her that's put you in it," he said referring to Izzy.

"But you are," Agnes cried. "Just by knowing that I will have to go and tell her, puts me in that exact position. Do you have no regard for anyone but yourself?"

Ari slammed the apple in his hand down on the table, "It's my mother!" he yelled. "There is no way that I will let her stay in the hands of her captors for one moment longer than I have to. I don't care you'll go and tattle to Izzy, go right ahead. But don't for one moment think that you can guilt trip me into staying, because I won't."

Aristide snatched up his bag and stormed out of the kitchen leaving Agnes in tears. She'd not been yelled at like that before – especially not by someone she looked up to so much. Her heart sank, being torn between her two cousins was not how she envisioned her place in the royal court.

Still, she'd promised Izzy that she would report to her any information about Aristide leaving Firestorm. So, she mustered up some courage and decided it was her duty to talk to the Queen as his actions affected everyone.

On her way out of the kitchen however, she stopped short. Aristide was leaning against the wall with his head in his hands – quiet sobs escaping.

She ran up to him forgetting his earlier outburst. "Oh, Ari. What's wrong?"

He lifted his head, and she could see his face was streaked with tears. "I'm sorry I yelled at you. It's not your fault," he said as another sob heaved from his chest.

Agnes ran a comforting hand down his arm. "It's okay," she said.

He shook her off. "No, it's not. I shouldn't have taken my frustrations out on you."

With a deep breath in and out, Agnes placed her hand on his arm again. "I know you think you need to go to her but think about it, there is nothing that you alone can do. By the time you get there it could take days to find her. The seas have been rough, it might take you a full day to even see the shores of Waterford. Then what? You'll magically know where she is being kept?" Agnes said hoping her voice sounded more soothing than it did accusatory. "Waterford isn't a small island. You could be searching for months."

"If that's what it takes," he said with a steel-like resolve.

"Ari, we don't have months. The Emperor will be here in a week. We can't do this without you," she said a lump forming in her throat.

Aristide stood tall and said, "I can do what I want. I am no longer a king – and last time I checked, there isn't a lockdown stopping ships from leaving the islands."

"Please reconsider. We need you here," she pleaded.

The look on his face was no longer that of her caring cousin, but that of a man with nothing left to lose and it frightened her. He wouldn't meet her eyes, "No. Now you can go and tell your Queen that I'm already gone. She won't be able to stop me nor should she try." With that Aristide picked up his bag and headed towards the open door leading to the path down to the harbour.

"DID YOU EVEN TRY TO stop him?" Izzy barked at her cousin when she was told of their meeting in the kitchen.

Agnes looked at the Queen incredulously. "No, I just let him go on his merry way with a pat on the back for good luck."

Sarcasm was new to Agnes, so she was not quite sure the Queen grasped it.

"Tell me you're kidding," Izzy responded.

Agnes let out a frustrated huff. "Of course, I tried to stop him. He wouldn't listen. I did everything I could, I practically begged him."

Izzy sank down on the sofa in her chambers. "Well, that's it," she said.

"What's it?" Agnes asked taking a seat beside her.

"You realise that without Aristide, we'll lose this war."

"Let's hope the training pays off then," Agnes replied.

Izzy shook her head. "I just don't think a single week of combat training is going to stop the onslaught that's headed our way. We might have powers, but they have the numbers to overpower us."

"What about the Gypsies?" asked Agnes.

Izzy looked sideways at Agnes, "You really think they're going to join us? I think the moment the battle hits our shores they'll retreat to the mountains. Honestly, I'm surprised they haven't already."

"You really think they'll run?" Agnes wondered.

Izzy nodded.

"Then why are you allowing them inside the walls of the castle if you don't think they'll stand by us and help?" she asked.

The Queen shifted on the couch obviously uncomfortable. "Why don't we have couches that are actually comfortable? Ugh. Because," she said. "I'm Queen, I have to be seen to be fair to every citizen of Lunacia regardless of my feelings."

"They aren't technically citizens though," Agnes replied.

"Actually," Izzy countered. "They are. They can't own land, but they are citizens – and for that reason they deserve our protection."

"Since when can't they own land?" Agnes asked.

"Since Jenta helped pass the bill that..." Izzy paused. Everything was coming into focus.

*As soon as Jenta passed that bill she received threatening letters signed by the head of the Gypsy Elders,* thought Izzy. Suddenly it all made sense and she knew who was to blame for Jenta's death.

"I have to go," Izzy said as she hastily got up and ran for the door.

ISABELLA RAN INTO THE great hall where the Gypsy Elders were already sleeping, a great ball of fire hovered in her palm.

A young Gypsy boy who'd been sleeping next to his grandmother woke at her hurried footsteps and tugged on her sleeve to wake her.

Slowly, the rest of the Gypsies in the hall began to stir, their eyes all fixing on the Fire Queen whose fireball had by now grown significantly larger.

"How dare you!" the Queen spat as she twirled the inferno around and around.

It was Minal, one of the elders that answered her, "How dare we what, Your Highness?" he asked incredulously as he rubbed sleep from his eyes, squinting in the wake of the burning light now suspended above their heads.

"I know it was one of you who murdered Councilwoman Jenta and to loosen your tongues, if I don't have a name by tomorrow night the lot of you will find yourselves on the wrong side of these walls by the stroke of midnight." The Queen caught sight of Nova who was now standing at one of the other entrances. "And you!" she spat at Nova. "You'll find yourself right back in the dungeons if you don't get back to the guestroom you were escorted to. I did not say you were permitted to roam the castle at your leisure."

An elderly man walked over to Nova and handed her a small pouch before she turned and left quickly.

"What did you just give her?" Izzy asked him.

"Just an herbal remedy to aid sleep, Your Highness. Nova said the energies in the room she was given were keeping her awake. She desired..." he said but the Queen cut him off.

"Don't give her anything else. If she leaves her room again without permission, I will send her straight back to the dungeons. Do not test me, I'm not in the mood," she paused, looking around at the rest of the Gypsies. "You have until midnight tomorrow night or you'll find my bite is indeed worse than my bark." And with that the fireball exploded and evaporated in a single moment leaving only ashy particles falling to the floor.

THE CLOCK IN THE GREAT hall struck midnight and chimes rang throughout the castle vibrating the glass in the windows. Izzy sat on the edge of her bed, adrenaline still pumping through her veins from her confrontation with the Gypsies.

She twirled a tendril of fire through her fingertips – the flame licking each nail as it passed onto the next. Letting out a sigh, Izzy closed her fist, extinguishing the fire and fell back onto the bed. Xander, had been watching her the whole time from his side of the bed and he shuffled forward to comfort her.

He reached out and placed a hand on her arm, but Izzy jerked away. "I don't want to be touched right now," she said.

Xander retracted his hand with a confused look on his face. "Sorry. I was just making sure you're okay."

Izzy huffed, "I'll be fine." She sat up and smoothed her raven curls back from her face. "Once I find out who murdered Jenta."

"I don't think the Gypsies will give up one of their own," he said.

"Oh, and then there's the fact that Aristide has decided to take off to Waterford to find his mother."

Xander face look more confused than ever.

"He didn't tell you?" she shook her head. "Of course, he didn't tell you."

Izzy filled her husband in on why Aristide relinquished his crown, and why he was leaving right when they needed him most.

"Well that's not exactly ideal," Xander said when Izzy had finished. "But I'm sure we will be fine here without him. You've got me you can turn to – remember that. I might not have been raised to be a King, but I know a thing or two about a thing or two," a cheeky smile creeping across his face.

Xander's smile was infectious – his silly grin, the way his tooth snagged on his bottom lip – Izzy felt like she was melting from the inside out. It had been quite some time since she'd simply looked at him and remembered why she fell in love with him. But he was missing the point.

"I don't just want him here for when the Emperor lands on our shores. I want him here so he can help train the Water Elementials. You and I both know he is one of the best users we have." A shocked sideways look from Xander told Izzy she needed to add, "Besides you of course," she smiled and tousled his hair earning herself a glare.

"It's fine. I get it. I know he's more suited to a teaching role than me. But do you really think this plan is going to work? It's not like we have an awful lot of time to prepare them. They're not soldiers Izzy."

His wife sighed. "I know they aren't, but they're all we have."

Xander moved to sit behind Izzy and wrapped his arms around her. "It's only a matter of days before he gets here, and that's if he and his ships don't catch favourable winds."

"I know. The truth is he could be here any day now. Which is why," she paused to unwrap Xander's arms from around her and stood up, "we need to start first thing tomorrow morning. Which reminds me, since Ari isn't here, you'll be taking over the training for the Water users."

"Izzy," Xander pleaded. "You know I'm not going to be any good at training people. I wouldn't even know where to start."

"Thank you, my love. I really appreciate your help," Izzy said and walked towards the washroom ignoring Xander's protests behind her. "Oh, and Xander..." she popped her head back through the door opening. "I expect that you'll have stopped complaining by morning," she winked and smiled at him.

"Are you saying that as my wife or my Queen?"

Izzy called back from the washroom a slight challenge in her voice. "Why don't we see what happens in the morning if I hear complaining still, my love. An angry wife, or a fiery Queen."

# 10

As the first rays of sunshine crept over the horizon, the castle grounds were already filled with the sounds of weapons striking each other and Elemental powers exploding as they all duelled. Izzy awoke to find Xander's side of the bed already empty, to her delight and relief. He'd obviously decided it was best to get an early start down with everyone else.

After climbing out of bed, Izzy decided she should find something less Queen-like to wear if she was going to be taking part in Elemential drills on the castle's training field. Looking at her wardrobe she decided a plain shift with riding pants and boots would have to do.

Izzy made her way down to the kitchen to grab something to eat. She'd forgotten to eat dinner the night before because her mind was busy trying to come to terms with Aristide's departure from his throne as well as everything else that was going on in the castle.

Walking down the hallway to the kitchen, she remembered Constance and Nova were still confined to their rooms. So, the Queen doubled back and took the left hallway that led to the wing of the castle that held the rogue princess and the All-Powerful Child.

Izzy took a deep breath before knocking on Constance's door. The way they'd left things wasn't the best, and she hoped that Constance would at least give her a chance to apologise. The Queen was beginning to feel as though she may have overreacted when they last spoke.

"Who is it?" Constance's muffled voice came through the door.

"It's Izzy," she said tentatively. "Can I come in so we can talk?" and as an afterthought she added, "Please?"

Silence. This wasn't good. Izzy knew she would still be mad, but still she'd hoped they could at least talk.

After a long moment, the lock on the door clicked and it swung open and there stood a visibly angry Constance on the other side.

"What do you want?" the Princess scowled at her.

Izzy stepped through the doorway causing Constance to take a step back to let the Queen past. "I came to apologise."

The other girl turned to face Izzy. "Is that so?"

"Can you please drop all the hostility and let's put this behind us?" Izzy pleaded.

"How am I supposed to react when the last time we spoke – if you could call it that - you confined me to my room and told me that I wasn't allowed to have my tea anymore because you didn't like it. Well, as far as I'm concerned, it's my life and it should be my choice," Constance said with her hands on her hips – a sullen look on her face.

"I know, and I'm sorry," Izzy said.

"Wow, a Queen that says sorry. That's a new one."

Izzy rolled her eyes. "Look, you're not the only thing I have to deal with right now, and I'd really appreciate it if you'd just accept my apology so we can all move on."

Constance recoiled. "I..." she stammered not knowing how to respond.

"Just get dressed and go down to the training field. You need to be with the others," Izzy said picking up a shift sitting on the dresser and throwing it at her cousin.

The princess caught it and nodded – still unsure what to say. Constance had already accepted the Queen's apology, though she wouldn't want to admit it so quickly. So, she hurriedly dressed and followed Izzy out the door.

"So, we are heading down to the training field?" Constance asked.

Izzy shook her head. "Not quite yet. I have one more stop to make before I come down. You go ahead though, and I'll catch up with you."

Constance nodded, said goodbye, and continued to the training field.

Izzy went to Nova's door which was right across the hall from Constance's room.

"Knock, knock," she called.

No answer.

Not this again, she thought.

"I'm coming in," Izzy yelled through the door.

She reached out for the doorknob but as soon as her fingers touched the metal, sparks zapped at her hand forcing Izzy to snatch her hand back in surprise.

"Nova? Can you let me in please?" Izzy asked in her sweetest voice.

The door opened and Izzy was greeted once again by the glare of an angry girl – it was clearly not her day.

*Oh, come on,* Izzy thought. *Is everyone angry with me?*

"Would you like to join us down in the training area?" She asked with as much sincerity as she could muster.

"Do you want me to use my powers or would you like me to just watch?" Nova asked sarcastically.

Izzy had almost forgotten that Nova had substantial powers. "Actually, I'd like you to use your powers without hurting anyone who is fighting on the same side as us. Can you manage that?"

Nova cocked her head and narrowed her eyes. "And what do I get in return?"

Izzy scoffed. "You get to help us all live – and you are living in considerable comfort I might add," she gestured to the room. Silk comforters adorned the lavish four poster bed with sheer curtains draped around the hand-carved wood. "Do you have any idea how many people wanted me to take your head after you attacked me?"

Nova knew she was pushing her luck, but she said it anyway. "I want to be allowed to move freely between the castle and the Gypsy lands when this is all over."

The Queen mulled it over. The possibility that the girl would want to maintain a relationship with the castle beyond this war was a step in the right direction for peace between the Gypsies and the Elementials. It was also a recipe for disaster to let the All-Powerful Child have free reign over where she went in the castle. "I'd like to think on that if it's okay with you. I'm sure we can come to a mutually satisfactory arrangement."

This satisfied Nova enough that she agreed to come along to the training field. So, the two of them walked down the winding staircase in a silence that seemed to stretch on forever.

When the training field came into view, they could see puffs of smoke and wisps of air and water being sent high up into the sky. Nova's eyes widened; she'd not seen Elementials use their powers in such a show before.

It had been many years since Isabella's father had mustered an army for battle. So long, that only one man remained of King Theodore's army – Maddox. He was of course getting on in years, but he still determined to prove his worth when the Emperor arrived, and Izzy was eternally grateful. They would need every skilled soldier they could get. Thankfully because of his age, he hadn't been affected by the sleeping curse. This meant that they had valuable insight into how a war would be fought on their home soil – something none of the reigning monarchs of Lunacia had experienced themselves.

Wet grass squelched under the Queen's feet as she marched over to where Agnes was standing with Constance on the side of the field. Without a word, Nova followed, and they took their place beside the other two girls and looked out at the Elementials and Gypsies busily training.

"Good morning," Agnes said all too cheerfully which earned her a quizzical look from Constance.

Agnes shrugged her shoulders at her and asked, "What?" Constance just shook her head.

"What's the plan for today?" Izzy asked Agnes, ignoring the two of them completely.

Agnes pointed to the Gypsies, "They're working on joining something together and then they're going to use that to draw the power from the ground. To be honest, I have no idea what they're doing but they're doing it." She moved her gaze to the Elementials who had positioned themselves on the other side of the field, making sure they were well away from the Gypsies. "And they're doing basic Elemential drills because some people are a little rusty and the rest are young. Our best Elementials are still sleeping so we are doing the best we can with what we have."

Izzy nodded and looked over towards Xander who was leading the drills. He may have shown some reluctance in being part of the training but standing out there. Izzy was lost in her own little world marvelling at how handsome her husband looked in his training clothes. It reminded her of when they'd first started courting at the games – back when life was simpler. Her cheeks began to grow hot as she remembered the last time, they were intimate. He'd whispered sweet nothings in her ear and caressed her body with his calloused hands.

"And if they don't, you know we're going to have a problem," Agnes said, but Izzy only caught the last half of it.

"Sorry what did you say?" the Queen asked.

Agnes pursed her lips before repeating, "Nova asked if we had any plans to join the training of Elementials and Gypsies together. I said that if we don't, we are going to have a problem."

"They'll never agree to work together," Nova said.

"When the Emperor gets here," Izzy started, "I don't think we will have much choice. It'll be us or them. There won't be a difference between Gypsies and Elementals for them. They'll kill us all the same."

Nova looked around at the high stone wall that bordered one side of the training field. "Are the walls like this the whole way around?"

"Why?" Agnes asked suspiciously.

"I might have an idea how we can fortify the walls more than they are already."

IZZY AND AGNES JOINED in the training with the other Elementials which left Constance and Nova on the sidelines watching.

"Have you eaten?" Constance asked and Nova shook her head. "Did you want to?" Nova shrugged her shoulders. This was getting Constance nowhere fast which was infuriating to her.

"Well, I'm going to get some food from the kitchen. If you want to join me, you're welcome to." The Princess said standing up and brushing the pieces of wet grass that had stuck to her skirts.

Nova got to her feet, "Do you think they'll have scones in the kitchen?" she asked sheepishly.

Constance smiled, "I'm sure they will."

The two girls got to the kitchen and sat down on one of the bench seats at the long wooden table that ran the length of the room. Constance grabbed a plate from the pile in the centre and served herself two scones, heaping cream on each and a fruit roll.

"You can grab whatever you want you know," she said to Nova with a mouthful of food.

Nova didn't have to be told twice as she reached out to pick up a scone. Constance having inhaled the two scones she'd grabbed went to get another and as they did their fingers touched. Suddenly fluorescent green sparks mixed with electricity jolted between the two girls making them flinch with the pain. Nova snatched her hand back, rubbing her fingertips to soothe them. They looked at each other in shock – they'd never reacted like that to another person's touch.

"What did you do that for?" Constance yelped.

Bewildered, Nova replied, "I didn't do anything. You did it."

"That was most definitely not me," the princess glared at Nova.

"I swear, I didn't do it."

"Then what just happened?" Constance asked. Her mind was starting to go fuzzy and a thrumming sensation in her hands was pushing her to reach out to Nova again.

Nova felt that same push and tentatively reached her fingers towards Constance.

As their hands were within an inch of each other's, once again green sparks began extending from their fingernails. This time they held steady and the sparks joined in the space between them and intertwined, growing upwards – the spirals zigging and zagging in and around each other.

"Whoa, what's happening?" Constance wondered staring at the light between them.

Nova followed the line of the green sparks and said, "I have no idea, but it feels normal, like this is what they're supposed to do. I'm not sure that even makes any sense."

"I get what you mean – it feels comforting and weirdly like finding home," said Constance.

Nova's eyes broke away from the light and caught sight of Constance's necklace – the half crescent moon. "Hey, that's mine! Give it back!" she reached out, grabbing it from the princess and severing the connection between them.

Constance pulled back and covered her necklace with her hand. "This is most definitely not yours," she said batting Nova away with her other hand.

"I had it when I came here. It was given to me by my mother when I was a child, but someone took it from me when I was in the dungeons. Give it back," she reached out again, and this time Constance stood up.

"I know," she said. "I'm the one that took it." Constance took the girl's necklace out of her pocket and handed it over to her.

Taking the necklace from her, Nova looked it over making sure it was the one she'd lost. "Well, thanks for stealing it, really nice of you," she said sarcasm etched her voice. "Why would you take mine if you've got one the same? Where did you get it from?"

Constance sat back down, and Nova joined her. "When I was very young, I was sent to the Northern Mainland."

"Why?" Nova interjected.

The other girl shrugged, "I'm not really sure. I wasn't ever told why I was sent there – only that I needed to train and drink my tea and..."

"What tea?" The mention of tea grabbed Nova's attention.

"Oh, just something my father used to send over for me to drink. He used to say it kept me focused and allowed my mind not to be swayed by outside forces. But anyway, he gave me the necklace..."

"Hang on," Nova interrupted again. "Your father gave it to you to drink? What did your mother say about you being given the tea?"

Constance was getting slightly annoyed with the constant interruptions. "Ugh, yes he gave it to me to drink and I never knew my mother. All I can remember from before I left to go to the Northern Mainland is my father keeping me at the Aerleon castle and then one day he decided to send me away."

"Did he tell you anything about your mother?" Nova asked. "Like, where she came from?"

Constance shook her head. "All I knew about her was that she lived on Aerleon for a time which is where she met my father. Then, after she had me, she left to come back to Firestorm to be with her family. My father never told me her name so I can't even look for her."

"So, when you left you were given the tea?" Nova asked, pieces were coming together in her mind – pieces that she didn't even know were missing. "Do you know what the tea was made from?"

"It was made with refined Uvvweeya powder. But that doesn't matter. Why are you so interested in the tea?" the Princess said pointedly.

As sweat started to form in the small of her back, the black silk on the bodice of Nova's dress began to stick making her even more uncomfortable in court clothing than she already was. "My mother gave me the same tea telling me the same thing. Except, she told me that it would help to control my excess of power – right before she gave me my necklace."

"So, your mother gave you that necklace?"

Nova put it around her neck and after she latched it, she took hold of the half-moon crescent. "She did. Actually, she decided not to come inside the castle walls when all of this started."

"Why not?"

Nova rolled her eyes, "She doesn't have the greatest relationship with your cousin."

The Princess let out a small laugh, "I'm not sure I do right now either. I kind of made her really angry when I asked for more tea – to which she said no."

Nova reached into her pocket and pulled out a small pouch. "You mean this tea?"

"I thought they took all your belongings from you when you were thrown into the dungeons. Where did you get that from?"

"My mother sent some extra with the other Elders in case it was needed. I think she foresaw I'd need it," Nova laughed getting up and walking over to the bench to get two teacups. "Would you like some?"

Constance had been feeling as though tiny bugs were crawling underneath her skin since she'd last had a drink of the sweet but tangy tea. It took all her resolve to remain calm as she nodded and said, "Yes please."

"I wonder," Nova said as she heaped two teaspoons of the tea powder into the boiling liquid in the kettle hanging over the fire.

Constance steadied herself and went to join the other girl. "You wonder what?"

Nova let a tendril of magic escape from her hand – and as she did, Constance subconsciously raised her own to catch it. "That's what I thought," Nova continued. "We're the same."

The Princess eyed the green swirls that ran over her hand – her eyes growing wide with confusion as she controlled where they travelled over, under and between her fingers. "What do you mean the same?"

"When I was in the dungeons, there was this old man that was constantly muttering about a prophecy. He seemed to think that there was more to it than what the Queen thought."

"I'm not sure what you mean," Constance said confused.

"Well," Nova continued handing the Princess a hot cup of the special tea. "He said that there was a whole section to it that she missed."

Constance's eyes narrowed. "What part?"

"Well, I didn't catch a lot of what he was saying because I was obviously stuck in my cell. But he seemed to repeat the same thing over and over. *Power twice does destruction hold, born on the full moon it was foretold. One Elemental heart, forever torn. To do what's right and be reborn.* And then he would continue muttering about other things, but I couldn't hear properly," Nova said taking the tendril of magic back from Constance's hand and extinguishing it in her own.

"What do you think it means?" the Princess asked.

"Do you know your birth date? You're sixteen, aren't you?" Nova prodded.

"This is ridiculous," Constance started. "And besides, just because I was born on a full moon doesn't mean I have powers."

"I knew it!" Nova exclaimed excitedly.

"What are you on about? Will you please fill me in on what's going on inside your head?" the Princess said.

Nova took a sip of her tea. "I'm saying that I think you're the other piece to this puzzle. I think you're the other All-Powerful Child."

Constance was so surprised she spat out the mouthful of tea she'd had in her mouth. "You've got to be kidding me, right?"

The look on Nova's face told her this was anything but a joke.

"We need to go and find my mother. She'll have the answers," Nova said. "We need to leave immediately."

"We are not leaving to ride off into the middle of the forest to look for your mother when the Emperor will be here any day," said Constance putting the half-drunk tea on the table.

"Do you actually think the Queen is going to be okay with you having this sort of power?"

Constance wasn't sure what to think. She'd always known that her father was the Air King, so it was possible that she had powers lurking deep down inside of her, but they'd never shown themselves until she'd stopped drinking her tea. "Wait!" the Princess said knocking the teacup out of Nova's hands as she went to take her first sip. "I think the tea has been binding our powers or whatever it is that we have."

Nova eyed the cup suspiciously. "That makes a lot of sense because that is definitely something that my mother would do."

"Okay," Constance said.

"Okay what?" asked Nova.

"I'll go with you to see your mother. But I'm going to make sure everyone knows where we are going. I'll leave them a note in my room. I don't really want to talk to Izzy right now, so a letter will have to do."

"Are you sure?"

"I've never been surer of anything in my life. I want answers. I need answers," the Princess said grabbing a handful of buns, some cheese and cured meat for their travels. "Let's go."

# 11

Pieces of dirt flew past Izzy's head and she ducked just in time to avoid a face full. "Hey, watch it," she yelled at Xander who was in stitches laughing at the young girl who'd accidentally thrown the dirt Izzy's way.

"I'm so sorry, Your Majesty," the young girl's cheeks were red with embarrassment.

"It's fine," the Queen said brushing away the few bits of grass and dirt that found themselves on her pants. "But don't take everything His Majesty says so literally. You need to feel your magic through to the tips of your fingers – don't be too eager to let it flow out of you into the ground. Otherwise you'll end up exploding things by accident."

The young girl nodded.

"Sorry Izzy," Xander called. "I'm not an Earth trainer. I have no idea what I'm doing."

"Who is the Elemental that we have pencilled in to train the Earth users?" the Queen asked.

Agnes was suddenly beside Izzy with an armful of paperwork. "Um," she said tentatively. "Me. But I'll be useless at training people. I don't have particularly strong powers as it is, so I don't really know what to teach them."

"Fine," Izzy said rubbing her temples. "But you need to find someone to replace you. Surely there is someone around that's still awake and has a sufficient grasp of their power that can take up the position?"

"We did invite one of the older Council members, but he didn't agree with what we're doing so he politely declined our invitation," Agnes said.

"It wasn't an invitation; it was as good as an order – I can't believe he's refusing," fury was building in Izzy's veins. She was so sick of the older Council members thinking they knew better than she did about how to run Firestorm. The crown didn't belong to them, but they still acted like it did. "Which one was it?"

Agnes rifled through the paperwork. "It was Davis," she said. "His reasoning behind not wanting to help was that he's too old and it would be bad for his heart."

"He's not even that old," Xander added.

"Ultimately," Izzy continued, putting up a hand to silence her husband, "It is his choice. We did say when we started this that whoever wanted to take part could. And those who didn't wouldn't have to, but I had expected the Council to lead by example – our citizens are scared enough." A look of resignation crossed her face. This was going to be much tougher than she wanted it to be.

On the field stood not even two hundred Elementials and even fewer Gypsies. Agnes was warring with herself over whether she should tell the Queen about Nova's plan to fortify the walls or not.

Agnes shifted the paperwork from one hand to the other as she tried to wipe the sweat from her palms on the side of her dress – a gesture that didn't escape Izzy's notice.

"Are you okay?" Izzy asked, half keeping an eye on the Elementials who had by now gone back to running through drills with Xander and the two other trainers.

Agnes' eyes shifted uneasily. "Nova said something to me earlier." Izzy raised an eyebrow. "Oh? And what was that."

Agnes pulled out one of the papers she was holding and handed it to the Queen. On it, was a simple diagram showing the castle walls. Below the drawing, one word. Uvvweeya.

"What in Luna's sake is this even supposed to mean?" Izzy asked confused.

"Look here," Agnes pointed to one of the points on the drawing. "Nova said that we should be putting Uvvweeya powder at all these points in some sort of sling shot device to throw at the Emperor's soldiers when they try and scale the walls."

"Agnes," the Queen said. "You know we don't have access to the Uvvweeya powder. Aerleon isn't letting any of our ships in. Even if we could get to Aerleon, they've moved the storage facility and we have no idea where it is now."

Agnes began kicking at the dirt at her feet avoiding eye contact with Izzy, "I know a way to get some," she said leaning in closer and talking in a whisper. "Nova said the Gypsies have a stockpile at one of their camps."

"Don't be daft, Cousin," Izzy said incredulously. "The amount we'd need to pull off something like this would be tonnes and tonnes. Not the measly amount that they'd have stored for Luna knows what reason."

"That's what I told her. But Nova said the Uvvweeya powder they've got has something else mixed with it that makes it more potent."

"They still wouldn't have the amount that we need though."

"Nova was sure they do," Agnes said pulling out another sheet of paper with a map of the forest on it. "Here," she pointed to a spot on the map. "This is where they keep it. Nova told me her mother stayed behind to protect it."

"Theodora?" Izzy remembered the old gypsy woman and how she always seemed quite reluctant to help the crown.

Agnes nodded.

"Well," Izzy said. "We need to pay Theodora a visit, but first where's Nova? I'd like her to come along, she can help negotiations."

The Queen and her cousin left the training fields and made their way towards the castle when one of the maids came running out. Her hair was dishevelled, and dirt caked her bare arms and face.

Izzy ran up to her placing her hands on the maid's arms – cold. They were so very cold. Now that she was closer, Izzy could see the girl's lips were blue and she was shivering.

"What happened?" the Queen asked panicked.

"I, I, I..." she stammered.

"It's okay," the Queen said gently, coaxing her story out of her.

The maid looked around as though she feared being seen. "I w-went to ch-check on the g-girls. And th-they were l-leaving."

Izzy called to one of the other servants that was nearby by to bring a blanket immediately.

"Come sit down," Izzy motioned to a nearby bench. "Who was leaving?"

The servant returned with a grey woollen blanket only moments later and Izzy draped it around the girl's shoulders. She then placed her hands underneath and willed them to generate just enough heat to warm the poor girl.

It took a few minutes for the maid to gather herself before she spoke again. "The Princess and the All-Powerful Child," she managed to get out without her teeth chattering. The warmth from the Queen's hands had begun to warm the girl's frozen body.

"What do you mean they were leaving?" Izzy was growing increasingly worried with each piece of the story from the maid.

"I went into the Princess' rooms to stoke the fire, and I saw her with Nova packing things into a bag. They didn't see me straight away and I overheard them speaking about which path to travel on to the gypsy camp."

"Why would Constance want to go to the gypsy camp?"

"I don't know, Your Majesty," the maid said. "But when they saw me, the All-Powerful Child told Constance to meet her down at the stables and that she would catch up. Once the Princess had left the room, she summoned a freezing wind that wrapped around me. It wouldn't let me go until just now. As soon as I was freed, I came straight to find you."

Izzy looked up at Agnes who was now standing in front of the bench where they sat.

"I told you she couldn't be trusted," Agnes said shaking her head. "I'll ready the horses."

"No," the Queen said with more force than she meant to. "Let them go. I may not trust Nova, but if Constance has gone with her willingly then she has every right to do so."

"But what about Nova?" Agnes pressed. "You can't allow her to just leave."

"Actually, I already said she could," Izzy said standing up. "I told her she could go between the castle and gypsy camp if she pleased. Although, she was supposed to help us fight the Emperor as part of that agreement. It might be a blessing in disguise if they aren't here when he and his army arrives."

"Are you sure?" asked Agnes.

"Yes," a small crowd had gathered around the Queen and the maid. "Now everyone please go back to training. We're nowhere near ready yet, and we are running out of time."

"WE WILL BE DOCKING in a few minutes, Your Majesty," the Ship's Master said to Aristide.

"Don't call me that. I'm not the king anymore," he said unrolling the map of Waterford.

"Sorry sire," the Ship's Master said. "Will you require anything of us once we have unloaded the ship? We were hoping to leave to go back to Firestorm immediately. My wife and son are sheltering there."

Ari looked up from the map at the man who clearly felt uneasy about being outside the Edenfore walls. "No, thank you. You do what you need to do," he said before rolling the map back up and shoving it in his bag.

Once the ship was brought into the harbour, Aristide scaled a rocky outcrop a short walk from the harbour. It was a closely guarded secret that it was the quickest way into the castle – one he didn't want anyone else knowing about. King Manu had constructed a series of tunnels when he first moved to Waterford – long before he became the king.

The tunnels were tidal and only accessible twice a day. Aristide looked back at the harbour. The tide was nearly all the way out, soon he would be able to make it into the castle unnoticed.

He pulled the map of Waterford from his rucksack again and sat himself down on a plateau of rocks – the smoothest of which he had chosen for his temporary camp. Laying the map down and securing it under a smaller rock so it didn't blow away, he looked around for some kindling.

The only wood he found was drenched from the last high tide. So, using his magic, he waved a hand at the small pile of sticks and drew all the water that had soaked its way into the wood's fibres out.

He didn't have the faintest clue where to start looking for his mother, but no one knew the island as well as he did. He supposed Xander might, but Ari didn't have the luxury of having the King with him on this mission.

Ari thought it best to continue thinking of it as a mission. If he stopped too long to think about the fact that it was his mother and not just someone in need of rescuing that he was searching for, it would certainly break his resolve – and that would do no one any good.

Once all the water particles were removed from the kindling, Ari took out the fire starter he'd brought with him. The fire starter was a neat little invention given to him by King John on his last birthday.

He'd once thought of it as a useless gift – given the fact that he was so often around fire users like Izzy, but now he saw its immense value.

A tiny spark leapt from the flint and caught on the kindling. As it began to smoke, Aristide used his water gift to control the water vapours in the air surrounding the fire to smother the smoke that drifted upwards and would likely give away his position.

He'd been rather lucky when leaving the harbour that no one had bothered him. Nor had they cared where he went as they were too busy trying to ready the ship to leave again.

Once his meagre flame had taken a hold, he added some more sticks and sat back on the smoothed rock behind him.

Removing the small rock from on top of his map, he spread the map out over the rock beside him.

He noted the few small villages on the opposite side of the island, but they were unlikely to be holding his mother there. Those villages were filled with fishermen and ladies that stitched and knit the nets. He had a nagging feeling that perhaps the kidnappers knew that the castle would be practically deserted, and they would hold her there. It seemed the most logical choice- who would look for a kidnapped woman in the castle?

Aristide wouldn't put it past some of his newer guards to be swayed into participating, especially if they were offered substantial amounts of gold to do so.

He let out a sigh. Ari knew exactly where they were holding her. In her quarters.

She'd not often used them, but the King's mother was always allocated rooms in the castle whether she was there or not.

The wind picked up and had started to howl through the rocky outcrop. Aristide put on the jacket he'd packed, stamped out his small fire and walked down closer to the tunnel entrance.

He could see the water was still too high to go in, but it wouldn't be long before there was enough room to swim through the entrance and continue up into the tunnel.

It had been many years since his father had shown him the tunnels. Aristide remembered being barely eight years old when his father pulled him from his bed in the dead of night. His father had told him there was something he had to see that no one else could know about. Manu told him it was imperative that the tunnels remained a secret in case he ever needed to escape the castle one day.

*Might not be an escape,* Ari thought. *But I definitely have use for them now.*

*His father held his small hand and led him down through to the cellar. When they reached the back wall, King Manu sent the two servants away and shut the door behind them locking it.*

*"Here," he'd said conspiratorially. "This is where you become privy to one of my most guarded secrets. I don't have many, but this one is possibly the most important for you to know."*

*Yeah well maybe the more important one should've been that you weren't my real father.* He thought bitterly. Aristide was still coming to terms with the man that raised him not actually being his father.

Ari also had another memory pop into his head where he'd overheard his mother chastising his father because she thought the King was going too easy on him. In hindsight it's maybe because Manu didn't think it right to be so hard on a boy that wasn't his own.

His mind drifted back to his first visit to the tunnels. Manu had shown him several other entrances after that first night – each one more dangerous to follow than the last. Ari had forgotten some of them over the years, having never visited them again – but he'd often come to the tidal tunnels as his escape from life at court. Sometimes he would simply sit on the outside of the cellar grate, listening to the servants gossiping. Other times he would use his magic to repel the water from around his head and swim as far as he could go on a single breath of fresh air – high tide or low never stopped him.

But today was different – the sea was rough, a storm brewing in the sky. The water was choppy, and his power alone couldn't compete with the force of the ocean beating against the rocks. Ari hadn't seen the seas so rough in several years.

The water was cold on Aristides stomach and legs as he waded into the tunnel. He knew the entrance to the cellar wasn't far up ahead - he only hoped the maids had forgotten to lock the grate when they all left in a hurry.

As luck would have it, they'd not locked it. It was exactly thirty-five steps from the tunnel entrance on the seaside to the grate. Manu had made sure he always counted his steps so that even in the dark, he would never lose his way. The grate was not the last stop on this tunnel's path – the dungeons and the waste room were further on, neither place he wished to swim to right now.

He stretched his hand out and grabbed hold of the grate. The last time he'd opened it was almost five years earlier. He hoped with all his might that it had not seized shut with rust.

With an echoing screech, the grate shifted, and Ari pulled it off dropping it to the side of the opening.

He'd been slightly slimmer the last time he'd used this small opening, but nonetheless, he was determined to fit through. Squeezing with all his might to get his muscled shoulders through the hole in the cavern, he finally dropped onto the cellar floor behind the barrels of wine that were left to age at the back of the dark room.

It was the perfect place for a secret entrance really – no one dared to move the old King's wine, else they would be detached from their head.

Aristide chuckled at the thought.

After brushing off the sand that had collected on his boots, Ari poked his head out to make sure the coast was clear. Not a sound came from the cellar, but he could hear voices coming from the room next door. Voices he didn't recognise – voices he knew must be from his mother's captors.

"Get the wine," one of the voices said.

"You get the wine," another argued.

"Both of you get the wine. And don't make me tell you again," the third said gruffly.

*Three of them.* Ari confirmed weighing up his options.

Aristide knew if he made his presence known it wouldn't go down well so he decided to stay hidden at least until the men moved on.

Heavy footsteps pounded towards the cellar door and Ari's heart thumped wildly in his chest – his wet hair plastered across his face: he was too scared to fix it in case his movements made a sound.

The cellar door creaked open and two men walked in.

Aristide sized them up. One of them was small and lithe, the other however was hefty and burly.

"Which one are we grabbing?" the smaller one said scratching his chin and looking around.

The oafish one shrugged. "I dunno. That one in the corner I suppose."

He'd pointed to the very barrel that Aristide was crouching behind.

Ari looked around quickly for somewhere else to go, although he knew full well that he was cornered like the skunk that once broke into their kitchen pantry.

"Well shit," Ari said. Though he wished he hadn't, because as soon as the words left his mouth, the men realised they weren't alone.

# 12

"Have you heard anything back yet?" Emily's maid asked her as they covertly hurried down the back steps of the Firestorm castle to head towards the dock.

"If I had," she sniped, "Do you think I'd tell you?"

"I thought with me helping you and all, you'd tell me things," the maid sounded hurt like a puppy being scolded for bringing mud inside.

"Ugh, just be quiet. I have to see some of the dock workers, and I don't want you opening your big mouth and ruining it," Emily said walking a little faster.

The girls arrived at the dock and Emily stood beside one of the stone buildings looking at the men who were working the yard. Her eyes followed one in particular – the Ship Master of the Delilah.

She'd watched earlier in the day when he'd set off with Aristide on board. Emily knew he was taking the former Water King back to his home island, but she wasn't sure why. In a time when Queen Isabella had called everyone to Firestorm, what business could he have back on Waterford?

What were they planning? She had to know.

Emily told the maid to stay where she was – it was better for her plans that the maid wasn't given the opportunity to say something that could unravel everything she'd worked so hard to implement.

The girl smoothed her dress, fixed her hat and gloves, and walked over to the Ship Master with the sweetest smile she could muster plastered on her face.

Emily was often underestimated because of her beauty – beautiful girls couldn't possibly be smart, at least that's what people thought. It was most certainly not the case for this girl. Her intelligence far outstripped her beauty and that was no easy feat.

The Ship Master saw her approaching and stopped unloading the crate from the bow of his ship. He brushed his hands clean on his trousers and jumped down onto the wooden dock that butted up against his ship. "Can I help you, Miss?" he asked.

"I surely hope so," Emily said sweetly. "I was wondering if you would be so kind as to tell me when Aristide would be coming back. I miss him terribly you see."

The man was unsure how to answer. Aristide had not given him any instruction to keep his journey a secret. In fact, he'd seemed to not care who knew he was leaving when he'd approached the Ship Master late the night before. But something about the girl and the way she spoke made him think that it was a bad idea to speak with her before checking with the young King.

"I'm sorry, Miss," he said looking back up to his ship. "I couldn't tell you anything about His Highness. I haven't seen him this afternoon," which wasn't entirely a lie. It had been morning still when he'd left the former Water King back on Waterford.

"Oh, now that is strange," Emily continued. "I thought for sure he would be coming back with much haste so that we might be engaged," saying it made her feel sick to her stomach. He was not her type. You see, what no one yet knew was that she preferred the company of females, not males.

"I'm sorry, Miss," the man said again. "I don't know what to tell you. I don't have any answers for you."

"We'll see about that," she said under her breath. With that she reached a tendril of her Sense magic into his mind to pluck the truth from it, since he was determined not to be forthcoming.

The man's eyes fluttered, his expression blank. He was blissfully unaware that his mind was being invaded.

Visions of Aristide's recent journey floated across the space between them and into her mind. She saw Ari sitting at the bow of the boat looking out over the water. He was looking at something on a piece of paper Emily couldn't quite make out. She could only see and know the things that the subject saw and knew themselves – clearly, he had no idea what Aristide was reading otherwise Emily would've seen it too.

Once they'd docked on Waterford, Emily watched through the Ship Master's eyes, as Aristide left the ship. Unfortunately, past the short conversation where Aristide had declined any further help – the Ship Master didn't watch where he went as he'd gone below deck.

"Rats," Emily said breaking the connection.

The man looked around, confused for a moment. "Sorry, I must've been daydreaming. What did you say?"

She plastered on her sweet smile again. "Oh, nothing. Thank you for your time," and she walked back to where her maid was waiting.

"Did you get the information you needed?" the maid asked eagerly.

"That's none of your concern," Emily snapped, still angry. "But I can tell you one thing, the Emperor's not going to be happy that he slipped through my fingers."

"What does he want Ari for?" the maid asked handing Emily a piece of fruit.

Emily always felt a little drained after using her powers. They weren't as strong as she made them out to be and it quite often left her feeling ill if she didn't have something sugary straight after using them.

"Look, there are some things you need to know, and that isn't one of them," Emily said biting into the sweet orange.

"Ari is so sweet though. How could you hurt him like that?"

Emily spun around on her heel to face the maid fury etched on her face. "I'm not doing anything except getting information for the

Emperor as far as you're concerned, and it's none of your business what that information is, or why he wants it. If you keep pestering me, I'm going to cut out your tongue."

"AGAIN," IZZY YELLED at the fledgling Fire users on the field. "I know you're tired, but you have to push through it."

Xander appeared at the Queen's side. "Don't you think everyone's had enough for one day?"

"I'll say when it's enough," she panted – the last drill was clearly one too many for the Queen. Her reserves were dangerously low.

"Much more training and they'll be on the floor, and that will take days to recover from if they do," he said. "And besides, we have time. They've already come so far today. Imagine where they'll be in a week's time."

"It's not good enough," her breathing now more ragged.

"Izzy!" Xander grabbed her by the arms and pulled her to face him. "Enough!"

She went slack in his arms – finally accepting she might be taking it a bit too far. "I just don't want to fail. So much has gone wrong lately, I don't want to add losing my entire country to the list."

"We're going to get through this," he comforted.

She smiled up at him, but he could see that she was just trying to put on a happy face for him.

"Listen," he said. "It's getting late. We've been out here all day. They need a break. They need food and a good night's rest. We'll start again early tomorrow. But tomorrow, we will only be training until lunchtime. They need recovery time as much as they need the training."

Izzy looked back at the Elementals still pushing out the drills, the Gypsies had long since left the field to eat and rest. "Fine," she agreed. "But tomorrow will be more intense. I'm not building an army of weaklings."

Xander pursed his lips. "What you might try doing tomorrow instead of running drills, is speak to the Gypsies about possibly joining us instead of them doing whatever it is that they've been doing all day. We need to unite our efforts, find a way to fight as one."

Izzy huffed in agreement. She knew the best chance they had was to work together – but it was something she was avoiding. She'd had enough confrontations with the Gypsies over the past few days to last a lifetime.

"WAIT," ARISTIDE THREW up his hands as the two men in the cellar shoved the barrel out of the way to reveal his hiding place.

The men clearly didn't recognise him judging by the looks on their faces.

"Who are you and what are you doing down here?" the smaller one said – he held a metal bar he'd found on a nearby shelf.

Aristide eyed the bar and looked between them waiting for the spark of recognition. When it didn't come, he realised he might be able to talk himself out of this. "The boss sent me down here to check out a noise he heard."

Confusion plagued their expressions. The big burly one picked up a plank from the floor and held it up in front of him. "What did you say?" he said, his lip curling into a snarl.

"I'm down here checking out a noise for the boss?" Ari said with a small questioning lilt, shrugging his shoulders.

The smaller guy nudged the bigger one. "Maybe he did," but the burly guy didn't seem convinced.

"How come we've never seen you before then?" he said.

Ari was never good at thinking on his feet, but this time he had to be. "Uh..." he said shifting his weight to his right foot trying to ease himself out of the corner without them noticing. "I'm new. I arrived this morning. The boss called me in to help out," he shuffled slightly sideways again.

"I don't remember being told about needing extra help. What's your name?" the big one asked planting himself in front of Ari.

"Well, that's the thing," Ari continued. "It was all a big secret. You know, the boss said he wanted to keep it on the down low."

The minute the words left his mouth, Ari knew he'd said the wrong thing. He wasn't entirely sure what part of it was wrong but the looks on the faces of the two guys, it was obvious he had stuffed up. Ari looked at the burly one and saw the plank he'd hefted in his hands coming straight for his face. The smaller of the two men reacted a second slower than his mate. All Aristide saw before his vision went black, was the smaller guy swinging his metal bar back and taking aim for Aristide's head. Before the bar connected though, the plank from the burly one connected with the side of Ari's face and suddenly stars followed by total darkness circled his vision.

IN THE LATE AFTERNOON sun crimson shafts of light filtered through the canopy of the forest as Nova and Constance walked their horses towards the Gypsy camp. They had passed where Nova thought it would be some time ago, and now they continued walking in the hopes that Theodora was hiding out at her childhood camp – the one near the waterfall where she had her first magical experience.

"Is it much farther?" Constance asked rubbing her sore back. They'd been riding for hours, and other than a quick stop to rest the horses, it had been continuous.

"It should be just up around this bend," Nova said pushing her horse slightly faster.

Dry sticks and leaves crunched under the horse's hooves, and for a while, that was the only sound they heard. The birds were quiet, and the animals had made themselves scarce giving Constance an uneasy feeling.

Noticing the Princess' discomfort, Nova decided to explain. "When we first made camp here," she said gesturing ahead. "My mother noticed something odd."

"What was it?" Constance asked intrigued and she hurried her horse up beside Nova's.

"Well," Nova continued. "No birds or animals would come inside the perimeter."

Constance looked around confused. "What perimeter? I don't see any fences or walls?"

"No, no. It's not like that. It's sort of invisible. It's basically an invisible border that we noticed the birds and other animals wouldn't cross. It's a circle. So, we set up camp inside it so we wouldn't have any issues with our food stores being pilfered by some hungry racoon or squirrel."

"But what's so special about it. Other than the animals not wanting to go inside it. What keeps them out?" the Princess asked.

Nova rode her horse to a nearby horizontal branch and dismounted. Giving the white mare a quick pat, she tied the reigns to the branch and motioned for Constance to do the same. "None of the elders were entirely sure what caused it – but no magic works inside the circle."

"How is that helpful?" the Princess said getting down from her horse.

Nova laughed. "Well, it isn't really, but without building anything permanent, we found it hard to protect our food. That's pretty much the only reason why we stayed, I think. I can smell smoke from a fire, I think Mother is cooking something – and I'm super hungry. I don't like the food at the castle."

The girls began walking through the thick trees towards the clearing where the smoke was coming from. Breaking through the tree line, they saw Theodora sitting next to the fire turning the handle of the rotisserie. The smell of meat was overwhelming, and Nova's mouth started to water.

"Mother?" Nova called.

Theodora whipped her head up. "What are you doing here?" she stood and moved as fast as she could – arms outstretched.

"I got out," Nova said returning the hug.

The old woman pulled back to look at her daughter. "But how? When you left and I couldn't stop you, I thought you were done for."

Tears were starting to fall down Nova's cheeks. "I know. It was so stupid. I don't know what I was thinking," her voice catching in her throat.

Theodora wiped a tear from her daughter's cheek with her thumb as her own fell in streams. "I thought you were dead."

Nova shook her head. "The Queen threw me in the dungeons and when I finally got the chance to talk to her I told her how sorry I was and how I had everything wrong. Then she let me out."

The old woman was dubious and had so many questions but a noise from behind her daughter caught her attention. "Who are you?" she asked Constance pointedly.

The Princess nervously inched closer – still unsure if she'd be welcomed into the Gypsy camp.

"Mother, this is Constance. She's a Princess and I have a feeling we have the same powers. We were hoping you could shed some light on why and how," said Nova linking her arm through Constance's when she got close enough.

Theodora's eyes shot open and she took a closer look at the girl standing next to her daughter. The crook of Constance's nose and the upward slant of her cat-like eyes matched her daughter's perfectly.

"This is impossible," the woman said – her eyes darting between them.

Nova glanced at Constance before looking back at her mother in confusion. "What do you mean?"

Theodora dropped her hands from her daughter's arms and shifted to stand in front of Constance. "I thought I'd lost you."

The Princess looked at Nova uncomfortably. "What is she talking about?"

Nova shook her head. "I have no idea. Mother, please start making sense."

The old Gypsy woman started to cry. "Nova, this is your sister."

The two girls in unison said. "Sister?!"

ARISTIDE FELT A SHARP pain across his temple – white spots floated under his closed eyelids as he saw only blackness in front of him.

Voices swirled around him – voices he recognised. He heard the two men from the cellar and another – his mother.

"Did you have to hit him so hard?" she said.

*Mother,* he thought. *You're alive.*

"We didn't know who he was Ma'am," the smaller man said.

"Iticus you and your brother are so stupid. His portrait is all over the castle. You walk past them every single day."

Iticus replied. "It's not my fault. Kit's the one that hit him."

"Don't throw me under the wave," Kit shot back angrily at his brother.

"You might've killed him," Aristide's mother said. "My poor boy. Things were not supposed to happen like this."

Ari heard her kneel beside him – he still hadn't opened his eyes, but he knew it was her. Her sweet coconut perfume washed over him reminding him of his childhood.

He felt her fingers caress his cheek. "Oh, my darling. Please come back to me," she said lovingly.

Aristide was still trying to piece everything together in his mind. How could she be completely fine? Did she evade her captors, or had they released her already?

His mother spoke to Kit and Iticus. "Go away you two. You've done enough for today. We still have much in the plan to execute – and I want to be here when my son wakes up."

"What do you want us to do next?" Kit asked.

Ari kept his breath steady. He remembered his father once telling him that true power came from information – and this was his chance to get information.

He heard his mother's silk dress rustle as she stood up and her voice got farther away. She said, "Take this and make sure it gets to Aerleon. The King needs to see it straight away and I want his response immediately."

*He's only a boy. What could he possibly have to say to my mother?"* Ari thought.

"Yes Ma'am," Kit said, and Aristide heard them leave the room.

His mother made her way back to where Ari was laying on what he assumed was the floor, and she sat down beside him. He felt her fingernails stroke his cheek up and down and he couldn't help but let his eyelids flutter at the tingling sensation.

"Oh, my darling boy. Ari?" she coaxed. "You're okay. You're here with me now – you're safe."

*Guess I can't really keep up this charade any longer,* he thought and let his eyes open.

He shifted off his shoulder and flat onto his back – the cold from the marble floor seeping deep into his bones. Ari groaned – the floor in the throne room he remembered, was not as inviting as it looked with its gold channels running through the marble lines. He'd often come to lay on its cool surface on the hottest of nights when growing up.

A fresh bolt of pain flooded his vision with more white spots – he lifted a hand to rub them from his eyes, but when he did, he felt something warm and wet on his fingers – blood.

"Here," his mother said bringing a wet cloth to his head. "Let me," she started dabbing at the wound on his head to clean it.

Aristide pushed himself up slowly onto his elbows, moving his head from side to side to free the kink from his neck.

"What's happening? I thought you were in trouble?" he asked looking her over from head to toe – not a scratch or mark on her.

"Later my darling," she said helping him to sit up fully. "For now, you must go to your chambers and rest."

Ari pulled his arm from her grip. "No! I demand to know now. What is going on here?"

"Fine," she said getting to her feet. "There was never a kidnapping. It was all a plot to get you back here. I knew the only reason you'd come would be if you thought that something had happened to me."

A look of pure astonishment appeared on his face. "You what?" he scrambled to stand – dizziness overwhelming his balance.

"Now just wait one minute," she said, her hands out in front of her defensively.

"What about my crown? You made me give up my crown!" Aristide was yelling now. "Why?"

"That was never supposed to be part of the plan. But you're not supposed to be the King, Ari. You were never supposed to be King. Even you have to admit that," she said.

"So, if not me, then who?"

"I don't know. But you're not of the royal blood. It's a sin against Luna to assume the throne without royal blood. I'm sorry."

He took a step towards her and she backed away. "Did you not think to come and speak to me about this directly?" his voice boomed across the throne room.

Her eyes darted left and right as if looking for someone to come and save her from her son's wrath. "My darling. Please. You wouldn't have listened."

"Maybe not, but I could've at least kept you and your crazy mind locked far away from any place you could spread your venom." He took another step closer to her and as he did, his mother realised she had nowhere left to go as she tripped on the steps of the dais.

Aristide loomed over her like a shadow. "Where are my guards?" he asked through gritted teeth – steam lifting from the sweat on his face in his fury.

"They're gone," she said lowering her gaze to the floor in resignation.

Aristide leant down to come face to face with the woman he called mother. "Where?" his voice as quiet as a mouse – but there was no mistaking the rage in his tone.

"They were killed on my orders," she flinched back from him raising her arm up in defence.

"Tell me one thing, *Mother*," spittle flying from his mouth on that last word, like venom from the deadly Water Snake. "Is it just the three of you left now?" a cruel smile tugging at the corner of his mouth – an idea forming.

She nodded.

His mother had not even seen him draw his sword – nor had she noticed he'd even been carrying it. But as he raised it, her eyes widening as she realised what he was about to do. The sword that was passed down from one king to the next by the Kings of Waterford, it was ironic that this would be the sword that would take her life.

The silver of his blade catching the light as he swung it and bought it down towards her. With one clean slice, her head skittered across the floor.

He regretted nothing.

Shortly after, her two lackeys returned and just as he did his own mother, he separated each of their heads from their bodies. On the floor of his throne room, the three bodies and their three heads lay in pools of blood. He'd contemplated using his magic to do away with them, but he felt using his sword was the justice his slain guards deserved.

Aristide grabbed his bag from the corner of the room where the two men had discarded it and left the room. He knew of one solitary ship that was still in his harbour. It was time he went back to Firestorm – back to the woman he loved and his family. Luna be damned and Waterford be damned – his home was with his family. The family that never went behind his back, the family that would never lie to him or ask unconscionable things of him.

# 13

"Don't you think you should've told Constance who her mother really is before she went traipsing off with the All-Powerful Child?" Xander asked picking at his fingernails as they sat on the terrace to watch the sunset.

"What good would it have done?" Izzy replied absentmindedly swirling her teaspoon in her coffee as she stared at the horizon. Any day now that line where the sea meets the sky will be dotted with the Emperor's ships – bringing certain death with them.

Izzy thought back to the day when she was walking along the dock and an old man approached her. He was a Sense user and he'd come with a warning. He'd told the Queen that the Emperor brought death to their doorstep - he wasn't wrong. In a few short days she would be telling her people to prepare themselves and ordering what remained of her army to defend their home – something she was not looking forward to.

"Well it might've been nice," he said shifting in the uncomfortable metal chair.

"Why?" she raised her eyebrows.

"For her to know she has a sister for one thing," Xander said.

Izzy had completely overlooked that fact. Her mind had been too preoccupied with other matters to be thinking about who was related to whom. "So, Constance has a half-sister – and not a very nice one might I add," she said finally placing the spoon down on her saucer.

Xander sensed her unease. "Look, you can't supervise everything all the time. You have to start delegating."

Izzy snapped her head up and glared at him. "You're kidding right? You are telling me to delegate when Uncle John and Aristide just *handed* me their crowns yesterday. For Luna's sake, there has to be something wrong with you."

Xander laughed – though he quickly realised he probably shouldn't have, given the smoke that was now seeping out of Isabella's ears. He clamped a hand over his mouth to quiet his chuckling, but resistance was futile – it just couldn't be helped. Something about his wife being angry was both hilarious and endearing all in one.

The Queen stood up, reached over, and slapped him square across the back of the shoulders. As soon as she had, she stopped – frozen in place.

"What is it?" Xander asked, following her gaze out into the harbour. "Can you see a ship?"

Izzy shook her head. "What? No. I just thought of something."

Xander stood to get a better look out into the harbour. "What?" He couldn't see anything.

"No, stop. It's not out there. I was just thinking – do you remember the night we went into Christian's room and took the journal?" she said, and he nodded.

"How could I forget?"

"Well, do you remember what it said about Constance?"

Xander shook his head.

Izzy let out a huff of air filled with the smoke that was building inside her with excitement. "I had almost forgotten. He said that Constance had a power that rivalled even mine. But since she arrived, she hasn't shown any signs that she even has powers."

"So, she's lying," Xander concluded.

Izzy shook her head. "I don't think she's been lying at all."

"So, Christian lied...in his journal – which makes no sense," Xander's head was starting to hurt and for the first time he got a glimpse into what it must feel like to be his wife. So many thoughts and questions all at once.

"I don't think he lied. It would make absolutely no sense for him to lie – Christian loved to brag but he also loved to be cryptic," she said.

Xander shrugged not knowing how else to respond.

The Queen continued. "I don't think she knows or at least remembers she has powers."

"How could she forget? It isn't like that kind of power is easily forgotten about," he added.

"There's a reason she was made to forget," Izzy said. "I think that's why she was permitted to return. If her magic is as strong as Christian hinted, then what happens when she remembers? She could go off without knowing how to control herself."

"You think she was planted here?"

Izzy nodded. "I think the Emperor knew her tea would only last so long – and once she ran out, her powers would start to come back. Just in time for his arrival."

"The tea was binding her powers. Wow. That's actually genius," he said rubbing his chin. Xander had forgotten to shave that morning, and his stubble was starting to itch.

"Without her memories, she'll have no clue how to control it and we could all be in the firing line."

The Queen picked up a small cloth from the table. She dipped it in the water from the vase in the centre of the table and dabbed it onto her husband's face – the redness from his constant scratching was giving him an angry red rash. Izzy made a mental note to remind him to shave before they hopped into bed later.

"So," she continued. "It wasn't Nova that we needed to be worried about at all – it was Constance."

Xander took the cloth from her and placed it on the table earning him a confused look. "Water user remember?" he said with a smile as he summoned a mask of water to coat his cheeks and chin cooling his skin. "Or both," he added as an afterthought.

"What do you mean both?" Izzy asked.

"Well," Xander said. "If Nova has powers, and she has a sister that also has powers, and...hang on a minute. I was down in the dungeons the other day taking Nova some extra blankets. I heard the old man down there talking about the prophecy."

"You mean the one we fulfilled already."

"I mean, the one that has more to it than we originally thought. I wrote it down somewhere. I meant to show you, but we've been so busy, and I didn't really think much of it. I'll go grab it, wait here," Xander said leaving the terrace.

A few moments later, he returned with his most current journal in hand and opened to the marked page.

Izzy read his entry and her jaw dropped in shock. "There's two All-Powerful Children?" She remembered reading something about this with Aristide some time back, but she'd brushed it off, meaning to come back to it when she had time to spare.

"I think that's what the prophecy is telling us," he said taking the journal from his wife and closing it.

"Do they know?" she asked, fear finding its way into her voice.

"I don't think so – but we have a problem if they find out from someone who does – namely Theodora. They've gone to see her."

"Ugh. Can I just get a break for two seconds? I know they have gone to see her; their maid came out to me earlier on the field remember? Are we sure that Theodora knows?" Izzy asked.

"Who do you think sees the prophecies? They don't come from us that's for sure," he said with a smile.

Honestly, Izzy hadn't ever thought about where the prophecies had originated. Of course, now that Xander said it, it was obvious that the Gypsies would be the ones who had the sight. It was part of their magic to walk the plains of existence.

WATER IN THE QUEEN'S garden fountain trickled slowly as Emily ran her fingers through its cool water. She'd been waiting a long time to hear from Aristide, and truth be told, she wasn't sure she would.

"Do you find it soothing? I know I do," a voice she didn't recognise spoke behind her.

Emily looked up to find a young woman standing at the edge of the path that joined to the fountain. "I'm sorry, do I know you?" she asked sweetly.

"Give it up girl. I know your plan, and you won't get away with it," she said.

Her heart skipped a beat. She knew telling her maid was a bad idea, but she'd needed someone to take the fall should everything go badly. "I'm sorry. I'm sure I have no idea what you're talking about," she said, the sweet smile not reaching her eyes.

"You know exactly what I'm talking about. You're trying to weasel your way into Ari's heart but all you really want is the crown. Many girls have tried before, none have gotten as close as you I'll admit, but they've tried," the young woman said coming to stand beside Emily at the fountain.

A spark of recognition flickered in Emily's mind. "You're Alina. Aristide's cousin."

The young woman smiled – a small chuckle escaping her mouth. "You're smart. I'll give you that."

"Aren't you supposed to be married and spending time with your new husband?" Emily asked.

Alina took a seat beside the other girl on the edge of the fountain. "There was, how shall I put it," she paused. "An unfortunate accident with a Gypsy curse. Oops," she chuckled again, this time not bothering to hide it.

"You caused the curse?" Emily hadn't seen that coming – and for a Sense user being surprised by something didn't happen often.

"See? I said that you were clever," Alina said checking inspecting her fingernails. "All it took was planting the seed with the Elders. They needed to think Isabella would never release their precious Nova."

"Why are you telling me this?" Emily asked. "And why can't I see into your mind?"

Alina held up the amulet she was wearing. "This takes care of you annoying Sense users. I can't have all my plans coming out into the open now, can I?"

Emily narrowed her eyes at the girl. "What do you want from me?"

The older girl again smiled sweetly at her, mirroring her expression of shock. "I want you to make sure Aristide doesn't take his throne back when all this is done."

Emily was confused. "Why? And how would I even do that."

"You'll marry him of course. He's already infatuated with you – you shouldn't find it hard to seal the deal." Alina reached her hand down into the water, cupping her hand to scoop up some of the cool water.

"And what if I don't?" Emily countered. She didn't like being told what to do, and it was never part of her plan to *actually* marry Aristide – she just wanted to toy with him just enough to cripple his kingdom ready for the Emperor to swoop in and claim it.

"Water is a funny thing isn't it." Alina said bringing tiny water spouts up from the fountain. "We need it to survive, but too much of it..." she let the water rise forming an umbrella over Emily's head. "And we die. It would be a shame for that to happen now wouldn't it?" her eyes bored into the other girl and all she could do was swallow and nod. "That's a good girl."

"Why do you not want him to take his throne back?" Emily dared to ask.

Alina raised an eyebrow and let the water slink back into the fountain leaving Emily completely dry. "Here I was thinking you were smart. Isn't it obvious? I want his throne. He wasn't even the King's son."

The older girl watched as she processed this latest information. "Oh," Alina said with a laugh. "You thought you were getting a legitimate king? That's so cute."

"He's your family. Why would you do that do him?" she couldn't help but ask.

Alina stood up waving her hand to remove all the droplets of water from the lap of her dress. "Because I can – and because I want to. Waterford needs a strong ruler. Something that you're too young and stupid to understand. Aristide, as intelligent as he may be, is not a strong ruler. He relies too much on Isabella and she is just as inexperienced as he is. Neither one of them know what they're doing, and it shows."

"And you think you're the person for the job? You're just as inexperienced as they are," Emily knew she was pushing her luck. "And besides, you're not even in line for the Waterford throne. You're Aristide's mother's sister's child...there is literally so many people in line before you, all of which will not just hand you the crown."

Alina scoffed. "When you grow up, you'll find there is more to life than pretty dresses and getting boys. Until now your antics have been amusing, but like I said, I'm onto you. Your plan to claw your way to the crown to advance your nothing of a family has been exposed. You work for me now. Do you understand?"

Emily could do nothing but let out the breath she'd been holding. When Alina had caught her off guard telling her she knew her plan, this was not the plan she'd expected to be revealed.

"Sure, I guess. But you're only telling me to do what I wanted anyway. I don't want to be a queen. All I want is for Aristide and me to get married and have children and live a happy life together," Emily said turning on the sweetness again.

"Ugh, you disgust me. Just get it done or you'll find yourself on my bad side – and you don't want to be on my bad side, trust me," Alina warned before leaving Emily alone at the fountain once again.

Once Alina was out of sight, Emily wiped the sweat from her forehead, relieved her true plans were still safe. She had heard of Alina before today and had been told about all her antics with the court gentlemen, but she'd not known just how cunning and manipulative she was. She had caught Emily off guard this time, but she wouldn't be outwitted or outsmarted by Alina, as long as her true mission stayed secret and Alina continued to believe Emily was simply after money and status.

# 14

"Did you hear Aristide is back?" Xander walked back into their rooms. He'd already gone down and had breakfast and left her sleeping, she was clearly exhausted from running training drills the day before.

She finished putting on her shirt and said, "No. When did he get back?" Izzy grabbed her hairbrush twirling it in her palm.

"Early this morning, I believe. I just saw him down in the dining hall," he said coming closer to her and taking the brush from her. "Here, sit," Xander led her to the stool at her dressing table and sat her down in front of the looking glass.

"Thank you," she said as he started running the brush through her raven curls. "I guess I'm still a bit depleted from yesterday."

He smiled. "We all are. But you really need to slow down a little bit. Did you even see our son last night?"

A wave of guilt washed over Izzy. In all the craziness of the previous day, she'd forgotten she promised the nursemaid she would visit before bed. Nothing was more important to her than her son, but somehow it had completely slipped her mind. Clearly, she'd been juggling too many things. "I think I need to take today off and spend some time with him," she said.

Xander handed his wife the brush so she could finish her hair. "I think that's a great idea. You really need it – and besides, we have everything handled down on the field. Nanu hasn't seen you in a few days either and I think it might be nice for the two of you to spend some quality time together with Emory."

Izzy nodded and continued to tie her hair up in a high bun.

Xander placed his calloused hands on her shoulders and worked his thumbs into her sore shoulders. She leaned back into his touch and groaned as he hit a painful spot.

"I think you ought to go see the Medica too for a proper massage," he said patting her shoulders before walking back towards the door. "I love you."

Izzy smiled up at him. "I love you too."

NANU STOOD HOLDING Emory kissing his soft little head – the wispy strands of his newborn hair curled down over his still fuzzy ears. It was something she'd never gotten to truly experience for herself, but Nanu had always considered herself a mother in so many other ways.

She was there when Isabella took her first steps and said her first words – and as much more than just her maid when she mourned the loss of her mother. Vivid memories flashed through her mind of the small girl clutching to her through the darkest moments one could ever live through. She remembered the night that stretched until dawn when the then Princess stood on her balcony beseeching the night sky and Luna to bring her mother back. The Princess had blamed herself for being born with the gift of Fire instead of Air – it was the element her mother had needed to keep life pumping through her mother's body. She had cried pleading and praying, but the Goddess did not appear to bring her mother back to her.

As Nanu looked down at the little miracle in her arms, he squirmed and opened his eyes and their bright blue found hers. His irises were the perfect blend of his mother's fire and his father's water. "Hello," Izzy said to Nanu when she arrived – the sound bringing the maid out of her daydream.

"Oh, good morning, Little One," the maid said handing Emory to her.

Izzy laid a gentle kiss on her son's forehead before cuddling him close and breathing in his baby smell. "Good morning, how was he last night? I'm sorry I didn't make it up here," she said – the guilt in her voice plain to hear.

"Oh, do not fret, Little One," Nanu said offering a smile. "We all do what we can in these times. No mind, there is always someone here to love him."

That reminded her, "Where is the nursemaid?" Izzy asked.

Nanu was folding blankets by the baby's change station. "Oh, she went down to get something to eat. I told her I would watch the little Prince."

"I don't blame you, Nanu," Izzy said changing the subject knowing Nanu was still feeling immense guilt that it was her own brother that was coming to bring their country to its knees.

The maid fell to her knees, put her head in her hands and wailed, "I am so sorry. I tried so hard to convince him not to come, but he would not listen."

Izzy placed her son into his rocking crib and knelt beside Nanu on the floor wrapping her arms around her. "I told you, I don't blame you. It's not your fault. You have been here your entire life. I know you tried. It's all we could ask that you try. It's not anyone's fault that he didn't listen."

"I don't even know why he wants Lunacia so badly," she said lifting her face from her hands – tears shone on the skin of her cheeks.

"It's anyone's guess really," Izzy said. "One thing we do know is that he is coming – and when he does get here," she said helping Nanu up, "I want you to be with Emory somewhere safe. I've organised with Agnes to take you down to the cellar."

The maid started to argue. "I must be with you..."

Izzy cut her off. "No! Emory is the most precious thing in the world to me, and you are the person I trust most with his safety."

"But I do not have magic in my veins like you do. How can I possibly protect him?" her eyes darting back and forth from the crib to the Queen.

Isabella laid a calming hand on the maid's shoulder, "You will protect him because he means as much to you as he does to me. Because in all these years that you've been by my side, I've never once doubted that there is nothing you wouldn't do to protect us."

The Queen went and laid another kiss on her sleeping baby's forehead. "But for now, I must go. Aristide has arrived back on Firestorm and I need to speak with him."

"I'M SO HAPPY YOU'RE back," Izzy exclaimed when she saw Aristide in the hall. Throwing her arms around his neck, he smiled and lowered his head into her neck. "I was getting worried you wouldn't."

He pulled back. "I wouldn't leave you here to fight the Emperor without me," a cheeky smile forming on his lips.

"Your Majesty!" A voice behind Aristide yelled gruffly making the two of them look quickly.

"What is it?" Aristide asked the soldier who smelled of sea water. He must have come from the harbour – a good explanation as to why he wasn't sleeping like the rest of them.

"My Queen," he said completely ignoring Aristide save for a quick glance in his direction.

Izzy stepped aside to receive him. "What can I do for you?" she asked.

"I think we should go and speak privately. It's a sensitive matter," he said nervously – his hands wringing the life from the tail of his scarf.

The Queen looked around – not another soul but she, Aristide and the soldier stood in the long hallway. "You can say what you need to here."

"I don't think that's wise, Your Majesty," he glanced once again at Aristide and back to the Queen.

"Oh, just get on with it," Ari was getting impatient.

The Queen nodded her consent.

The soldier stammered for a moment, not knowing whether he should continue before finally saying, "It appears there has been an issue on Waterford," he paused – again glancing between the two of them awkwardly.

Aristide's blood ran cold. *How could they know already?* he thought.

"Go on," Izzy said sensing his hesitation.

"My Lady, the King's mother is dead," he said almost flinching away from Ari.

Izzy immediately went to console Ari, but he just stood there, his face void of all emotion. Instead, she said to the soldier, "Can you please leave us. As you can imagine this is quite distressing news."

The soldier shifted his feet uncomfortably. "I'm sorry, Your Majesty. There's more."

She gestured for him to continue.

"Um, well..." the soldier hesitated. "It was King, I mean Prince Aristide who killed her."

Izzy spun on her heel to face Ari. "Is this true?" but before she had even asked, she knew it was true. His head hung low and his shoulders drooped. "Why?"

"She faked her kidnapping so that I would relinquish my throne," he said lifting his gaze.

"She what?" Izzy was dumfounded.

The soldier still stood next to the two of them as if waiting for something more.

"Was there anything else?" Izzy asked him curtly.

His eyes darted again. "The Law of Sovereignty no longer applies since he stepped down from the crown."

Izzy squinted at the soldier trying to find the meaning behind his words – so he continued.

"I'm here to arrest the Prince for the murder of his mother, by order of the Council," he finished finally finding some semblance of strength in his voice.

"You most certainly will not," Isabella boomed – the tone in her voice reminding her of her father when he got angry.

"I'm sorry, Your Majesty. It's by order of the Council. Not even you can overrule this," and with that he pulled power blocking manacles from his belt as three more soldiers suddenly appeared out of nowhere providing back up, but Ari wasn't going to fight.

He was guilty and he knew it. Prepared to accept the consequences for his temper getting the better of him, he touched his cousin on the shoulder and nodded, then he put his hands out and the guard shackled his hands in the manacles – all the while, listening to Izzy's cries of protest.

IZZY BURST THROUGH the doors of the Council chambers – smoke coming from her skin, her fury mounting. "How could you," she spat at them.

"I'm sorry, Your Majesty?" Davis said quizzically. "We're in the middle of a meeting."

Five members of the Council sat along a U-shaped meeting table with papers strewn in front of them. The room was a rectangle shape with exposed wooden beams across the ceiling, each of the many windows along the back wall stained glass, depicting a ruler from times gone by.

"I don't care," she yelled. "You can't just put out an order to arrest Aristide."

"Oh, we can," Davis said removing his spectacles and placing them on the desk in front of him. "And we did. He murdered his mother. We have eyewitnesses."

"Like whom?" Izzy asked.

"Me," Alina said casually as she entered behind Izzy.

"Why didn't you come to me first?" she asked, baffled.

Alina stepped around so that she was standing in front of the Queen and looked her up and down. "You really think you would've made a rational decision as a ruler?" she laughed. "Doubtful. You let your emotions get the better of you quite often. Just look at how you handled the whole Christian fiasco."

Izzy growled. "What's that supposed to mean. Her fists clenched at her sides – she could feel the magic coursing through her veins, flowing down to her hands just waiting to explode out.

"Well," Alina said in an infuriatingly chirpy voice. "I'm just saying electrifying him like that wasn't exactly your most composed moment as ruler. Especially in front of all those people."

The Queen lunged at the girl, her heart thumping in her ears. The moment her hands touched the girl's bare skin, she let out a screech of pain. Izzy immediately let go from the shock of the noise to see a severe burn in the shape of her hand on Alina's upper arm.

"You burnt me!" she shrieked, as tears fell down her cheeks from the pain – the sleeve of her dress singed and ragged now having been caught under the edge of the Queen's grip.

"I, I'm sorry," Izzy started not sure what to do. "I didn't mean to."

"You need to control your power," Alina cried clutching her burnt arm.

Davis and another woman from the Council rushed around to tend to Alina's injury.

"She burnt me on purpose," Alina told them, tears still running down her face.

Izzy protested. "I didn't. I swear."

Xander rushed in the door. "I just heard what happened..." but before he could continue, he saw Alina in tears and a distraught Izzy. No one looked up from the commotion, but he could see how flustered Izzy was, so he hurried to her side and grabbed her scolding hot hands that were glowing bright red.

With a wave of cool water, he coated her palms to try to soothe the fire burning deep inside her.

After a moment, Izzy's eyes stopped darting around the room and focussed on her husband. "Thank you," she said pulling her hands back from him. He released her hands from the water back into tiny particles that disappeared into nothing with a swish of his hand.

"Don't think you're getting away with this?" Alina screeched at the Queen – Davis whispered something in her ear. "What?" she cried. "Just because she is the Queen doesn't mean that she can get away with burning people."

Davis interjected. "Actually, it does. The same sovereignty law that has made it the law to arrest Aristide, in fact protects Isabella from prosecution on this matter."

"Alina, I really didn't mean to do it. I'm so sorry. Please forgive me," the Queen pleaded.

"Enough," Xander said stepping between the two girls. "Alina, you need to leave. Go up to the Medica and get your arm seen to." He took hold of Izzy's hand and led her to a seat at the Council table.

"What are you doing?" a Councilwoman asked them.

"We are going to talk about why you felt the need to arrest Aristide," he said calmly.

Izzy started crying. Nothing was going right for her. She'd tried repeatedly to stay strong, but it was all getting too much. She felt her hands once again burning up until Xander interlaced his fingers with hers sending cool water over them.

"As we previously told you, the Sovereignty law no longer applies to him. I'm sorry there is nothing you can do to overturn this ruling," Davis said. "You can lodge an appeal after his trial, but with him being accused of Jenta's murder too, we don't believe it is promising."

"He had nothing to do with Jenta's murder," Izzy yelled at the woman.

The woman sighed, "Surely you can see the connection. He was the person to find Jenta's body, and the two killings were much the same in the way that their heads were removed from their bodies."

"You've got to be kidding me," Izzy started. "Just because he found her doesn't mean he killed her."

"There was no indication of anyone else entering or exiting her room on the night of her death," Davis said. "The evidence against him is overwhelming."

"We'll see about that at his trial," Izzy muttered under her breath.

"What was that, Your Majesty?" the Councilwoman asked.

Izzy rolled her eyes and stood up – the tears no longer falling as a deep rage took their place. "Nothing. Xander, let's go."

THE DUNGEONS SMELT exactly how Izzy remembered it – faeces and an intense musty aroma from the pig pen outside wafted in through metal grates. The monotonous sound of dripping water was giving her a headache as they walked down the cobblestone hallway towards the cell where Aristide was being kept.

"I hope they didn't rough him up too badly," Xander said mostly to himself.

Izzy didn't respond. She felt so guilt-ridden that Ari was even in this position. There was no way it was her fault, but it still plagued her. She now wondered why in Luna's name he had killed her. Izzy knew that Aristide had never had a close relationship with his mother, but this seemed such an extreme response, even for him.

They arrived at his cell – it was much nicer than the one Nova was given. This one at least had a proper bed and a water trough so he could wash himself.

Standing looking out the window nestled in the back wall of the cell was Firestorm's newest prisoner. Still dressed in his sailing gear, he made no effort to hide his worry. His hair was mussed from him running his hands through it repeatedly and his eyes looked weary and swollen, but not from tears.

"Ari?" Izzy padded closer to the bars of his cell.

He turned. "Oh, hi," the smile not reaching his eyes.

"Why did you do it? Why would you kill your own mother, Ari?" Izzy asked.

Aristide walked up to the bars grabbing hold – his knuckles turning white from the strain. "She blackmailed me into giving up my crown."

That wasn't what Izzy was expecting at all. No one from the Council had any more information about what had happened to Ari's mother except that he'd struck her with his sword.

Astonished, she didn't know what to say.

"Cousin, slicing off her head might've been a little bit of an overreaction though don't you think?" Xander said shoving his hands into his pockets.

"Don't you have somewhere else to be?" Ari glared at Xander.

"Aristide!" Izzy chided. "What is wrong with you?"

"Nothing. Just leave me alone," he said and lifted his hand up toward the roof bringing up a solid wall of water.

"I guess he's done talking," Xander said.

"There has to be more to this," Izzy added turning to walk away.

Xander followed. "How do you mean?"

"Something doesn't add up. He killed his own mother. That's not normal no matter how angry you are at someone," she said pushing open the rusted metal gate at the end of the path and stepping out onto the sodden grass. "Does this grass ever dry out?"

"Not that I've ever seen," Xander said asking her hand to stop her from slipping. "What are we going to do about Ari?"

Izzy let out a huff. "There's nothing we can do. He doesn't want to talk to us, and we can't force him."

"But we need him to help with training and especially when the Emperor gets here," he pursed his lips.

"We are just going to have to do this without him. His trial has no set date yet because the Council wants to wait until the threat of invasion is over. I don't think we will see Ari out of the dungeons anytime soon."

"THEY'RE LOOKING GOOD," Agnes said to Izzy and Xander when they arrived at the training field. "Where's Ari?" she asked, looking past them. "I heard he'd come back. I was expecting him to be down here already."

Xander and the Queen looked at each other before she said, "He's down in the dungeons."

Agnes looked puzzled. "What's he doing down there? I didn't think we had many prisoners right now."

"Um," Izzy looked to her husband for support.

"He's *in* the dungeons," Xander stressed – Agnes continuing to look perplexed by the statement. "He's a prisoner."

Agnes dropped the stack of papers she was holding – the wind immediately picked them up and spread them across the field, her jaw dropped in shock.

"It's a long story. One that I'm sure you'll hear amongst the gossip that is constant in the court, but for now, we really need to call a meeting," Izzy said. "One with every nobleman that's still awake and all the members of the Council."

"My paperwork," Agnes cried coming out of her shocked state and running onto the field after it.

Izzy shook her head. "That girl worries me sometimes," a faint smile crossing her lips.

Xander picked up her hand and hooked it around his elbow. "Things are a bit of a mess, aren't they?"

"When you say "things," are you referring to Max being held hostage, Nova and Constance going missing, Aristide in the dungeons, the Emperor coming or there being another All-Powerful Child supposedly wandering about the kingdom?"

Xander tilted his head to the side, "You forgot about Jenta's murder."

"You can't honestly think that Ari killed her," Izzy said pointedly.

"No. I don't – but he did have motive. She was one of the only people who knew of his true parentage. I'm not sure anyone still alive knows who his real father is. Maybe he wanted to keep it that way?" Xander said.

"Possibly – there's just no way he would do something like that. He's a good person, not a murderer," she shook the thought out of her head. "Either way, I have more pressing issues to worry about. I need to figure out what our plan of attack is for when the Emperor and his ships get here. I don't have room in my brain right now to think of more than one thing at a time and considering this will be the difference between life and death for us, I'm going to go work on a plan. Are you coming?"

"I am," Xander said pausing on the overhead walkway that crossed over the dungeons.

"What are you waiting for?" Izzy said annoyed.

"I just had a thought," he said with a puzzled look on his face. "Ari just used magic."

"So?" said Izzy.

"In the dungeons..." Xander was waiting for the coin to drop.

"Oh," She said after a moment. "How? No one is supposed to be able to use magic down there. It's the reason why they're such effective dungeons."

"Exactly," he said continuing along the walkway. "But I think he is too upset to have figured that out yet – and I'm not going to tell the guards, or the Council."

Izzy thought on it for a moment. Her duty as the Queen was to her subjects and their safety – and she still wasn't convinced Aristide was even a threat. "Neither will I," she said at last.

# 15

"Well that was stupid wasn't it?" Alina mocked her cousin through the cell bars. She leaned on them facing out and away from him. "If I were you, I would've made sure no one was watching before committing murder."

"I don't want to talk to you Alina," Aristide said not moving from the bed in his cell.

"Oh, but you don't have a choice. I'm here and you're there," she gestured to their positions. "And there's nothing you can do about it."

Ari's glare was like knives piercing right through a heart. "It is because of you that I'm in here."

"Come now Cousin, we all know that I didn't tell a lie. I would never lie about something so important. You know that," she said sweetly.

He stood up and started to pace the cell. "You didn't have to tell them at all."

Alina ran her sharp fingernails along the rusted metal of the bars. "Aw Cousin, where's the fun in that."

"It was all your idea," he rushed at the bars causing Alina to jump back quickly. "You're the one who's been after my crown this entire time."

"And people said you were stupid," she taunted him. "Anyway, I must go. There is only so long a cat can play with a mouse before it gets bored."

"You really are a piece of work, you know that?" he said through gritted teeth.

She let out a guttural laugh. "Thank you. That's truly kind of you."

Ari punched the bars out of frustration – blood immediately welled on his knuckles. "Get out!" he yelled.

"Suit yourself – but just know, when this is all over, you'd better start treating me with a little more respect – since I'll be your Queen and all," she turned to leave but paused. Giggling she said, "Silly me, you won't be alive to see that. I wonder if Queen Isabella will electrocute you like she did Christian. Now that would be a spectacle. Never mind, I'll be too busy trying on my new crowns to care."

THE WIND ALONG THE channel howled and Maximus, tied to the mast leaned over trying to capture some of the water that had collected in a tarp in his mouth. He'd now spent two thousand and forty-four days as a prisoner of the Emperor – each day felt as though it lasted an eternity.

He was the sole surviving crew member from his fleet of five ships – the civilian passengers were taken to the Northern Mainland to be sold into slavery. Max had no idea what had happened to them past that point. His crew were herded onto one of his ships and tied up in rows – women and men alike. There they stayed tied up on their knees for two days and nights before the Emperor's men grew sick of hearing their complaints and sliced their necks. Max remembered being held by one of the officers and no matter how much he wanted to look away, he couldn't. He watched the life leave their eyes and the magic leave their souls and floating up to the skies and back to Luna.

Having watched everyone, he'd left Lunacia with die, his ships were taken to the Northern Mainland, as was he. He was thrown into a cell and left there, alone. The only time he saw another person – or rather their hand, was when the meagre tray of food was shoved through the small metal flap in the door to his cell.

And that was where he had remained until a week ago when he was dragged from the dark cell into the light and thrown on another ship. Max's eyes burned and watered for two days from the sudden and blinding light he was now sitting in. He'd been thrown onto the deck and tied to the mast – deck hands and officers of the Emperor's army alike throwing insults at him as they passed. That wasn't the only thing they threw though. Max looked down at his feet. Bits of old food clung to his boots and pieces of broken glass littered the deck beneath his feet.

"Oi, don't be falling asleep there," one of the deck hands called to him. "We're meeting up with The Emperor's ship in a few hours."

"Shove it. You fat bastard!" Maximus called back.

"Oh ho, listen here," the man said to another beside him. "He thinks he's clever with his name calling."

"Let me out of this rope and I'll show you just how clever I really am," Max said – his cheeky smile was wide, revealing his canine teeth.

"Nice try," he said.

The men kept heckling him, but Max ignored it. He couldn't help but look out towards the Lunacian islands and wonder what had been happening for the past five and a half years since he'd made the worst decision of his life.

He thought about how when he was on Lunacia, he'd always thought life would be better out across the open sea – boy was he so very wrong.

It had been his greatest dream to sail the seas to find new land – to have the excitement of being the first person to ever lay eyes on the water's edge of the fabled lands to the south or the west.

The moment he'd set sail away from Lunacia, it had been as though nothing would ever go wrong again. The wind through his hair and the sound of the water slapping the ship's hull was everything he imagined the afterlife to be like.

They'd had such a good run on their departure – the tides and the wind favoured them, the crew were happy and eager to work hard. Three days later and everything turned on its head.

A storm blew in from the North-East – heading for them head on. There was no way they would've seen the fifty ships coming for them with the seas so rough, but with all the Sense users on board, Max wondered why no one had been given a warning.

The Emperor's ships pulled alongside theirs and soldiers swung from ropes down from their much higher decks down onto that of the five Lunacian ships. Chaos ensued and those who didn't die, were taken captive and later killed. Max, however, was beaten by soldiers and healed by a Gypsy woman who travelled with them, and then beaten again. This vicious cycle continued for many days and nights aboard his ship. Max was forced to watch as the Emperor's soldiers killed his friends and raped the women – leaving the children to cry before they too were given the sweet kiss of death from their blades.

Tears fell from Max's eyes as he remembered everything he'd gone through to get to this moment. This moment as he stood tied to the mast of the Emperor's second largest ship just waiting to watch his home burn.

What terrified him most was the fact they would assume he had perished long ago. But here he was on his way back home and when the Lunacian people fought back – and he knew they would, he would either watch them all be slaughtered, or he would go down in flames on this very deck, attached to this very mast without ever having the chance to reveal himself and be saved.

IZZY SAT ON HER FATHER'S chair in his study and wondered how long this would feel like his study instead of her own. So many things had happened since her father had passed away. None of which she felt the least bit equipped to deal with.

A knock came at the door and Alina poked her head in.

"What can I do for you?" Izzy said, her voice raspy with exhaustion.

Alina practically skipped in – Izzy eyed her with suspicion.

"I'd like to have a quick word with you if I might?" she chirped, taking a seat opposite The Queen.

Izzy motioned for her to go on.

"It's such a shame about our Aunt is it not?" she said, her eyes void of emotion.

The Queen surveyed the girl. Her dress was a pale blue silk with beading running over the bodice. Lace lined her cleavage giving the illusion she was demure and not the notorious flirt Izzy knew her to be. Her hair was swept up off her neck in a mess of curls – a sapphire pin holding it all together.

"Can you make it quick please?" Izzy was sorting through some paperwork on her desk and trying to sound uninterested.

Alina always liked to be the centre of attention, so without Izzy's full attention, her anger was starting to flare. "I would like," she began tersely before reigning herself in, "To talk about the Waterford crown. As you know, I'm now first in line since Aristide's unfortunate downfall."

Izzy placed her paperwork down and leant back in her chair crossing her arms. "If you're about to ask me to give you the crown, then you may as well leave. I have no intention of handing out any crowns to people they don't belong to."

"But Aristide has been arrested for murder!" Alina protested.

Izzy held up a hand to silence her. "And I most certainly wouldn't give the crown to the very person who is the reason why he may never be allowed to have his crown back," Izzy stood and walked towards the door Alina had entered through. "I used to think you were nice, I guess I was wrong. Now if you would kindly leave, I have a battle plan to form."

Alina wanted to argue but she knew if it came to blows, no one was stronger than the fabled Fire Queen, especially her with her weak Water magic, and so she left.

Izzy returned to her desk and waited for Xander to join her. A few minutes later, as she was busily reading the weather report from the harbour for the next few days, she heard the door beside her creak open. Xander would be coming in from their rooms so she didn't lift her gaze. She would greet him once she'd finished reading.

Something sharp and cold caught Izzy's neck and she was pulled back into her chair. Air fought to get past whatever it was blocking it. She tried to tilt her head up to look at whoever was restraining her, but the force of being pulled into the high back of the chair stopped her. Someone reached from behind her chair and grabbed her arms, yanking them down and holding her wrists so tight she thought her hands would pop off.

She couldn't scream and her magic needed fresh air in her lungs to have any sort of effect – all fires need oxygen. Black spots clouded her eyes and her vision swirled. Everything inside her was screaming as ragged gasps escaped her throat. Izzy's lungs were aching, and her eyes were wide with fear. Despite the pain, she began to thrash underneath what she'd now worked out to be wire at her throat.

Izzy kicked her legs and raised her feet up to the desk. She hooked her boots on the curved edge of the desktop and kicked against it rocking herself back in the chair. Whoever was behind her chair screamed out in pain – the back of her father's heavy chair jamming them between the stone wall. They let go of her hands and immediately the chair started to rock forwards again.

With another mighty kick, Izzy tumbled backwards, rolling onto the floor. The wire around her neck slipping loose as the man holding it was thrown out of the way. She scrambled out of the way and took a deep breath that felt like she was inhaling knives.

In her veins she felt the fire building – adrenaline taking the place of strength.

Streams of fire burst from her fingertips and she aimed them at the two men who were scrambling to get out from underneath the chair and onto their feet. Izzy didn't see their faces until their bodies were alight with fire. Screams echoed from them between the flames and the Queen backed away as tried to run at her. Her hands remained outstretched towards the two men, willing the fire to consume them on the spot but not spread through the castle.

Another rush of power coursed through her and the inferno engulfing the men flamed brighter. Their screams had long stopped, and their charcoaled heaps lay twisted together, flames still playing on their bodies.

Xander came crashing through the door having heard Izzy screaming – she hadn't even realised she was.

Water flooded the study and the bodies, extinguishing the flames. Xander sent several waves over pieces of furniture to stop them burning before turning to his wife, sure nothing else would catch alight or continue to burn. "What happened?" he asked embracing her.

A cold expression across her face. "These two men just tried to kill me," her voice was hoarse and raspy.

"Who were they?" Xander asked. He'd tried to get a look at their faces, but they were beyond recognition now.

"I don't know. They didn't use magic, but that doesn't mean they didn't have any," she said. "Nanu?" Izzy yelled loudly, her voice still croaking and gravelly.

A moment later the maid ran into the study.

"Tell the soldiers that the castle is officially on lockdown. No one in or out without my permission. Anyone who doesn't normally reside inside the castle is to join the Gypsies and the other Elementals outside the building. Lock the gates. If someone wants to leave let them. If someone wants to get in, kill them," she said wiping the soot that had mixed with her blood on neck – a thin but deep cut ran across her neck in a line from ear to ear.

"But Little One, what about Constance and the other girl? They've gone to the Gypsy camp. If they return, I'll instruct the soldiers to let them in," the maid said sure of her words.

"If someone wants to get in, kill them!" Izzy repeated rubbing her throat and looking at Nanu without blinking. Izzy eyed the two men, "I wonder who they're working for. Now that they're dead, I won't be able to find out who."

"You're a Queen," Xander said summoning a sphere of water between his hands. "Everyone wants to kill you for one reason or another. Does it really matter?"

"I guess not," she said.

# 16

The ship that Max was being held on sailed through the channel between Firestorm and Terrania. Several hours passed and he watched as the sun moved across the sky growing steadily lower on the horizon. His skin was dry, and his lips were chapped after days of being exposed to the elements. Each time he tried to access his power, he felt nothing. It had been years since he'd reached into the depths of his soul to bring it to life. The years he spent prisoner in the Emperor's fortress he'd never had a need to use it because he had been alone, there were no thoughts but his own to hear.

The days continued to pass after moving through the channel and finally the Emperor's other ships were spotted in the distance. They littered the sea like ants swarming on the crumbs left on a picnic blanket. When Max finally looked up, he saw over the side of the ship a monstrous hull butt up against the boat he was on, it was clearly the Emperor's. Max had come to learn that the Emperor had very particular tastes, and as such he knew that he would only sail on the largest and most opulent of ships in his fleet.

Ropes were cast between the two lashing them together and Max shifted as best he could so that he was standing up straight. There is no way he was going to show any weakness to the man who had destroyed his life.

Once the ships were lashed together Max saw the deckhands on the taller of the two ships manoeuvred the gangway over the side and down on to the ship he was on. With a loud thwack the gangway landed on the railing and deckhands rushed in to tie it down securely.

Chattering amongst the deckhands petered out as a commotion on the deck of the much bigger ship filtered down to them – the

Emperor was coming. People hustled and bustled making sure everything was perfect, and in its place. No one wanted to suffer the wrath of an angry Emperor.

From Max's vantage point he could see only the bottom of his robes – red brocade with gold filigree along the hem flowed in the stiff breeze. He wore shiny black shoes that ended in a severe point and they clicked with each step he took toward the gangway.

Coming into view, Max saw The Emperor's flat top hat with tassels hanging down the side of his face. His black moustache pointed at each side was a stark contrast to his ice-blue eyes – a colour not often seen in people with dark-coloured skin.

He exuded absolute power with each step he took towards the bridge between his two ships – slaves trailing after him, lifting his long robes as he walked. Taking a step onto the gangway, he shoved the slaves aside and they landed on their backs. One of them clutched at his arm in pain and seeing this one of the soldiers walked up kicking him further out of the way.

Max shook his head trying to move his matted, unkempt hair out of his eyes. His beard knotted and grubby hung limply down to his chest, one of the many signs of the many harsh years that he'd spent living in captivity. He struggled to see through the dreadlocked pieces that were filled with grime and oil, but he tried his best.

The Emperor moved slowly along the steeply angled gangway – one of the rare times he was forced to hold his own robes up. Every single movement deliberate and calculated until at last, he stepped down onto the smaller ship.

Max steeled his face and straightened his shoulders as much as his bindings would allow – he would not appear weak to this monster.

"You're still alive," the Emperor said to Max with disdain.

"No thanks to you," Max replied, venom in his words.

"Don't be like that," the Emperor continued. "Have I not let you live these past five years? I could have left you to the same fate as your little crew."

Max spat at the Emperor, it landed squarely on the lapel of his ridiculous robe. Gasps from those assembled filled the silence. The Emperor looked down at the saliva, calmly taking off his robe and throwing it aside. It landed in a heap at the feet of one of his soldiers.

"That was one of your less intelligent decisions, Maximus. I warn you, do not make that mistake again." Out of nowhere, another coat appeared behind him. He reached his arms out and the slave deftly shrugged it on, carefully pulling up to his shoulders. "Now," he continued. "What are we going to do with you?"

Max stayed silent – he wanted to scream and shout and spit everything he had at the man, but his lack of energy and severe thirst made it all too much effort.

The Emperor smacked his lips together. "I might just throw you over the side. How does that sound?"

Max started to protest, and the Emperor began laughing. They both knew that the water was far too cold to survive more than five minutes and even if one could, they were too far from land. Sharks and monsters from the deep would take you if the cold didn't. Max slumped with resignation – it wasn't looking good for him.

"Or maybe I will give you some of this to drink," he held up a vial that he'd pulled from his inner pocket. The bright green liquid glowed with a light as blinding as the sun that Max had to look away. "It is interesting isn't it?" the Emperor continued. "This special potion will burn your vocal cords which means you'll be unable to talk for about a week."

Max's eyes grew wide.

"Then, maybe I will send you back to Firestorm and have my spies report on how nobody knows who you are. It will be quite entertaining for me to say the least." He gestured to one of the slaves he'd shoved earlier to take the vial from him.

As the slave moved tentatively closer, the Emperor shoved it into his chest, his hands barely coming up in time to grab hold of it before it dropped.

"I'm going to give you three goblets of water to choose from – you look thirsty, my friend," he said, a cruel smile on his face.

Max narrowed his eyes. "What's the catch?"

The Emperor let out a guttural laugh throwing his head back, the tassels on his hat swinging back and forth. "Maybe you aren't so stupid after all, Princeling. One of the goblets will have the poison in it. Which one, I'm not telling – that choice is up to you."

"That's barbaric," Max said shaking his head.

"You will need to drink water eventually Princeling, so the choice is yours. By my calculations, it's been two days since you were given anything. You must be feeling desperate for water by now."

Max had given little thought to his situation until the Emperor brought it up. Suddenly the cracks on his lips began to sting and his tongue felt two sizes too big for his mouth. He tried swallowing but it felt like a ball of cotton wool was stuck in his throat. It felt like razor blades were piercing his throat all the way to his stomach, slicing an agonising path with each attempt to swallow. "I will not bend to you," Max said to the Emperor, hoping he had injected enough conviction to be taken seriously.

"We shall see," the Emperor said smiling. The servant returned with three goblets placing them in front of Max.

An unexpected pang of desire niggled at Max, and the urge to just reach out and blindly choose a goblet and start drinking was overwhelming save for the fact his hands were still tied to the mast. He turned his head away to try and get rid of the burning desire.

The Emperor said, "I will leave you and your new friends alone to get better acquainted." He looked down at the three goblets that had been placed on a crate near Max. "Do let one of the deckhands know if you'd like to have a drink from one of them. I am sure they will gladly help you. It'll be interesting to see which of the three you choose and whether you've chosen wisely or foolishly.

The older man cast his gaze to the sky, dark clouds were starting to form, and he continued, "Fashion a tarp over the Princeling. We wouldn't want him to get any ideas about quenching his thirst with this rain, not after I've gone to the troubling of giving him goblets of water to drink from."

*Damn it,* Max thought.

THE SUN'S RAYS FILTERED through the sails and cast a dull glow on the goblets in front of Max. He had spent the last four hours staring at them. His eyes and mouth were bone dry and as much as he tried to resist, the inescapable heat from the boat's deck beckoned him to call for the deckhand to bring one of them to his lips so that he might take a drink.

But which one would he choose? The decision had been weighing on him heavily. On one hand, he could taste the sweetness that was fresh water and finally quench his thirst. On the other hand, he was running the risk of choosing wrongly and losing his voice for a week. He'd even considered drinking all three knowing he would lose his voice but get some much-needed water, just so he would be taken back to Firestorm.

He missed his home. Max had no idea it had been five years until the Emperor told him earlier.

Five years! Five years he'd spent in a dark moss-covered room hidden away from all civilisation. Five years he'd spent clawing at every inch of the stone walls trying to find purchase on a loose brick in the walls. Try as he might though, the walls were rock solid and there was no escape to be found. Despite not being able to see his way around the cell for the most part, there was one hour a day when a bright white light would be illuminated inside his cell. The servants would come, sweep, and mop up his mess, they'd scrub the walls clean and leave again, taking the light with them. There was no lavatory in his cell which made the first few days very awkward for him when the cleaners arrived. Though he'd eventually realised that was the purpose of their daily visit to his cell – to clean.

Max thought it strange that the Emperor was so concerned with the cleanliness of his dungeons. Why wouldn't he just put in a lavatory or waste receptacle? It perplexed him, but eventually it became his norm, and he craved the company for that hour, even though they didn't speak to him at all. They came, they cleaned, and they left – every day at the same time.

The goblets called to him – each one becoming more enticing. Max wrestled with himself – he didn't know which fate was worse. Staying on board with the Emperor and his men or being thrown back on Lunacia with no voice and bearing no resemblance to his former self.

His greatest worry: that his brothers wouldn't recognise him. He'd missed Manu so much and the thought of seeing him again made Max want to cry – except he had no moisture left even for tears. Theodore would be welcoming but he knew he would be chastised for losing the ships. Despite all of that though, he looked forward to seeing him – John too.

Christian would ridicule him, finding any reason possible to insult him, so maybe there was one brother he was not looking forward to seeing.

His niece Isabella would be all grown up by now, the thought comforted him, but none of this took away from the persistent dry feeling in his throat.

Max attempted to lick his lips; dry flakes of skin sticking to his tongue. His vision swirled from dehydration – white spots appearing in the air in front of him.

He couldn't go on any longer, he called for one of the deckhands.

"Finally caved, have ya?" the deckhand asked walking over to him.

"Just give me the middle one," Max said desperately.

The deckhand picked up the goblet and asked, "Are you sure?"

"No. But I need water," He replied gingerly putting his lips on the rounded edge of the metal goblet.

As soon as the cool liquid touched his tongue, sweet relief washed over him.

He swallowed down the first mouthful, some of the water spilling out of his mouth and dripping down his chin.

After the second mouthful, his chin began to burn, and he began coughing and spluttering.

"No!" he tried to scream his eyes wide with fear, but nothing came out.

His throat burned as if someone had pushed a hot poker down it – and no matter how many times he tried to make a noise; nothing came out.

Silent sobs wracked his body. How could he be so unlucky?

Max remained tied to the mast until the near-full moon was high in the night sky. His neck ached from hours staring up at stars. – he wondered how many of his ancestors were looking down on him and shaking their heads in dismay at just how stupid he'd been to drink from any of the goblets.

The Emperor's ship had remained lashed to the smaller one and Max kept looking at the gangway, almost hoping he that something, anything would happen just to relieve his boredom.

His knees ached and he kept shifting his weight from one foot to the other to try and stop the pins and needles, to no avail. Suddenly a sound from the Emperor's ship made him jump and he jerked his head up – a lone figure stepped out of the shadows and up onto the plank.

Max's eyes were still sore from being exposed to so much light after years of being held captive in the darkness, so identifying the figure was difficult. He watched as they walked down the gangway and slowly stepped onto the smaller ship. Max could just make out it was a man wearing tight long pants, a long sleeve shirt and ankle-high boots.

Slowly, he walked over towards the mast where Max was tied. Max stretched his neck and wriggled his wrists, trying to ready himself for whatever was coming.

"My men tell me you could not help but have a drink," it was the Emperor – not at all who Max had expected. For him to be out here in regular clothing and without his entourage was very odd. "There is a small boat tied to my ship you know," he said. "I am going to untie you now, and you are going to walk up that plank and then climb down the other side of my ship and get into the small boat." Max could do nothing but stare at the man's beady eyes. "Once you are in that little boat, you will row yourself to Firestorm. What you do from there is up to you," a vicious smile stretched from ear to ear on his skinny face, his cheekbones more pronounced as his lips pulled back revealing yellowed teeth.

The Emperor took a knife from his back pocket and sliced through the thick ropes that wrapped around Max's chest and wrists. As the ropes fell to the deck, Max grabbed his wrists and tried massaging the feeling back in and the pain out.

"You are wasting time. I didn't tell my guards that I was coming over to see you, but it will only be a matter of time before they notice I am no longer in my chambers and they come to ensure I am safe. If they find you no longer in your restraints, there will be many questions." His thick accent made it difficult for Max to understand every word, but he understood enough to know it was time for him to go.

He tried to say something but again nothing came out, a sharp reminder that even if he did manage to make it back to Firestorm in one piece, he would be unable to tell anyone who he was – not that anyone would believe him enough to let him inside the castle to his family.

The small boat rocked as he gingerly stepped into it. He heard a commotion above him – his absence had clearly been discovered. Picking up the small knife that lay beside him on the floor of the boat, he cut the rope that tied it to the grand ship and gave the oars an almighty heave shifting his small boat away from the larger ship and out into the open waters.

A feeling of excitement bubbled up inside of him – he was going to see his home again, his family.

"THEY'RE NOT STRONG enough," Izzy said to Agnes the following morning as they watched on beside the training field.

Agnes sent a sideways glance towards her, "They'll be fine. You need to relax more."

"Hi," a perky Alina said walking up to them.

They greeted each other with a hug and a kiss on each cheek.

"How have you been?" Agnes asked her, unaware of the recent exchange between her and the Queen. "I haven't seen you since... well, since you were here on Firestorm right before Christian's trial." Izzy stood behind Agnes as she and Alina talked, smiling ruefully as she recalled the last time that she'd had words with the girl in her study. Izzy completely distrusts Alina, and she hopes one day soon Agnes comes to realise just how dangerous Alina is too.

Alina brought her hand up and throwing her hair over her shoulders responded, "I've been well," her eyes darting away from her

Agnes to gaze at her and back so quickly Izzy almost missed it – almost.

"Where have you been for the past week?" Agnes questioned the girl as she hefted her paperwork into her other arm .

"Oh," she said smiling. "I've been around. I was on Aerleon until the um, incident happened with Aristide and his mother."

"Yes," said Agnes, "we are so sorry for your loss."

"Yes, it's terribly sad. Anyway," Alina said waving her hand as if dismissing the conversation. "I just wanted to come down and say hello. I'm off to settle into my rooms now before you know who comes. I don't want my maids to have to leave during the siege because they didn't gather everything I needed."

"You aren't going to help us fight?" Agnes asked surprised. She thought that surely everyone would be wanting to protect Lunacia. But perhaps that was just being naïve.

"Oh, come on, you both know that's not my style. By the way Izzy, how's your neck? I heard things got a bit tight for you yesterday. I'm sure you're going to be just fine though – you always are," she said and walked away waving her fingers goodbye over her shoulder.

"Well that was strange," Agnes said after she was out of earshot. "What did she mean about your neck, and things getting a bit tight?" she asked.

Izzy tugged at the scarf she had fastened around her neck concealing the wound from her attack. "I pay no mind to most of what Alina says, but I think we're going to be better off with her out of the way when the Emperor arrives. She'd just be yet another thing for one of us to worry about."

MAX HAD ROWED HIS SMALL boat without a break right through the night and now, as the sun's heat beat down on him from directly above his head the shores of Firestorm came into view on the horizon. He estimated it would take him another day and night of rowing to reach it but seeing the end goal somehow made the pain in his muscles and the ache in his heart vanish – he was going to make it.

He'd found a flask of water and a small bag of rations buried underneath the bench seat of the small boat. Slowly, he pulled out a hard biscuit – his arms felt like jelly after the long night rowing as hard and far as he could from the Emperor's ship.

Biting into the biscuit, he laid back on the floor of the boat to stretch the muscles his back. He was sure he'd only lasted this long because of the adrenaline coursing through his veins.

After resting for a short time, he gathered up the oars and continued rowing toward his home.

Five years was an exceptionally long time. A lump catching in his throat – so many emotions were threatening to be released. He'd spent so much time alone with no one there to listen when he spoke, and now...more silent sobs came from deep within. His home was in sight once again but would the last five years he had endured leave him so that he could enjoy being here again. Or had he escaped only to bring the torment he had endured with him?

THE NEXT AFTERNOON, Izzy and Agnes walked down the long hall to the Queen's study to look over the finished battle plans once more before sending it to the separate groups within the castle. Agnes was dragging her feet – exhaustion written all over her face as she mentally tried to work the aches from her muscles.

"You ought to go soak in the bath after this, Agnes," Izzy said noticing how tired her cousin was.

"Oh, I definitely will be. I went earlier and picked up a special powder the Medica said to pop in the water," Agnes reached for the door to the study, stopping short when she saw it was already ajar.

The Terranian princess slowly turned her head to Izzy – pointing at the already open door, bringing a finger to her mouth to quiet further conversation in case whoever was in there heard.

Izzy remembered locking the door when she'd left earlier. She pushed past Agnes and laid her palm flat against the door ready to push it further open – fire mixed with adrenaline ignited within her.

A faint rustling sound came from within, Izzy and Agnes held their breaths. They stopped and huddled close to the door to see if they could hear more – the rustling of paper grew louder, and a woman's voice groaned.

Agnes looked at the Queen puzzled. Izzy however had had quite enough of listening to someone invade the privacy and sanctity of the Queen's study, and being the impatient Queen she was, she opened the door and walked right on in.

The girl standing there was not who she expected – it was Emily. She'd been caught red handed going through the paperwork on the Queen's desk.

"I should've seen this coming," Emily said putting her hands on her hips and letting out a huff.

In the blink of an eye, it was Agnes who shot forward – Emily was now pinned against the stone pillar between the windows behind the desk, a small dagger at her throat.

The girl's hands went up in surrender. "Calm down. I was just looking for a piece of charcoal to write a letter."

Agnes narrowed her eyes; she could smell a lie. She pressed the dagger's blade into the girls throat just a little more, making her flinch back even though she had nowhere to go. "Do you want to try that again?"

Izzy had never seen so much fury from Agnes before, she wasn't quite sure what she would do. "Agnes don't kill her," she said.

Emily looked to the Queen, "Thank you. Now if you'll kindly let me go." Her eyes shot to the dagger and back up to meet Agnes' eyes.

The Queen said, "Oh, I didn't say she should release you. I said she couldn't kill you...yet."

"Okay, okay," Emily tried to wriggle under the blade's edge.

"Who are you working for?" Agnes asked, fury in her eyes. "Who were the two men that tried to kill the Queen?"

Dust and dirt from the floor started to rise out of the carpet in a haze around them making it difficult for the Queen to see – a clear sign that Agnes was much angrier than she appeared.

Emily looked confused, "What two men?"

"Don't lie to me," yelled Agnes, the dagger pressing the tip of the blade into flesh of her neck, blood oozing from under the blade.

A tear fell down the girl's cheek. "I'm not. I don't know anything about them," she cried, her voice quieter than before.

"Agnes," Izzy said walking closer. "I think she's telling the truth."

"Not the whole truth," Agnes pressed the dagger harder – more lines of blood ran down Emily's neck. "I also want to know why you were seen down at the dock asking questions about when Aristide would be coming back."

"I didn't want to work for him. He made me do it. I swear I didn't want to," Emily started sobbing as Agnes releasing the pressure stepped back, leaving the girl against the bricks – the cloud of dirt dropping back to the floor.

Izzy stood in front of the girl, "And who are you referring to when you say 'he'?" she asked, pulling a handkerchief from her pocket, and handing it to Emily – the blood now ran down to the top of her dress.

Emily took the handkerchief, gingerly pressing it to her neck wincing. "The Emperor. He..." she paused, "I am his property."

"You'd want to start explaining a little quicker. My dagger is getting impatient again," Agnes said tossing it up in the air and catching its handle over and over.

"Would you be quiet?" Izzy rounded on Agnes. "Go on," she said to Emily, privately horrified at her referring to herself as property.

"When I was a little girl, the Emperor took my father hostage and killed my mother. I was sent to live with Nadia and her family under the guise of being their ward. All the while I was expected to work for the Emperor as a spy. I was supposed to gain information on any topic he found interesting until he decides he is of no more use. It's been nine years and still he holds him hostage."

"That's terrible," Agnes said, her demeanour softening.

Emily nodded. "I'm not even sure if he is still alive."

"How horrible for you – but why didn't you come and tell me this? We could've worked together and fed him lies. He would never have known," said Izzy.

"I don't know," Emily cried. "Because I'm not very smart and all I could think about was my father. If I had have been found out he would've killed him. I couldn't take that risk."

Izzy led the girl to her father's big old chair and sat her down. "I understand."

"You do?" Agnes said, confusion etched in her voice.

A sideways glance from Izzy told Agnes she should stop talking.

"Just tell me one thing," Izzy said, her voice becoming serious. "Was it real with Aristide? Why were you down at the dock asking questions about him? This is my kingdom; you won't be able to get much past me."

The girl paused before answering Izzy, she knew she needed to convince her of her feelings for the royal. But as Emily stood trying to form a response, she couldn't help but think of the awkward young man who was so obviously smitten with her. Maybe she could love a man if he were like Ari. He wasn't a terrible tyrant like the Emperor; he seemed bashful, sweet even. Maybe she didn't hate him the way she had wanted to when she was given this assignment by the Emperor.

Emily looked at Izzy and nodded. "We have only just started to get to know each other – but yes, I believe it is real – and as far as what I was doing down at the dock...it started out as me trying to do the Emperor's work by creating a rift between the Lunacian rulers. But in the end, all I really cared about was if he was safe and coming back."

"So, he was part of your plan?" Izzy pressed further. "To get to me?"

The girl's head dropped. "In the beginning yes but not anymore. The second I started to feel something for him, I stopped reporting to the Emperor about him. I just couldn't bring myself to hurt him like that."

"So, the day the two of you met, looking at the paintings..." Izzy continued for her.

Emily nodded, "I had to go away from him. He was just being too sweet, and I was questioning myself and what I was doing."

Agnes laughed. "And here we were thinking it was just because his story about the dragon was so ridiculous."

The girl smiled from Izzy to Agnes. "Well, there was that, but it was at that point that I decided I was going to leave him out of every-thing, and so I did."

"So, what did you report to the Emperor?" Izzy pushed on.

Emily stood up. "Only bits and pieces. Not anything of sub-stance, I swear."

"What now?" Agnes asked looking at Izzy.

Izzy thought for a moment. "You know I really can't let this go," she said, a hint of sadness in her voice.

The girl's expression changed from one of relief at finally unbur-dening herself, to one of resignation. "I know."

"Come with me," Izzy said. "I know someone who will be very happy to see you," she led the girl out of her study and down to the dungeons – soldiers trailing right behind to ensure she didn't get any ideas.

As it happened, the cell right next to Aristide's was empty. After assuring her that it would only be temporary until everything settled down, she left them there to catch up. Emily had some truths to reveal and Aristide had some explaining to do of his own.

# 17

The moment Max tied his small boat to the dock, swords were pointed at his throat – a welcome he was expecting given his current appearance – the grubby, soiled clothes, his matted and unkempt hair and beard. Seven guards stood around him ordering him to slowly exit the boat and kneel on the dock.

"Identify yourself," one of them ordered.

Max threw up his hands up in surrender.

"Speak now or find yourself on the wrong end of a blade," another said.

The Prince, panicking, gestured as best he could that he couldn't speak – the guards looking from Max and back to each other stood there unsure what to do.

One of them deciding he wasn't going to be the one to make the decision turns to the others and asks, "Well, what do we do with him? We've been given orders."

"Technically he hasn't gone inside the castle walls yet, plus he's a mute. What harm could he possibly cause?" the one that spoke first said. He turned back to Max. "Are you here to seek refuge?"

Max nodded furiously.

"Can you work?" a third soldier asked lowering his blade.

Again, Max nodded, trying to smile and at that exact moment exhaustion washed over him. His legs gave out from under him and he fell onto the dock, his knees taking the impact with a crunch.

"Follow Phillip here, he'll take you to work somewhere you'll be useful," the third soldier continued. "After that you can rest until tomorrow. But you'll pull your weight, do you understand?" A sharp nod of understanding from Max, he pulled himself up and followed the soldier back to their camp.

Max would have to wait a little bit longer to find a way inside the castle walls because without a voice to explain himself, his options were limited. For now, working as a soldier's hand was as good as it was going to get, and he was certainly happy to be back on dry land in Lunacia and not in a small dark room or tied to the mast of a ship in the blistering sun.

"DO THEY STILL NOT REALISE we all need to work together?" she said exasperated throwing her arms up in disbelief seeing the Gypsies and Elementals were still segregating themselves on the training field.

She marched herself over to where the Gypsy Elders were gathered off to the side – her palms growing hot in frustration.

"Good afternoon, Your Majesty," Theodora's sister Rosa said eyeing the frazzled Queen up and down.

"Why won't you join in?" Izzy huffed at her.

Darius, one of the gypsy men, joined them. "Your Majesty," he started, "You know there are laws against our magic, don't you?"

Izzy's eyes grew wide and she stared at him in disbelief. "What? That's ridiculous. There aren't laws against magic."

"Ah, but there is," he said. "Your father was the one who crafted them."

"Is this the reason why your people are not training with everyone else? Fear?" she couldn't believe it. "Agnes," she called back over her shoulder and a minute later the Princess was standing by her side. "Go and gather the Council, we have a law to change." She turned back to the Gypsies, "Now please join in the training. I'm going to change the law right now. You have nothing to fear from using your magic to help us defend our beautiful Lunacia. Together."

The Elders smiled and nodding said, "Thank you, Your Majesty."

"Well, what are you waiting for?" Izzy said gesturing to the field – the gypsies immediately went to their groups to explain there will be no more threat of punishment for using their magic in the presence of Elementals.

The Queen watched as, for the first time Gypsies and Elementals alike began to blend their magic together. Their magic intertwining like the limbs from two vastly different trees coming together as one. Finally, they were helping each other, finally enemies were becoming allies.

FOR THE NEXT FEW DAYS, Izzy and Agnes continued to put the Elementals through their drills from morning to night with little rest. Minal, Darius and Rosa learned new techniques from the Elementials, as they did from the Gypsies. Things were looking up and for the first time since the threat was laid upon them, Izzy felt pride wash over her. Her people had come together – mostly.

There was still the issue of the dwindling food. The Emperor was due to arrive the very next day and by all estimations, there was only two days of food left in all of Edenfore. People were starting to revolt; they were refusing to train until they were given more rations. Xander was busy in the storeroom trying desperately to keep the peace and prevent looting – he'd even gone as far as sleeping in there of a night just to guard the stores. These new duties for Xander were making it difficult for Izzy to spend any time with him and even more difficult for Xander to spend any time with their son.

Izzy had snuck away to the nursery as many times as she could in the last few days to see Emory, but she knew the time was drawing near that she would have to send Nanu with him down into the catacombs below the dungeons for their safety.

Looking out over the training field, Izzy watched the sun fall lower and lower until it was just a sliver laying across the top of the horizon. Tomorrow the Emperor would be on their shores and they had two options fight or surrender and there was no way she was giving up her kingdom, her country without a fight. It would be do or die for the citizens of Lunacia.

"Did you find us more food?" Rosa hobbled over to where Izzy was standing.

*Not this again,* she thought. "No. I didn't," Izzy rolled her eyes. "You know, we are all in the same position here," Izzy said as she felt her stomach gurgle from hunger.

Everyone in the castle had now been reduced to half rations – the royal family included. Izzy didn't want her people to think their leaders were eating sumptuous feasts whilst ordinary citizens were being fed the bare minimum. Right now, she could not afford any extra tensions or reasons for hostility amongst the citizenry.

"Our magic comes from the ground, the elements, and the world around us. We cannot be expected to be at our strongest without proper sustenance," a crowd of Gypsies and Elementials alike were gathering behind them listening eagerly.

Izzy saw this and lifted her chin in a show of strength, despite feeling weaker than she had done in years after day after day training and using her Fire element. "I want everybody to listen," she said to the crowd. "Rosa here has approached me about getting more rations. Those of you who would like more rations please form a line to my left," she gestured to her left-hand side and tentatively people began moving over and before long they all had.

Once everyone had made their way to the line, Izzy pausing for a moment looking at them and started shaking her head. "Okay, now as you should all be able to understand, there is limited food. So those of you who are willing to forfeit your rations so that others may have the full rations they're demanding please move to make a line on my right." No one moved. "Because," she continued, "You must realise, now we are all on half rations. So those of you who wish to have full rations you must stand here and look across at the face of the person you are taking any rations from. It is simple maths – if you want more, someone must have none."

Again, no one moved but a quiet hum of murmurs started amongst them.

"Now do you understand?" she asked looking at them all her face a wall of steel. "There isn't any extra food. We are all hungry. If you want more, it must come from somewhere, rather it must come from someone. If you continue to press me on the matter, perhaps I will start choosing people to move over to this side," as she gestured to the empty space to her right. "Or, you could just stop your complaining, get back to training or whatever it is that you're doing to help us tomorrow and realise that I am not your enemy," with that Izzy walked away and up the stairs that led up to the top of the wall.

Arriving at the section of wall that looked out over the water, Izzy saw Xander standing there with his eyeglass looking out at the ocean.

"Hi," she said coming up behind him and wrapping her arms around his waist. "I thought you were down in the storeroom."

He brought one hand down from the eyeglass and laced his fingers through hers – his hand cold to the touch causing Izzy to jump.

"How long have you been up here?" she said with a shiver.

Xander smiled pulling her around in front of him and laying his arms over her shoulders. "A while," he smiled.

Izzy took a deep breath in and relaxed back against his chest – his intoxicating scent of pine trees and cranberries finding its way around to her and making her slightly lightheaded.

They stood together with Izzy looking down below at the harbour for the longest time. The people below were still working hard to bring all the small boats to shore and tie them down. Xander on the other hand kept his spy glass to his eye, scanning the open waters.

"Wait a minute," Xander said letting go of Izzy and stepping closer to the edge of the wall.

Izzy nearly tripped over when Xander shoved her aside. "Hey. Watch it!" she shouted indignantly at him. She straightened herself up and waited for his apology, but there was none – a look of worry firmly affixed to his face. "What is it? What do you see?"

He handed her the spyglass, worry etched all over his face. Izzy grabbed it from him and tentatively raised it to her eye and looked out at the ocean.

Just as she focussed her eye down the tube, she heard Xander say, "We're out of time. They're already here." With that he took off running, leaving Izzy staring out at the blanket of ships appearing on the horizon. The Emperor was upon them and they could only hope they'd done enough. Izzy's blood ran cold for the first time in her life. Her powers were depleted from another long day of training – and others she knew would be feeling the same.

SHARDS OF GLASS SPLINTERED to the ground, the light rippling and bending through them in multi-coloured fractals as they fell. Izzy could do nothing but watch the chaos that was unfolding inside the castle walls. Panic had gripped Edenfore as the news of the Emperor's early arrival spread like wildfire through the people.

The sleeping soldiers and nobles had finally started to wake – those that were furthest away from where the curse was laid awoke first, but it wasn't enough. Izzy tried to calculate how many were ready and able to fight. She shook her head knowing that even if they all woke up, the Emperor would still have significantly more men at his disposal. By the time they'd all been roused from their slumber they would be cutting it fine.

But they had magic, and with that thought she clung to the hope that their training would be enough.

Rosa and Minal approached handing her a vial. The Queen reached out her hand and took it from them absentmindedly, unable to tear her eyes away from the pandemonium below. It took her only a moment to realise that the two Gypsies were talking to her. "Sorry, what did you say?"

"When the time comes, throw this," Minal said.

Izzy turned her hand over to see the bright orange vial in her hand. "What is it?"

"We have given some to the other nobles. It's just something that will help you if you are in dire need," Rosa said. "But do not use it unless you absolutely must," her eyes were a grim warning.

"Okay," Izzy said stuffing it in her pocket. "You should go and get into position. We have at most two hours before they arrive."

The two Gypsies left Izzy standing alone on the wall – her hand in her pocket, fingers caressing the ridges of the cork in the vial. It was time.

The Queen ran to the nursery where Nanu was hurriedly packing things in a satchel. "Nanu!" Izzy said. As soon as the maid saw her, she passed Prince Emory into Izzy's arms so she could continue grabbing things from around the room.

"I am so sorry, Little One. We were going to go earlier, but the little Prince was having such a lovely sleep I did not want to disturb him. I fear now it is too late," she was becoming hysterical.

Emory lay calmly in his mother's arms as Izzy moved closer to the maid to calm her. "There is still time. You don't need his toys; he is too young to play with them. Leave them, come now. The nursemaid is on her way down to the catacombs now – I saw her on my way here. She will meet you there."

Izzy lowered her head, breathing in the scent of her son for what could possibly be the last time. That sweet milky scent all young babies had mixed with the salty smell she was sure he'd inherited from his father; a Water user warmed her heart. She never wanted to forget the way he smelled, and she hoped he'd never have to endure a life without her there by his side.

"Come now," Izzy handed Emory to the maid. "It's time."

The Queen led them to a hidden door in her study that would take them to the secret entrance to the catacombs that sat below the dungeons. Nanu reached for the latch to the secret door – she had learned of its existence long ago when she cared for Izzy as a young princess. Izzy stopped her, taking one last moment to lean down and give her son a final kiss. She hugged Nanu just before she slipped through the door into the dark corridor and Izzy quietly closed it behind her sending up a quiet pray of protection to Luna as she did.

"GET UP MAN!" A GRUFF voice yelled at Max. He'd finally come to rest on a makeshift bunk behind one of the beached fishing boats.

Grunting, he rolled over, away from the pestering – it was his official break time and Max planned to use every minute of it to catch up on sleep.

A sharp pain in his sides caused him to tumble off the stretcher – the man had kicked him, and hard.

His voice was starting to come back, but not as much as he'd hoped. Max managed to find some soap at the camp, but no razor or scissors to cut off his mane-like beard and matted hair. He sat up and raked his dirty hands through his knotted locks – tying them back with a piece of cloth he'd torn from his shirt and looked up at the man with a defiant glare.

"The ships are here. Get up! I won't tell you again maggot. Next time's the whip," and the soldier left to wake more sleeping men.

*Here already?* Max thought. He was sure he had more time – more time to get inside the walls of Edenfore and find his way to Isabella.

It had hit him like a tonne of bricks when he'd learned his brother Theodore had passed away – unable to show his true feelings, he'd worked through his pain in silence.

Max rushed over to the armoury tent that had been set up on the coral beach next to the harbour. Grabbing a suit of armour and a sword, he was sure someone would stop him, but as he reached for the armour and sword, daggers, and a helmet along with boots and gloves were thrust at him.

Throwing on the armour as quickly as he could, he was suddenly reminded just how heavy the steel vests were. It had been many years since he'd donned the battle armour of Lunacia – and even then, it was only ever for show at regal events and ceremonies.

"You there!" a gruff voice yelled at him. "Go with this lot," he pointed to a line of soldiers walking down the beach – Max followed with one last look back at the wall he so desperately wished to be on the other side of.

"YOU MUST GO NOW, OR you won't make it back in time," Theodora said to the girls as they warmed their hands over the fire – the air quickly becoming frigid because they were so deep in the forest.

Constance looked up at the sky, her vision was still slightly blurred from the detoxifying tea her mother had given her earlier to rid her system of the Uvvweeya tea. The first glimpse of the full moon shone through the trees as the sun and moon mirrored each other on opposite sides of the sky – one coming up, one going down. Lost in the stillness, she thought back to her arrival in the forest – the first time she'd laid eyes upon her mother. A smile spread across her face.

She'd spent so long with the Emperor on the Northern Mainland not knowing where she came from or what she really was. Before moving north, all she'd been told about her life was that she was born on a full moon.

The story of the Goddesses was still new to her; her mother having told her of it only days ago, but somehow, she saw herself in that sky – her sister too. The two of them parted by oceans and their lives forced to be lived travelling in different directions.

Nova grabbed her coat from the hanging rack on the side of the wagon and untied their horses bringing them closer to where Constance was at the fire. "Have you got everything, sister?" she asked.

Constance still couldn't believe she had a sister let alone a twin. Nor could she believe the power that she held inside her was real – power that could only be unlocked with the help of her sister.

# 18

Three days had passed and as cannon fire continued to rain down on the castle, Izzy screamed to the nearest guards to go and release Aristide from the dungeons. The Water users needed all the help they could get and Xander's powers were starting to run dry – along with everyone else's.

"We're trying, Your Majesty but the keys have gone missing," he yelled back over the deafening explosions.

Another blast hit a mere thirty feet from where they were standing. The thundering crack reaching them at the same time as the shockwave threw them backwards. Rubble and blood mixed on the ground, a dark red paste that covered everything – Izzy wasn't even sure whose side it came from.

Rosa rushed in behind Izzy to help her to her feet. "Little Queen," she said. "The Water King has been released. My family went down to seek shelter from the attack and saw the Lady Alina leaving with the keys. She told us you'd requested them, but as soon as the soldiers came down to free him on King Xander's orders, we knew she was lying so my family set to work unlocking his cell door."

Izzy searched, desperately hoping to see Ari, assuming he'd come with the old woman – but she saw no sign of him. "Where is he?"

"He said he had to go back to his rooms to get something and that he would join the fight shortly," she said.

The Queen was about to thank Rosa when an arrow, flying through the air, pierced her in the chest. One of the Emperor's soldiers had managed to scale the castle wall and had taken aim at the Gypsy woman, killing her with one loose of his bow - behind him, many more were following. The Lunacian army taking him out as soon as the arrow had left his bow.

Looking around, Izzy saw a bow and quiver laying against the stone bricks and after gently laying the old woman down, she quickly picked it up and slung the quiver over her back.

Holding the bow up, an arrow nocked and at the ready, Izzy stalked along the wall towards the steps leading down to the harbour shooting off flaming arrow after flaming arrow at the Emperor's soldiers that dared stand in her path.

At the bottom of the steps and after a short argument about her safety, a failing line of the Lunacian army eventually let her pass. Although Izzy was going to pass them regardless of what they said. She made her way further down the steps and out onto the rocky outcrop below – to her left was the main path that led to the marina.

"They're still out of range," Aristide's voice came from behind her.

She spun on her heels and ran to hug him. "I'm so sorry," she cried into his shoulder.

"Water under the bridge. We have other things to worry about now – like living through today," he said pushing her back and pulling something out of his pocket.

"What's that?" she asked ducking as another canon ball whistled overhead.

"Don't think, just drink," as he shoved the vial into her hands.

"I'm not going to drink this just because you tell me to. I want to know what it is," she pushed the vial back at him.

Aristide let out a groan. "It's the same thing you were drugged with that enhanced your powers. What you did to Christian is what you need to do to the Emperor's ships..." he paused looking out to sea. "But on a much larger scale. They're too far out for any of our powers to reach the ships. We've only just been holding them back because they've been landing in such small numbers. But they're getting set to release a lot more landing boats and we don't have enough

Elementials and Gypsies combined to fight off that many at once,"
shoving the vial back at her he said once again. "Now drink."

Izzy looked down at the vial in her hands. "Are you sure this is
going to work?" she asked taking the cork out and raising it to her
lips.

"No. Not at all – but we don't have any other choice right now.
You're the only one with enough power, and we've been saving it until now, but even you need more. This is more concentrated than
what you were given last time. It should give your power the boost
you need."

She put her lips to the glass and gulped back the tangy yellow
liquid – she felt a slight burn as it went down her throat and into her
stomach.

Immediately she could feel tingling sensation spreading through
her body, right down to her fingertips – she felt her power growing
stronger with each passing second.

The dark grey of the cannon smoke and the waning light of dusk
grew gloomier as she raised her palms up to the sky – just as she had
when her uncle challenged her. Small sparks flew from her fingertips,
sizzling and cracking as they arced in the air.

"Are you sure?" she looked up at Aristide.

He looked at her and simply nodded.

With that, Izzy delved deep down inside of herself to the core of
her power, reaching down as far as she knew how to. The now bottomless pit of her power beckoning for her to release it. Pulling the
power up as she felt herself climbing out of that place deep within
her once again, she lifted her head and looked up into the sky.

Black clouds teeming with lightning rolled in above the Emperor's fleet of ships. Soldiers from both sides stopped fighting and
gawked at the madness happening overhead – those who'd seen the
execution began running for cover.

Izzy felt her power pushing against her skin, waiting to be set free. Sounds of thunder replaced the cannon fire as it ceased on every ship – every pair of eyes now fixed on the swirling sky.

"NOW!" Aristide screamed over the loud rumbling. "DO IT NOW!"

Taking a deep breath in, Izzy let loose every emotion and every skerrick of power she'd been holding in. There were so many moments that challenged her as a Queen and as a woman – so many moments recently that should've broken her but didn't. So, she let loose every feeling of inadequacy, the stress she'd been holding in for weeks, every time she was told she knew nothing and shouldn't rule because she was a woman. She drew on her feelings of hate for the Emperor and what he'd reduced her people to. But mostly she drew on the love she held for her son, a son who she would never see again if this failed. So, failure was not an option.

Lightning snaked down from the clouds striking every single ship and setting it spectacularly ablaze. One by one the smaller ships succumbed to the flames so hot they burnt a brilliant blue that could be seen all the way to shore.

"It's not going to be enough," Izzy panted. She could feel herself slipping into a daze – the overload of power making her vision swirl. The Queen dropping to her knees tried catching her breath, taking in heaving gulps of air.

"What are you doing?" Ari cried catching her. "Get up."

But she couldn't. Her legs had gone weak and black spots were clawing their way in front of her eyes. She'd somehow hit the bottom of her bottomless pit.

"No, no, no," Ari was there holding her as her knees gave out from under her. "Izzy!" he whimpered, "You're our only hope. You need to get back up. Just one more time, there's only a few ships left. Izzy!" But it was too late she'd fallen into a slumber caused by the overload of Uvvweeya in her system.

Aristide picked her up and cradled her in his arms – suddenly reminded of the times he used to hold her when she was just a baby, even though he was so young himself. He'd never forget her bouncy raven curls or her chubby little cheeks. He couldn't help but smile, tears forming at the memory even though the battle had resumed, and swords began clanging and crashing around them again.

"Izzy!" Xander yelled rushing up to them as Aristide carried her back behind the wall. "What happened?" he asked caressing her cheek, worry etched on his face.

Aristide filled him in and Xander's shoulders drooped, the realisation that without his formidable wife, they were done for.

Edenfore had endured three days of this siege already. They had been without food since the first day, but despite that the fire in their hearts continued to burn bright.

"How long will she be out?" Xander asked.

Ari shrugged, "Theodora said it was very potent. Possibly a day, perhaps even a week. There's no way to tell."

Suddenly, the night sky blazed into day. Confused, Aristide and Xander left Izzy in the care of one of the Medica nurses and ran back up to the top of the wall.

There, on the edge of the rocky outcrop stood Nova and Constance hand in hand, a bright light radiating from their very skin and shooting into the sky like an explosion of sunlight.

"What in Luna's name are they doing?" Xander exclaimed, turning to Aristide in surprise.

Ari shrugged; his eyes keenly fixed on the girls.

Their hair, flowing wildly in the heavy wind was luminous and glowing brightly. Between them, the copper and obsidian strands weaving together in radiant spirals of fire, water, earth, and air rising and falling, burning, and steaming all at once in a brilliant show of magic and power.

Lunacian soldiers along the dock were spent – their magic close to depleted, their arms heavy from the effort of lifting and swinging their swords in battle for days. Grime and dirt caked their faces and armour, the constant onslaught from the Emperor's army unrelenting. Every minute a new landing boat would bring still more of these invaders to shore. No sooner had the Lunacian army disposed of one lot, another would be there, ready to take their place.

Nova and Constance began walking towards the wooden pier that led to the end of the harbour – their hands still joined and their hair now a flurry of each element.

Behind Aristide and Xander, Izzy appeared – limping up to meet them with the help of one of the nurses.

"Izzy!" Xander cried, taking over from the nurse, and helping his wife to stand with them. "You're awake."

The Queen nodded and tossed a can of Waterford salve at her cousin. "The nurse put some on my tongue – apparently we've found an antidote."

But the young men didn't have a chance to process this new revelation because at that precise moment Izzy spied the two girls on the pier.

"What is going on?" she said shaking her head in disbelief.

The only ship remaining was the Emperor's and it sailed closer to shore, as if he knew the Lunacian forces had been worn down and were poised for defeat.

The mighty sails were raised, and they billowed out as they caught a perfect wind and the ship lurched forward carving a path through the water.

"What are they doing?" Ari asked in shock. "If they land, we're done for. He must have a thousand men still on that ship."

It sailed closer and closer and the seconds ticked by it was as if the world had been somehow paused in time. The world blurred and

Izzy wasn't sure if it was real or if she was experiencing residual side effects from the enhanced Uvvweeya that was still in her system.

Swords clanked and explosions boomed, and cannon fire continued raining down on the castle from the few smaller ships that had narrowly escaped Izzy's fire. They were still just out of range of their Elemental magic making it difficult for the lines of younger and older Elementals that remained to be useful. The castle walls had taken a beating, Lunacia's only losses on the wall were from the direct hits from the cannon fire and the odd soldier who had managed to scale the walls, surviving long enough to take out one or two Lunacians.

The Gypsy clans gathered along the beach behind the harbour joining hands in a long line, their melodious chant rising above the sounds of metal clashing and screams from the soldiers.

Izzy looked from the Gypsies to the girls not noticing Theodora had arrived to stand beside her until she spoke. "I'm sorry I didn't tell you," she said.

"Didn't tell me what?" Izzy replied confused.

She inclined her head towards Constance and Nova – the light intensifying around them in bright blue and green hues.

"They're my daughters," she said.

Izzy had been suspicious about Nova for a while, but Constance shocked her. "Wait a minute. *Constance* is the second All-Powerful Child?"

The old woman nodded, "Now you know why it was kept a secret for so long."

"Christian only talked about one pregnancy in his journals."

Theodora smiled. "He wrote the truth, there was only one pregnancy. They're twins."

The pieces started to fit together like a puzzle in her mind. Izzy repeated the prophecy quietly.

"*Power twice does destruction hole, born on the full moon it was foretold. One Elemental heart forever torn, to do what's right and be reborn.*"

She paused and then said to the old woman, "What I don't understand is the last part."

Before the woman could answer, a loud crack came from the direction of the pier. Instinctively Izzy ducked but she was not yet steady on her feet and she fell against the stone wall.

The Emperor's ship came crashing into the end of harbour – wood and debris flying everywhere. Gone was his care to protect his ship, this was clearly a last-ditch effort to take control.

Peering over the wall, Izzy's mouth dropped open. Down below it was absolute carnage. Soldiers from the Emperor's ship were flung overboard upon impact, their mangled bodies a sea of red and gold amongst the pieces of broken wood and fallen pylons.

The Queen was on her feet and running down the stairs before she could even think about what she was doing, Ari and Xander right behind her.

Soldiers began spilling over the sides of the demolished ship, their swords drawn with fury in their eyes.

Lightning crackled at Izzy's fingertips, fire forming at the end of each spark.

Suddenly she remembered the orange vial in her pocket and without missing a beat she pulled it out. Nova and Constance were right in front of her, the light still shining from them like some sort of protective bubble around them.

Izzy stretched out her empty hand and pushed her way past the twins. The swarm of soldiers from the Emperor's ship now getting dangerously close to the girls.

Uncorking the vial with her teeth, Izzy hurled it forward and pivoted back around and ran to the twins pushing them backwards. The moment it connected with the ground orange smoke filled the air.

A vibration started deep down in Izzy's bones making her violently ill all over the wooden dock. Her stomach gurgled and bile rose in her throat – the vibration not easing.

Wiping the sick from her chin, Izzy looked up at the twins – now no longer alone on the dock.

The last sliver of the sun disappeared behind a cloud of ash and smoke – fading away to reveal a too-close full moon high up in the sky.

Izzy moved around behind the girls – all four of them. The twins had somehow doubled themselves in some kind of astral projection – the vibrations holding their astral bodies.

It was common knowledge that Gypsies could walk the plains of existence, but what they were seeing was on a whole other level. The Queen now stood behind the twins; her feet planted in shock.

The vibrations grew more intense and the Emperor's soldiers who were coming towards them slowed. Confusion etched on all their faces, they stopped and looked at each other a mere twenty feet from the girls.

A thunderous crack followed by brilliant white light exploded from Nova and Constance – hands grabbed Izzy and pulled her back onto the dock.

Izzy fought to get out from under the body that laid on top of her – fabric from the person's clothing on top of her over her face obscuring her vision.

Wood popped and warped, the sound sending shivers through Izzy's bones. It was an unholy sound, the sound of collapse, death, and destruction. Still, the Queen couldn't get out from underneath the body pinning her to the ground. A wave of pure light and force swept out like liquid spilling from the twins in all directions. It did not discriminate as soldiers on both sides were crushed from the inside by the sheer might of it.

Then the light dissipated like smoke evaporating in the wind leaving only darkness. Izzy finally managing to free one of her trapped arms, gave the person on top of her a great shove. Clawing out from underneath their weight Izzy saw it was Agnes who'd pulled her back. It was Agnes who lay on top of her, not moving.

"Agnes!" the Queen screamed, picking up the girl's limp shoulders and laying her across her lap.

A small flutter of her eyelids told Izzy that she still clung to life – but only barely.

"Agnes, stay with me," she pulled her closer to her chest, the warmth on the Queen's legs spread and she knew it was blood spilling out from the girl's back.

Desperately she looked around hoping someone else could help, but alas, only the twins were there.

Violent sobs wretched from Izzy and the tears streamed down her cheeks. "We were supposed to watch our children grow from our rocking chairs as old women," she cried, trying to blink the tears away. "Don't leave me. You are more than my cousin – you're my best friend. Please," she begged.

Another flutter and Agnes slowly opened her eyes and tried to speak, blood trickling from the corners of her mouth.

"Agnes?" Izzy shifted sitting her more upright.

"My powers aren't that strong," she choked out past the blood.

"It's okay. You don't need to talk," Izzy brought her palm to Agnes' cheek.

Agnes used what little strength she had left to place her hand over Izzy's. "But I told you, I'd stand and fight with you anyway."

Life left her glassy eyes and Isabella fought past her sobs to place her fingers over Agnes' eyelids to lower them shut.

Moments or perhaps they were hours passed, she wasn't sure. Izzy didn't want to believe her cousin; her best friend was truly gone.

She hoped that her eyes would miraculously open again and she would be okay.

It was not to be so.

Slowly and gently, Izzy lowered Agnes' body down and stood – small pieces of debris and dust covering her skirt.

She looked towards the castle – Lunacian soldiers helping Gypsies along the shoreline back behind the wall.

Turning her head, the twins stood between Edenfore and the Emperor. He stood atop a mountain of his soldiers' remains – a look of apprehension on his normally proud face.

Nova and Constance, still standing, hands linked let go and stepped to aside revealing Isabella to the Emperor.

Izzy was now standing, her fists clenched at her sides. Flames mixed with lightning sheathed her hands, spreading up her arms.

"You!" she spat at him.

The Emperor stepped down the mountain of bodies as if they were nothing more than stone steps, removing his long flowing cloak as he did in a pile at the top.

"Where is my Uncle?" she asked through gritted her teeth as she started to raise her hands.

The man smiled and his white teeth glowed shockingly bright against his dark skin. "Has he not made himself known? Oh, that's right. I took his voice from him."

"You're going to need to speed this up a little," Izzy said, the inferno around her hands growing even more ferocious. "I'm not sure how much longer I can control this."

The Emperor rolled his eyes strolling ever closer. "I put him on a boat and sent him back to Lunacia days ago. Could it be he didn't make it? Or perhaps he arrived, and I managed to kill him in the battle anyway. Would that not be poetic?"

Izzy dared to look over her shoulder back at the castle, a stupid naïve move. The Emperor rushed at her, dagger in hand.

He made it a mere foot away from her before she turned back and reaching her hand out connecting the lightning and fire to the tip of his outstretched dagger. The electricity ran up his arms and coursed through his veins his insides sizzling with the heat and his eyes darted open in surprise.

In that moment he was no longer the Emperor, he was simply Chino, Nanu's brother. Fear swam in his eyes and Izzy extinguished her fire, catching him by his elbows as he fell. There was no undoing her lightning, no undoing the blaze that burnt its way through his body. It would only be a matter of moments before it reached his heart, stopping it forever.

Izzy may have caught him as he fell, but it was not out of mercy. No, she did it so she could watch the life leave his eyes, so she could be there to make sure that light didn't return. After everything he'd put her and her people through, she wanted to be certain.

His eyes rolled back in his skull and Isabella smiled though it didn't reach her eyes. "I hope you suffer," and she dropped him where they stood – watching him writhe in pain until his convulsions were reduced to twitches, and finally after a minute he was still.

# 19

The Emperor was dead, and the first thing that went through Izzy's mind wasn't that her people were now safe. No, it was how could she possibly explain to Nanu that she, her Little One, had killed her brother. A lump caught in her throat just thinking about how she would even word that impossible sentence.

Agnes' body was collected by a group of nurses shortly after the Emperor died. Izzy could do nothing to help – her strength so completely drained, so she just stood back and watched. Xander coming to comfort her, tears falling down his own cheeks.

The white sheet used to cover her body was lifted by an Air user and draped gently over her body on the stretcher – silence engulfing everyone as it did. The former king, John had been sent word of the death of his daughter, but he was not expected to get the letter until early tomorrow. Knowing he would be on a ship over to Firestorm straight away meant Agnes would be taken to the citadel and put on display for mourning until her funeral could be arranged.

The Emperor's remaining few ships had turned around, catching favourable winds away from the islands of Lunacia as fast as the winds would allow the moment the wave of light had decimated their army. Izzy stood in silence looking over the mountain of bodies as the last of their sails disappeared over the horizon.

A huge sigh of relief came from Xander as he tightened his arms around Izzy's waist. "We did it," he didn't sound excited though – more just stating a fact.

"We did – but it's not over just yet," Izzy said turning to face him she raised her hands and placed them on his chest. Her lips so close to his that she could feel the coolness of his breath.

Xander leaned down closer so that their lips were all but touching and said. "How so?"

"Tomorrow," Izzy said. Standing up on her toes to close the gap, she pushed her lips to his and they melted into each other, their kiss deepening and the world disappeared around them.

THE NEXT MORNING, ISABELLA ran down the hall desperate to see her son.

Nanu had settled back in with Emory just before midnight once they were sure the threat was over. Izzy being so drained from the battle needed to go and sleep off the rest of the Uvvweeya in her system before she trusted herself holding her precious baby.

The maid told Izzy that Emory had been upset down in the catacombs many times. Nanu told her how she noticed a small wisp of power coming from the infant – he had conjured a water bubble above his head – she was sure he was using it to calm himself because when he did it, he giggled and calmed at once. She'd told the Queen that it was only a small show of power, but nonetheless a show of power that young would mean wonderful things for him as he grows.

Izzy hugged Nanu, thanked her and sent her off for some much-needed rest. She looked tired and for the first time Izzy noticed how frail she was becoming. After Nanu went back to her rooms, Izzy kissed Emory on the top of his small head and handed him to the nursemaid. It was time she went to see Agnes.

Up the long winding path to the Citadel that sat atop the highest peak of Mount Ember, Izzy couldn't help but smile at all the flowers blooming along the edges of the stone walkway. She ran her fingers through the tops of the blossoms, their sweet scent floating up, engulfing Izzy's senses. Seeing a flat top rock off to the side, she sat down to soak in the moment.

Butterflies fluttered over the petals and bees collected their pollen, ready to turn it into the sweet honey that would feed their hives. Birds drank the nectar and beat their tiny wings and as Izzy sat watching all these little creatures, she wondered if her life would ever be that simple.

But it was time, she left the rock and finished the walk up to the Citadel – the last time she'd ventured up this far was for her father's funeral. Izzy used to think she would be sad forever. She didn't get over the loss of her father, no, but she'd learned to live with it. In some respects, she'd healed and rebuilt herself from the inside out.

She felt something brush her hand and jumped – but looking down there was nothing there except the flower she'd picked to bring to Agnes. Agnes loved flowers of all kinds; she'd said it was nature's way of putting a little bit of beauty back in everyone's lives. As she continued, she wondered if it was her father walking beside her, or perhaps her Uncle Manu.

Pushing open the giant metal framed wooden doors, Izzy taking a deep breath, stepped over the threshold. The musty, old smell of the long since dead hit her full force like a wave crashing on the sand causing her to stumble backwards.

Recovering herself, Izzy stepped inside and closed the creaking doors behind her, shutting out the direct sunlight so that the only illumination streamed in through the stained-glass windows lining each wall.

In front of her on the flat marble block was a peaceful looking Agnes dressed in her finest dress, her blonde ringlets draped across her shoulders.

It was so hard for Izzy to put one foot in front of the other to take those final ten steps it took to get to her cousin. She simply could not think of a word strong enough to describe the pain of losing a loved one – she wondered if she ever would.

"If I could give you a flower for every time I had thought of you since last night, I bet you would have enough to walk in a garden of beauty forever," Izzy said through her sniffles as she laid the blue flower on Agnes' chest. "I'll miss our talks, your level-headedness and..." she sighed. "I'll just miss you."

Izzy leaned over and laid a kiss on Agnes' cheek, her own warmth leaving a small puff of smoke against Agnes' now cold skin. As the Fire Queen left the Earth Princess one last time, there were no more tears left to cry – only memories of their time together remained.

After leaving the Citadel, Izzy knew it was time to face the other nobles and the Council. She had a lot to explain – starting with why Aristide was released from the dungeons.

The meeting had been scheduled for later that afternoon – why it was set for the day after the battle had finished, she would never understand. Though she knew that the nobles and Council members were nowhere near the front line, so they didn't have anything to recover from. They didn't care that Agnes had died, or that Xander was nursing what was surely a broken arm – though he'd never admit that it hurt at all.

Izzy huffed and muttered curse words to herself as she tied her blue silk sleeves onto her dress, readying herself to be scrutinized and undermined once again by the people that were supposed to be taking orders from her. In one hour, she would have to put her grief for Agnes aside, she would have to play the part of being the Queen of Firestorm. Truth be told, all she really wanted to do was hold her son and rock him to sleep on the wooden rocking chair that sat in his nursery – to forget everything else but the two of them.

IN THE THRONE ROOM, Izzy stood looking out the side window down over the decimated harbour. What was left of the Emperor's ship lay scattered over the dock – the three large masts laying broken and bent over the still dark water.

Broken pieces of the hull splintered off in every direction making it difficult for Izzy to see where the original ship had been. Bodies still littered the harbour and beach – Lunacians and Northerners alike. The Lunacian soldiers were slowly gathering the Northerners up and throwing them on a huge pile waiting to be burned. For the dead Lunacians, it was the families who were down there searching for their loved ones. Once found, the family would collect the body and return to their villages to conduct their own funeral services – sending their dead off the way they wished according to their beliefs.

She could hear behind her the room was beginning to fill. People of noble blood as well as commoners dragging their feet as the exhaustion of not sleeping or eating properly for days weighed heavily on them – their voices were barely audible. Just because the war was over, didn't mean the food shortage was.

Izzy's head was pounding, and no matter how much water she drank, it did nothing to abate her hunger. There was only one person in the castle that was given extra rations and that was Emory's nursemaid – protect the heir. No one would dare argue that point. Izzy thought of her son and his sweet almost-smile. *Any day now,* she thought.

"Order, order," Davis said hitting his gavel on the table, snapping Izzy out of her daydream.

The Queen left the window and took her seat on her throne. Her feet were heavy, and her eyes drooped, nothing but food could help her now. The room grew quiet and all eyes were fixed on her.

Davis stood. "We have several items on the agenda for today's meeting."

All too official, Izzy rolled her eyes earning a giggle from a small girl at the front of the crowd.

He continued. "Item number one; the food shortage. We have received word that a ship from Terrania will be bringing a shipment of Cactona plant over to us. Though it is poisonous when raw, it can be cooked and consumed until we have had a chance to get back out to the farmland and harvest what can be harvested. It will be here later tonight."

"How will it be rationed?" A voice from the crowd called out. Izzy recognised it as Jackson. She'd not seen him since he fell victim to the curse. She smiled, glad to see he had survived the battle.

The rest of the crowd mumbled their support for his question.

"Everyone will receive five rations, young or old, Gypsy or Elemential. This should be enough to last through till after the harvest. Now if you don't mind, this is not question time. All questions should be reserved until the end," his tone sharp.

Izzy looked around the room, people appeared to be happy with this solution. She did worry however, that when the time came to rationing the Cactona plant out, that people would become greedy and violent, but she hoped for their sake they kept their calm.

Davis kept speaking, "Item number two; the trial of Aristide Lunakeep has been set for tomorrow after morning meal. All noblemen are to present themselves to the throne room to be part of the judging panel. No exceptions will be accepted."

"Wait a minute," Izzy interrupted getting to her feet she walked over to where Davis and the other Council members were to the right of the dais. "I demand a voice in the trial," she'd almost forgotten that Ari had been arrested again the moment things had settled after the battle. He was in the Medica tent helping tend to the wounded when soldiers came and arrested him by order of the Council.

She looked at the other Council members who were now shaking their heads. A woman stood up, "I'm sorry, Your Majesty. A member of the royal family cannot take part in a trial unless they are called as a witness." The woman looked almost sad at having to be the bearer of such unwelcome news.

"When this is all over, I have a fair idea of what laws I'm changing first," Izzy said returning to her throne. She sat down in frustration and crossed her arms.

"If you are finished, Your Majesty," Davis said looking over the top of his spectacles. "I would like to continue."

Izzy nodded indignantly and waved her hand in a sarcastic flourish.

"Item number three;" Davis said looking over the paperwork in front of him sending a sideways glance at the Queen. "A new trade agreement between Waterford and the Firestorm Gypsies is to be put to vote."

This time the crowd grew unsettled in a negative way – voices calling for the Gypsies to be cast out from inside the castle walls permanently.

That was about all Izzy could take. Getting to her feet, she spoke to the assembled group. "Do you actually have any idea why we won this war?" she looked down into the crowd, seeing Nova and Constance joining the back rows hoping to come in unnoticed. No one answered her. "We won this war because of the Gypsies. There is no way we could have won it without them. Do you know why? Because it was their vial of a Uvvweeya mixture that I took that gave me the strength to kill the Emperor. But even more than that, it was those two girls there," she put her hand out to Nova and Constance.

They tried to sink back behind a few old men and women, but they'd already been spotted. Izzy gestured for them to come forward.

The girls shyly made their way to stand in front of Izzy, dropping into a low curtsy.

"Rise," she said to the girls. They did, coming to stand beside the Queen. She then turned to the crowd. "These two are the reason we are still alive. They took out the army. They are the reason we are all standing here alive today." As soon as the words came out of her mouth, she remembered Agnes and how she wasn't so lucky, Izzy's face softened. "They are half Gypsy and half Elemental and yet you treat them as heroes, but their Gypsy families as less than human. I will not have it."

Shock radiated out from the crowd. They'd clearly not known the truth about the twins.

"Are you waiting for some sort of divine intervention before you see that we are no better than them?" she pointed at the small group of Gypsies huddling in the back. "Because if you were, I'm quite sure that we've seen it already when they wiped out the army that landed on our shores. In fact," she paused. "I am making a new law, effective immediately. All Gypsies are to be given full citizen rights. No longer will use of their magic be a crime. That includes the right to own land and to trade on any of the three islands I am currently Queen of. All those in favour say, 'aye,'" she had meant only to put it to the Council, but everyone in the room shouted in unison, "aye" – the Council echoing it mere moments after everyone else in the room.

"Good," she said, "Motion carried." Izzy wasn't sure if that's what she was supposed to say or not, but it sounded good. "I also propose that Nova and Constance be awarded their rightful titles as Princesses of Lunacia."

This earned her rapturous cheers.

Xander appeared beside her handing her a small tiara – one that had clearly come from her own collection. She could see a second in his hands and realised what he meant for her to do.

"Kneel," she said to them and they did. Their dresses fanned out over the floor – blue on Constance and red on Nova. "I hereby bestow upon you, your birthright to be forever known as Princesses of Lunacia and heirs to the Aerleon throne should its current King produce no heirs of his own." She placed the tiara in her hands, on Constance's head, followed by placing the second on Nova's.

When the small, impromptu ceremony was finished, Nova and Constance re-joined the crowd – their new tiaras sparkling wildly on their heads.

Davis cleared his throat. "If that is everything, Your Majesty?" he asked Izzy and she nodded with a smile. "Then we shall close this meeting. Any other matters should be addressed at our next Council meeting," and he lifted his gavel marking the end of the meeting.

"What about the Waterford crown?" a voice came from the back of the crowd.

Izzy looked up to find Alina walking through the crowd.

"What about it?" the Queen said.

"It should be mine," the said putting her hands on her hips.

Izzy couldn't help but let out a guttural laugh at the stupidity of the girl's assertions. "You're kidding right? You don't even have any royal blood and you expect me to hand you the crown that belongs to Aristide? I don't think so. Get out!"

"It should be mine!" Alina screeched. She tore the amulet from her neck and threw it to the floor – the amber stone glittering in the sunlight that beamed through the windows. "He lied to me."

"Who lied to you?" Izzy dared to ask.

"The Emperor. He told me wearing the amulet would secure me the Waterford throne. He told me if I wore it, I wouldn't have Sense users reading my mind to know his plan, and when the time came and he had taken Lunacia, he would give me Waterford to rule as a Queen," she was crying now. "Everything I've done, and you give these two mongrel-blooded, half-breeds a title and I've still got nothing."

Izzy couldn't help but stare at her dumbfounded. She'd known there was someone within Lunacia who had somehow been communicating with the Emperor, but she didn't expect that person to be Alina. Truth be told, she thought the girl was too stupid to be behind such a cunning plan. "You will continue to have nothing," Izzy eventually said. "Guards, take her to the dungeons."

Alina could be heard from all the way down the corridor as they dragged her out kicking and screaming.

Davis looked around. "Are we done?" he asked hesitantly.

Izzy nodded and he banged the gavel.

THE DUNGEONS WERE DARKER than Xander remembered them – and wetter. He'd come in the hopes of talking with Aristide to get a better understanding of what his defence would be at the trial.

He leaned against the bars, knocking his arm, causing him to wince – remembering the exact moment he'd rammed it into a Northern soldier and heard something crack.

"Are you here to bestow your pity on me?" Ari said shifting on his cot.

Xander shook his head. "No. I'm actually wanting to know how we plan to get you out of this place – without killing anyone," he inclined his head towards the old man who was pottering around at the end of the walkway, muttering to himself as usual.

"I don't think there's much chance of that," Ari said laying back down and looking up to the roof where vines were growing in through the small window up high.

"What makes you say that?"

"I cannot deny that I killed my mother," he said exhaling a long breath.

"Yeah, that was unexpected I will say," Xander replied not sure what else to say.

Aristide rolled over towards his cousin. "Life used to be so much simpler didn't it? When Lunacia only had one ruler."

Xander pursed his lips. "Things will always change – even if we don't want them to. It is an unpleasant fact of life, and not one we can do anything about. We just have to learn to go with the flow," a smile crept across his face, delighted with his ridiculous play on words.

Ari rolled his eyes. "That was bad, even for you, Cousin."

"Look, I'll be there tomorrow to help in any way I can – and whatever happens, I know Izzy won't let you die. She will find a way to get you out of here and back on your throne."

He shook his head. "It was never my throne."

"Of course, it was. You were raised to become Waterford's King," Xander said.

"You know full well that the only legitimate heir to the throne is dead," Ari said thinking of his younger brother who died shortly after birth.

Xander nodded. "Without you, Waterford will not continue to be the strong island nation it once was. You must know this. Even if you don't think it is rightfully yours, the people think it is – and it is for them that we do any of this. Please think about it."

Ari licked his lips. "I will, but for now I just want to be alone with my thoughts, and my regrets."

He lifted his palm and once again raised the wall of water up in front of the bars to seal himself inside the cell, only dropping it once Xander had exited the dungeons.

# 20

It was the morning of Aristide's trial and Izzy sat in the kitchen trying to eat something even though her stomach churned. The cooked Cactona plant sat on a plate in front of her, its meat dripping a lime green ooze that was ever so off-putting. She screwed up her nose and turned it away, but that didn't take the smell away.

Izzy was lost in thought, there were so many things that even as Queen she couldn't fix. There had to be a way for Aristide to claim diplomatic immunity for his mother's murder. She'd gotten word that even though Aristide denied murdering Jenta, he couldn't be charged with it because he was still King at the time it occurred. Izzy was confident on that one.

They may have won against The Emperor, but nothing could repair the heartache she still held inside. One cousin dead and another imprisoned – Izzy had lost two of her most trustworthy advisers.

A rustle at the door made Izzy snap out of her daydream. It was coming from the other side of the door that lead to the vegetable patch. Knowing that the garden and kitchen staff were sent out to work with the farmers on the harvest, Izzy grabbed a metal poker from the hearth.

She edged over towards the door – the rustling now joined by clanging and banging sounds.

Placing her hand on the old wooden door, Izzy inched her finger closer to the latch.

Something crashed into the door on the other side causing it to shift and wobble. Izzy shrieked and jumped back.

"Who's there," she held the poker up defensively with one hand, the metal starting to glow from the heat – the other hand reaching towards the latch.

Tentatively she unlocked it and quickly pulled the door open inwards. A man appeared, his beard covered in strands of cabbage, his face otherwise caked with dirt.

Still holding the glowing poker up, Izzy asked. "Can I help you?"

The man whirled around and dropped the half-eaten cabbage he was holding – hands immediately going up in surprise.

"What are you doing in here?" Izzy yelled at him, "This garden is private. It's for members of the royal family only." But just as the words finished coming out of her mouth, she saw a glint in the man's eyes that she'd seen many years ago, "Do I know you?"

Until that point, he'd not said a word, but his facial expression changed, and he nodded. He took a step forward and instead of keeping her guard up, Izzy lowered the hot poker.

She had definitely seen those eyes before. Izzy was unsure if he had been a past contestant at the games, or if he was simply a desperate merchant she'd seen down at the dock.

"Did you want to come inside?" by now she was almost sure he was harmless. Though she had her magic if he wasn't.

The man nodded and raked his left hand through his hair, still not uttering a single word.

As he stepped nearer to the Queen to walk past her and come inside, Izzy stopped him – a man she used to know fixed his hair the same way. It was rare to be a left-handed Elemental.

"Are you...?" she was unable to finish her sentence, but the man's eyes lit up.

He turned to Izzy, face hopeful.

The Queen tilted her head to the side. It couldn't be. Her Uncle Max was a prisoner of the Emperor. He was on the ships when they burned. Lunacian soldiers found no prisoners on the main ship, so she'd assumed he'd been killed long ago, and he had never been on the ships like the Emperor had claimed.

But his eyes told a different truth. The second that she got close enough to get a better look at him, she knew. It was him. It had to be.

"Uncle Max?" she asked, her voice almost a whisper. "Is it really you?"

A beaming smile crossed his face and he nodded. His hands came up to his throat and instantly his face changed to that of despondency.

Izzy was trying to grasp his meaning. Eventually she realised he couldn't talk. "Your voice?" and he nodded.

Jumping into his arms she clung to him not caring about the stench of rotten fish or dried blood that caked his clothing. She held him tightly, fearing that if she let him go, he would disappear again.

"I can't believe it's you. Will your voice come back?" she asked, tears falling down both of their cheeks.

Izzy felt his nod against the top of her head and couldn't help but smile even wider.

It only took a minute for Izzy to calm down enough to realise just how truly horrendous Max smelled. "You need to take a bath," she waved her hand in front of her nose jokingly.

He shrugged, a small look of embarrassment causing his cheeks to turn red – visible even under the dirt and grime.

Izzy took Max up to his old rooms – it hadn't been touched in the many years since he'd been gone. Except for the maids buzzing around, who'd rushed up and got the bath started as soon as Izzy informed them of Max's return, it all looked the same.

Max ran his fingers along the dust covered table that sat in the entryway of his chamber – particles floating up into the air. Each one of them was its own snowflake in the beam of sunlight coming through the partially drawn curtains. Home, he was finally home. Though he did agree he really needed a bath.

"I'll come see you later today. I have something I need to be at, but as soon as it's done," she said.

Max cocked his head.

Grasping his meaning, Izzy continued, "Aristide is on trial for the murder of his mother." Max inhaled quickly. "I know," she said. "A lot has happened since you left. But don't worry, I'll catch you up as soon as I get back."

He smiled and Izzy left him to his much-needed bath. It was time for her to get ready to attend the trial.

ARISTIDE COULDN'T THINK straight. Soldiers had come into his cell to place the shackles on his wrists about thirty minutes prior, and his wrists were already starting to hurt. He rubbed them repeatedly, hoping the action would soothe them – it didn't.

Something had occurred to him just before dawn as he lay on the threadbare mattress. He'd used his magic down in the cell – several times. From everything he'd ever been taught, that shouldn't have been possible. It was said that the dungeons had been built with special bricks that had some sort of ingredient added to them in the manufacturing process that cancelled out all magic. Ari had tested that theory again of course – before they'd shackled him.

The shackles were supposed to have been made with the same ingredient – to make sure that even when prisoners were outside the dungeons, their magic would still be nullified.

He could feel his magic coursing through his veins right up until the moment the latch caught on the shackles – confirming his theory. Either the magic in the bricks had finally waned, or something else had caused it to no longer be effective.

"I'm sorry," Emily's voice came from the cell next to his.

"What for?" He stood up and walked to the wall that joined their two cells.

Ari could hear her lean up against the bricks – the beading on her dress scraping against the stone as she slid down to the floor. "Just that you have to go through this."

"Thank you, but it is what it is," he said.

"Ari?" she called. "Can you make me a promise?"

He made a small sound of agreeance.

"If we both ever get out of here, will you marry me?" Aristide could hear the smile in her voice, and he couldn't help but grin himself.

Moments passed and Aristide still hadn't replied making Emily even more nervous than she was asking the question.

Finally, he replied. "I promise."

Nerves fluttered in his stomach and he placed his palm against the bricks just wishing he could touch her.

"I don't want to get married straight away though. I mean, we really only just met, but I already know I don't ever want to let you go," she added as if it were an afterthought.

Ari chuckled, "Whenever is absolutely fine with me." They'd spent the entire night delving deep into each other's pasts, revealing some of their deepest and most guarded secrets. Emily had thought secretly to herself that all this time she believed she preferred women. But the truth felt nearer to, when you're under the thumb of such a vile man like the Emperor, you'd cling to someone who was thoroughly opposite of them. "We will have the rest of our lives together, there's no need to rush a single thing," he heard her sigh in relief through the bricks.

The sound of keys jingled from down the corridor.

"I guess it's time," Ari said.

"Please come back to me," Emily choked out.

"I'll try," a key slid into the lock on his cell and Ari turned away from the wall that separated him from the future he hoped he'd live to see.

Guards came in and gently urged Aristide to come with them. There was no point in him fighting them, so he went willingly.

It was a long walk up the pathway from the dungeons to the wing of the castle where the Council chambers were. The sun was beating down relentlessly causing Ari to sweat even though winter should be well and truly on its way.

The light burned his eyes – he'd only been put back in the dungeons for a day, but already his eyes had adjusted to the change in light causing him to squint.

Soldiers opened the gate and let Aristide and his guards through – the creaking sending chills up his spine. Across the courtyard where flowers bloomed everywhere stood Izzy – her face sombre.

"Hello, Cousin," she said taking a few steps towards him.

The guards escorting Aristide stepped between him and the Queen.

"Oh, stop it. He's no threat to me," she said shoving them out of the way with her elbows as she pushed past them to hug him.

Aristide lift his shackled hands over head her and embraced her thinking back to the day in the courtyard when he saw her sitting on the bench reading. She'd been so innocent back then – in fact, so had he. It was a different time, one he longed to return to.

"C'mon now," one of the guards said giving Ari's manacles a sharp yank.

After being taken inside, Ari was seated behind a long waist high wall – it's three sides only allowing for one possible direction of escape: backwards, straight into the guards. Not that he planned to, but he was always one to keep his options open.

Isabella took a seat next to Xander behind him and next to them sat Nova and Constance – all four faces were grim. The room slowly filled with Noblemen and people simply there to gawk at the trial.

It wasn't long before Davis commanded Jackson to begin the proceedings.

He cleared his throat, "Good morning, Your Majesties," he inclined his head to Isabella and Xander. "And to all others present. This is the trial of Aristide Fen Lunakeep. The charges are as follows; one count of murder- the victim his mother on the island of Waterford, one count of concealing and supplying an illicit drug and the third and final count is the murder of Councilwoman Jenta."

Izzy looked at Xander in confusion. "The vial he gave to you," he whispered in her ear.

"No, it's not that," she whispered back. "I was under the impression that the law couldn't touch him for Jenta's murder because he was King at the time of her murder."

"He's not King anymore though," Xander replied.

Izzy was grasping at straws and she knew it, but she couldn't help but interrupt. "I ordered him to get me the vial, so you can scratch that off your list right now," she said standing. Her voice surprisingly level considering how much rage was building inside her.

Davis looked down over his glasses. "There will be time to refute the charges, Your Majesty. Now is not that time," he looked to Jackson who was clearly uncomfortable at the Councilman's tone with the Queen. "Please continue."

"Aristide Fen Lunakeep, please stand to plead to these charges."

Ari stood slowly, the manacles becoming heavy around his wrists.

Jackson continued, "How do you plead?"

Looking around quickly at Izzy, he said, "Guilty."

Gasps of shock echoed around the room, Izzy clamping a hand over her mouth to stop herself from screaming.

"Then we will continue," Davis said. "You may be seated," he said pointing at the chair behind Ari.

Izzy couldn't remember much of the trial. There was evidence given and statements made – none of which gave any confidence that Aristide would be found not guilty of any charge.

Davis and the other Council members finally took leave to deliberate their decision – Aristide was sweating profusely, nervously waiting for them to return.

It was almost an hour before they ambled back into the room and took their seats – their movements felt like slow-motion. Every breath in and out taking an eternity to complete.

Papers rustled as the Council sat, busying their hands awaiting Davis to read out their verdict.

Eventually, Davis stood and cleared his throat. The chatter throughout the room fell silent, it seemed even the birds outside ceased their singing.

"Well then, we shall get right to the point. On the count of concealing and suppling an illicit drug, we find Aristide Fen Lunakeep, not guilty. Even though he has pleaded guilty, the Queen has claimed the Law of Sovereignty and as such his actions were a direct order from, Her Majesty," Davis shifted his spectacles on his nose and continued looking at his paperwork.

Aristide's shoulders visibly dropped – Izzy had moved to sit right behind him and reached out to lay a hand upon his back. His breaths were short and shallow, and Izzy could feel his heartbeat thumping through his shoulder blades. She had to do something, if only the Law of Sovereignty extended to Aristide after giving up his crown – he would be untouchable. An idea was forming in Izzy's head as Davis started to speak again.

"On the second charge, that of the murder of his mother, we find him guil..." Davis was cut off.

The Queen stood and shouted. "Wait! I proclaim that Aristide Fen Lunakeep from this moment forth is King of Waterford," she drew in a breath. "And so, the Law of Sovereignty applies."

The room suddenly erupted, Davis looked to the other Council members. It was a woman that stood and spoke. "Very well, Your Majesty. However, he was not the King at the time of the murder. So, the Law of Sovereignty doesn't apply. It will, however, prevent King Aristide from being put to death, though it will not stop him from being imprisoned indefinitely."

"No!" Izzy cried out. "You can't."

Davis sat back down in his chair and leaned back causing it to creak. "But we can, and we will."

Someone shifted behind Izzy, their footsteps coming up behind her. Beside her, Nova appeared.

She looked at Aristide, "I cannot let you suffer for something I caused," said Nova.

Confused and surprised, Izzy's mouth dropped open as she watched Nova step further forward towards the Council bench.

"What is the meaning of this outburst?" Davis started.

"Hear me out," Nova went on. "It was me who killed your Council woman Jenta, though I did not know it at the time."

It was Aristide's turn to be in shock. Of all the things the half-breed girl could've said, this was the furthest from what he expected to come out of her mouth.

"When I arrived in Edenfore, I was furious that our lands were slowly being taken and that we were not permitted to own any for ourselves. I lashed out at the Queen thinking it was her fault – of course it wasn't. Once I was in the dungeons, I was no longer allowed to drink the tea my mother had been giving to me since I was a child," Nova pulled a small pouch out of her pocket and walked up to the bench, putting it gently in front of Davis. "Unbeknownst to me, this Uvvweeya extract, which is fashioned into a tea, bound the powers I never knew I possessed."

"This is ridiculous," Davis yelled. "Seize her!" he called to the guards, but not one moved as Izzy had held up her hand to stay them.

"I want to hear her out," the Queen said. She could feel the anger growing but as a Queen, she had to know all of the information to form her opinion – something her father always stressed upon her.

"Thank you," Nova said to Izzy. "Once my body got the Uvvweeya out of its system, I started having very vivid dreams. I was of course still mad about what Jenta had done, and one night I dreamt that I was in her rooms and I enacted my revenge on her. It was only later that I'd found out it wasn't just a dream, and that one of the powers my mother had bound, was my ability to astral project."

"And you admit this freely?" the other Councilwoman asked.

Nova nodded.

"Then we have no choice but to release Aristide from custody and arrest you in his place and sentence you to die," Davis said.

"Wait," the Queen said. "I propose a different sentence."

Soft murmurs broke the silence, followed quickly by shushing as the majority listened eagerly on.

"Nova and her sister were instrumental in us defeating The Emperor. They are literally the only reason why we were not overrun by the army. Her actions are not excused by what she did for our nation, but perhaps they have earned her a little bit of grace in the sentencing."

Davis didn't speak, but he uncrossed his arms and leant forward showing his interest in hearing more.

Izzy went on, "I propose that Nova's powers be bound using the Uvvweeya tea. Forever to live with the consequences of her actions but, nevertheless, to live...as a free woman and citizen of Lunacia."

The crowd voiced their agreement and Nova mouthed the words 'thank you' to the Queen, to which she inclined her head with a slight smile.

Davis and the other members of the Council had no choice but to agree and he banged his gavel to pass the sentence.

Constance sighed in relief. She'd only just found out she wasn't as alone in this world as she once thought she was, and this Princess wasn't ready to lose her sister quite so soon.

NANU ROCKED BABY EMORY to sleep in the large wooden rocking chair on the balcony of the nursery – a blanket draped over her knees to protect her from the draft coming in with the afternoon tide.

She'd received word through a maid that Aristide had been pardoned and set free and knew it was only a matter of time before Izzy would be coming through the door to see her son.

Smiling down at his little face, the tiny baby gurgled and wriggled making himself more comfortable under the tightly wrapped swaddle.

Nanu was hesitant to move, her old bones were aching, and the child had just nodded off when she heard the door to the nursery open.

"Is he sleeping?" Izzy whispered coming into view.

Nanu nodded.

"Are you okay?" the Queen said to her friend. Her skin looked more ashen than usual – the maid's eyes dull.

"I am just tired, Little One," Nanu replied, though not convincingly.

Izzy reached out and gently took Emory from her and walked him inside to his crib. His eyelashes fell heavy on his cheeks and with a kiss, she lay him down.

The Queen walked back out to the balcony where Nanu still sat and they shared a smile. It was a smile of relief. It had been many months of upheaval for them and now, they could finally relax.

"We did it," Izzy said to her.

Nanu inclined her head. "You did it," she corrected sighing heavily.

Izzy turned and leant over the railing that looked out over the harbour. So many memories in this very spot flashed through her mind.

Once, when she was just a small girl, Nanu and her had played hide and seek. Izzy had thought it was a good hiding place and ran out on to the balcony thinking the maid wouldn't check there. Only when she'd gone outside, the doors had locked behind her. For ten minutes Izzy sat out on the balcony and cried – but of course it wasn't long before Nanu found her and comforted her until her tears stopped.

"He would be very proud of you," the maid said of her father. "*I* am very proud of you."

Izzy smiled, "I don't know if I've ever said this to you, but I love you," she turned to look at Nanu, but her eyes were closed.

"Nanu?" the Queen said to the sleeping maid. "Would you like me to help you to your rooms?"

But the maid didn't answer. Izzy walked closer to her and sat down on the stool beside the chair, taking her hand.

Her fingers tightened around the maid's fingers. She knew what this meant. Nanu had once told her that she wouldn't leave her until she knew everything would be okay.

There had been enough loss in the past few days to last Izzy a lifetime, but somehow, she wasn't scared or even sad. Nanu had been getting older for some time and her body would only hold out for so long. She'd seen many things in her life, and taught Izzy a great deal more about how to be the woman she so hoped she would be.

Nanu's breath slowed – her chest moving less and less with every passing moment.

"It's okay Nanu. You can go. Find your mother once more," Izzy said, her eyes stinging as tears formed, though she didn't dare blink them away.

Her breathing slowed more until finally, it stopped.

Izzy fell onto Nanu's lap and sobbed. A minute later, Nanu took a ragged breath and The Queen shot up – hope in her eyes as she searched the maid's face for any sign of life.

But it was not to be. There were no more breaths, ragged or otherwise – the rise and fall of her chest had stopped. She was gone.

# Epilogue

Nanu's funeral was a private affair – just as she had requested when Izzy and she had spoken about it many years before.

The Queen wore a crown of flowers and carried one of the many colourful headscarves Nanu would always wear as she walked up alone to the Citadel.

There was a small grassy outcrop behind the stone building where Nanu took Isabella on the day of her mother's funeral. The young girl, then eight, clung to the dress of her maid looking out at the ocean. It was the spot they would often come to when they visited the Queen's mother Martha in her tomb.

This was the place Izzy had decided to bury Nanu – the place they shared as their little secret.

Izzy had her men dig the grave and they carried her body up in the dead of night, just as Nanu asked – she did not want a fuss.

A lone man stood beside the wooden box that encased the maid and waited there to lower her down once Izzy had said her final goodbyes.

Pulling the crown of flowers from her head, she placed it on the lacquered wood and placed a kiss to her fingers before pressing them to the coffin.

She nodded to the man that she was finished, and he turned the lever that released the straps to lower her down.

In silence, Izzy watched until the dirt was returned to the earth atop the woman she'd known as her second mother – the woman who shaped her into the Queen she had become.

There were no more tears left to cry – only memories to rejoice in.

"I will miss her deeply," a soft voice said from behind Izzy.

"As will I," she replied before realising who the voice belonged to.

She spun around so fast she nearly tripped on the uneven ground, unable to believe her ears or her eyes.

There stood Agnes – alive and right in front of her.

"But I watched you die. I-I held you as you did," Izzy stammered.

Agnes smiled. "You did – but sometimes magic finds a way," she said reaching out to hug her cousin.

After the longest time, Izzy broke their embrace. "No magic has that kind of power. Does it?" Izzy asked, still unsure if she should believe her eyes.

"It was the prophecy," Agnes said leading her cousin to sit on the ledge at the back of the building.

"I still don't understand," Izzy shook her head.

"Theodora didn't get the chance to explain it to you fully. Power twice does destruction hold, born on the full moon it was foretold. One Elemental heart forever torn, to do what's right and be reborn." She took a breath in, "Power twice as you worked out was the twins – they were born on a full moon. But it was the second part you didn't know," Agnes said taking the Queen's hand.

"I'm guessing you're the reborn one – but how?"

"When Nova and Constance were about to release their wave of power, I was standing at the shore. I knew you would be right in the firing line so I ran as fast as I could to you. But I was torn, I knew that if I didn't get to you in time that we might both perish, but I had to try. I had to do what was right. I had to save my Queen. So, I ran, I barely made it to you in time to pull you down and lay on top of you. I had known the moment I grabbed you, that it would take my life. I didn't know, however, that I would be reborn, but I was okay with dying if it meant you lived."

"It still makes no sense though," said Izzy shaking her head. "What sort of magic could possibly be strong enough to bring back the dead?"

"The castle did it. Well," she paused. "Not exactly the castle, but what was under it. There was very ancient magic deep down in the castle. It appears it knew some time ago that it would be needed, and it collected and syphoned its magic into me. That's what brought me back."

"That would explain why Aristide was able to use his magic in the dungeons."

Agnes nodded, "I saw a great many things while I was on the other side. One of which being that you still cannot allow Elementials and Gypsies to have children. We got lucky this time, but there will come a time in the future when Lunacia won't be so lucky. The All-Powerful Child will come again, but not in your lifetime."

Hope inside Izzy flared, "Did you see my mother?"

"No," she sighed. "I didn't see anyone from our time. Only five ancient beings that once called Lunacia home, but we can talk about that more later. For now, I would like to go home – if that's okay."

Izzy laughed, "I think you've earned at least that," she said hugging her cousin once more.

"And besides, my neck is really sore from laying on that marble block for so long – I'd really like to have a nice hot bath in a Terranian bath house."

The girls walked back down the path towards the castle hand in hand – the wind throwing their hair out behind them like a scene from one of the paintings on the walls of the castle.

NOVA TOOK THE UVVWEEYA tea from the guard outside her room as she had done every morning. In the two weeks since the trial. She had without fail drunk it every day at sunset.

The taste was more bitter than she was used to, and it now left a foul taste in her mouth, something she didn't notice once upon a time when she was drinking it every day.

She set the empty teacup down on her bedside and climbed under the covers. Another night of drifting into loneliness awaited her. Her head started to swirl, and spots floated in front of her eyes even when she closed them.

No one really understood fully what effect the Uvvweeya tea would have on the All-Powerful Child, and Nova never said.

Constance knew it was more serious than she was letting on, because the moment the first dose touched her sister's lips, their twin bond was severed – no longer were they able to join hands and bring the day into the night – no matter how hard they tried.

So as Nova lay there under the too-soft covers staring into the nothingness in front of her, she realised the Uvvweeya had been the flower that made her realise her powers – but also what would bind them for eternity.

*The Uvvweeya has many uses,* she thought. *But for me it has only one. It is my flower of solitude.*

# Acknowledgments

O nce again, I find myself here writing thank you to the many people who helped bring this book to life.

To my mother and father – Mum, I'm sorry I made you wait until release date to read this. I know how much it bugged you not knowing what happened next. Your support for my writing means the world to me and I hope you love this book as much as you loved the first.

Dad, even though YA fantasy isn't something you would read normally, thank you for reading Kingdom of Stone anyway.

To Jasmin – Thank you for keeping me on track and telling me I needed to go sit down and write. I'm sure this book would never have been finished if you hadn't. You kept me sane when I was fretting about my story and you offered valuable feedback on bits and pieces – all whilst trying not to find out the ending so you could still be surprised as a reader. You're the sister I never had and I'm so proud to call you my friend.

To Hannely – As always, your covers are absolutely stunning. I still can't believe they are attached to my books. There are not enough words to express how dear they are to my heart and how much you've really brought this series to life through the covers. Thank you.

To my Auntie Jeanette – Who knew you'd become a fan of Young Adult Fantasy and bring your friends with you? I will be forever grateful for all of your support.

My editor Samantha – You amaze me. Living with a chronic illness is extremely tough, but your commitment to this series, and to be editing while sitting in hospital for your weekly treatments just astounds me. We have known each other for many, many years and I can still say – I know no one stronger!

There were so many times during the writing of this book that you pulled me out of the pit I'd fallen in to. You pushed me past my writer's block, and we had many laughs about how my brain just couldn't "do words" sometimes because I was so creatively spent. Yet, you were there, and you kept me moving along.

The funniest moment throughout the process of this book was possibly when two months before its release, I told you I wanted to write and release another book in a week. Maybe we were crazy, in fact that was definitely crazy – but we somehow did it and (Not so) Average Addie was born – reaching number one Bestselling Book for Children's Paranormal Fantasy on Amazon in its first few days of release. Something I'm sure we will be forever proud of.

Through the gifs and the ah-ha moments, to the many times you messaged me saying "I think you've contradicted yourself here." I could not have ever asked for a better editor and friend than you. You "get" my writing and my books would surely be a hot mess without you. Thank you.

To my husband – one day our children will be big enough to look after themselves, but right now, they're not and I want you to know I appreciate all those times I worked late, and you got up to the baby if she cried or rocked her to sleep while I kept working on this book. You are the reason I can continue to be able to do what I do. Thank you – I love you.

Finally, to all my readers – I'm so happy to be able to share Lunacia with all of you. I've said it before, but this series has been in the works for so long I'd started to lose hope that it would ever become a reality. I love hearing your thoughts on my books and I adore all the artwork and character adaptations I've been sent. I hope you enjoyed Flower of Solitude and I can't wait to share the next instalment with you.

As an independent author reviews mean more than you could ever realise. So, if you enjoyed Flower of Solitude, please head over to Amazon or Goodreads and leave a review.

I ALSO HAVE A NEWSLETTER that has giveaways and free stories for you to read that I send out from time to time

You can sign up at www.kathrynleeauthor.com

# About the Author

Kathryn Lee is a young adult fantasy author living in Darwin, Australia. She has two young daughters, a military husband, two Border Collies and a cat without a tail. Kathryn enjoys playing her soprano cornet in a brass band and in the afternoons she teaches private singing, brass and piano lessons

Read more at https://www.kathrynleeauthor.com/.